Lemon Chiffon Larceny

HONEYPIE MYSTERIES

JOANN KEDER

Cover Art: Molly Burton, Cozy Cover Designs

Editor: The Editing Fairy

ISBN: 978-1-953270-40-5

Characters

Honeypie Chiffon Sweetwater: owner of the Honeypie Diner, formerly her grandmother's restaurant

Dexter Jenkins: her fourteen-year-old son who hates everything

Tildie Bunce: Dexter's best friend

Minty: new chef at the diner

Booker Danno: Misty Cove Police Chief

Sullivan Sweetwater: H.P.'s father and Dex's grandfather

Gwen Folds: coroner, and owner of The Final Press Cleaners

Gram Gram: H.P.'s beloved grandmother and former owner of the Honeypie Diner

For Shauna
Thank you for your love and support. Your light shines
bright.

Liars don't run out of breath, they run out of audience.
-anonymous

Chapter One

H.P. Sweetwater scrubbed the last streak of grime from the stainless-steel counter, her arms aching from the effort. The harder she scrubbed, the more the image of a body floating in Lake It or Leave It lake persisted in her mind. She straightened up, shoving dark strands of hair behind her ear as she surveyed The Honeypie Diner's kitchen with pride. It practically gleamed under the fluorescent lights.

"You missed a spot, Hun Bun. It's over to your right," a disembodied voice remarked. "But that's not the reason you're working so hard, is it?" The familiar, comforting sound of an old woman caused Honeypie, or H.P. as she preferred, to shift her attention to the crack of cold air coming from the walk-in cooler. Anyone else would have slammed the door shut and lamented the waste of energy, especially if they were scrimping to fund a new roof for their home.

The distant sound of an ambulance sent chills up H.P.'s spine. For a fleeting moment, she hoped it meant the poor woman, whose bright green dress ballooned up like a flotation device, was still alive. Unfortunately, ever since moving to Misty Cove, she'd become an unlikely expert on the recently deceased. "You're the one who's dead, Gram Gram. Shouldn't you have the lowdown on any new arrivals?"

A rush of warm air greeted H.P. at the door, causing her brunette curls to rise. She closed her eyes and let the feeling of love wash over her.

"I haven't earned the ability to see everything yet, and I'll thank you not to take that tone with me. I may be dead but I'm still your grandmother."

A cold burst of wind replaced the warmth, causing Honeypie's lips to rubberize. It was a stern reminder that, dead or alive, there was one person who remained in control. "Okay! Geez!"

She propped the walk-in door open, using an overturned bucket with the words, "Luscious Lou's Lemons" emblazoned on the side. It was her seating of choice when engaging in conversation with her namesake, Honeypie Sweetwater. For a fleeting moment, she thought about her increasingly large electric bill. Between replacing the roof on her home and dealing with a slowdown in customers, she had to pinch every penny. At least it took her mind off that bloated image... but only for a brief minute.

A shimmering light appeared between two heads of lettuce and giant-sized carrots, coming into focus as the image of her grandmother. It was not the way she'd looked, all prim and proper, in her casket. No, this version of her grandmother was stunning. She wore bright pink lipstick and her hair was changed into one of several fashionable styles. Gram Gram never bothered much with her hair during her life. She just didn't have the time. Her eyes still sparkled with mischief. "You got those peepers from me, my darling Hun Bun!" she would say.

After her untimely passing, Honeypie Sweetwater, or "Gram Gram" as she was known lovingly to her sizable brood of grandchildren, couldn't quite leave her prized Honeypie Diner and her favorite granddaughter behind. When she wasn't enjoying the company of a famous departed soul, she resided in the walk-in, always managing to offer H.P. supportive advice.

H.P. used the back of her hand to wipe her forehead before turning to view the ethereal vision that always took her breath away. "You know that propping the walk-in door open is a luxury I can't afford right now. If you were any other ghost, I'd have to put my foot down."

"Egads, If I didn't know any better, my darling, I'd think you were having money troubles. Please don't tell me you've run through all the cash I left you."

H.P. gulped. "No, it's nothing like that." Her grandmother, while living, always had an uncanny knack for uncovering the truth. Some things never changed. "The money is safely tucked away in the bank, earning lots of interest."

She'd decided the sizable inheritance would cover her son, Dexter's college tuition. There was no touching it until he was eighteen, no matter how many buckets she had to fill with the relentless winter rains.

"To answer your earlier question, Gwennie and me were out for our early morning walk when a stray cat ran across the path. We followed it, thinking it may be in need of medical attention. You know that Gwen's mother is a cat fanatic..."

"Keep it moving, darling. I don't have all eternity to listen to this story."

"Sorry. We came out of the clearing and that's when we saw this bloated body..." Her voice faltered before she added, "Her eyes were staring straight up and the expression on her face was..." H.P. paused, trying to erase that picture from her mind. It wasn't working. "That poor woman experienced something horrible before she died. Her mouth was open, like she was trying to yell for help. It was just awful, Gram Gram. I called the police while Gwen went to get the coroner's truck. I felt bad for leaving, but..."

"Anybody you knew?"

H.P. shook her head, trying to block out the vacant green eyes on the poor woman's face.

It didn't work.

H.P. glanced up at the clock, remembering that her teenaged son, Dexter was on bucket duty before school. No doubt she'd come home to another soggy mess from the leak in the ceiling if she didn't make a quick trip across the lawn that separated her home from the diner.

"Did you hire a new chef yet? I really liked the last gentleman. He was a gorgeous, tall drink of whiskey." Gram Gram's ethereal appearance changed from gold to bright red and puffs of red tinted air formed tiny hearts that framed her face.

"Minty. He offered to work for free. You always taught me that if something sounds too good to be true, it probably is." She let out a loud sigh. "Can we pick up this conversation tomorrow?"

Gram Gram's glittering gold dress swished in front of H.P.'s face as she swooped down from the ceiling. Gram Gram's expression and her aura darkened. "Hire the man, sweetheart. You have enough to worry about, so take the gift he's offering. And Hun Bun? You're poking at a hornet's nest. The body you found this morning is someone else's problems, not yours. Probably one with more bees than honey."

Before H.P. could respond, the diner's door flew open, and her son, Dex, appeared, looking as though he'd just seen a ghost.

Chapter Two

Dexter and Tildie burst through the swinging kitchen doors of the kitchen.

"Mom! Tildie and I—there was a guy—and blood everywhere—"

"Follow me home and we'll talk. I need a few hours away from work."

H.P. stared longingly at the walk-in before guiding the teens out the door. Gram Gram's former home, the one she left H.P. in her will, was right across the lawn from the diner.

"Mom... Mom... Mom! You wouldn't believe who we just—ow!" Tildie Bunce, a brown-eyed beauty who was also Dexter's best friend, elbowed him in his ribs.

"Can I take off my shoes first, kids?" She glanced at the bucket in the middle of the living room. It was full. Shaking her head, she directed her attention to the excitement in the room. "Take deep breaths, my darlings," H.P. cooed as she sat down. The most cognizant information would come from Tildie, so she focused on Dexter's best friend. H.P. loved Tildie Bunce like the girl was her own child.

"Mom... Mom, the craziest thing happened on our way home from school!"

Although she loved her son with all her heart, he could spend all day telling a story before admitting, "Oh, wait, that's not it." Tildie, however, was a Brightwood Scholarship winner every year since the first grade, which only proved she was a "right to the point" kind of girl.

Tildie elbowed Dex again and sighed. "Ms. Sweetwater, allow me. We found an injured man in the alley between Scheddy Street and Blackberry. He had a serious head wound. No ID. Dexter performed a perfunctory check for oozing blood and broken bones before my father showed up and called the ambulance."

H.P.'s heart raced. "What? Who was it? Is he all right?"

"There is patient confidentiality, Ms. Sweetwater. We won't know unless he makes his treatment public knowledge," Tildie replied calmly. "But the man motioned for Dexter to lean in close before the ambulance came. He whispered something about recognizing his attacker."

H.P. folded her arms across her chest to prevent the kids from seeing them shake. Today had already been too much.

Dex, shifting nervously, added, "And uh... he said the attacker was you, Mom."

The room fell silent. For a long moment, all H.P. could hear was the ticking of the clock. "Me? That's impossible."

Dex shrugged, avoiding her gaze. "He was out of it. Maybe he was confused." H.P. sank into the couch. But as she did, something caught her eye: it was a glittery, golden residue clinging to the soles of Dex's sneakers.

"What's that on your shoes?"

"Huh?" Dex lifted one clown-sized shoe and inspected the bottom. "Oh, probably got it from the alley. Looked like some weird glitter in the dirt. Tildie said it was from cheap makeup or something."

H.P.'s stomach tightened. She could recognize that shimmer anywhere—the same glittery aura Gram Gram surrounded herself with.

"Dex, honey, go get something for the two of you to drink."

"Uh-huh," Dex mumbled as he disappeared into the kitchen.

He maneuvered deftly around the full bucket. When they were alone, H.P. turned to Tildie, taking her delicate hands and looking into her eyes. "Start from the beginning, sweetie."

"Dexter and I were on our way home from school," Tildie began, "when your son challenged me to a race. Tsk." Tildie shook her head as she folded her arms across her chest. "Your boy here hasn't learned it's never wise to accept a challenge you know you won't win."

H.P. had yet to find something Tildie DIDN'T excel in. Poor Dex never learned his lesson.

"No, you said, 'Dexter, are you up for a wager?'" Dexter handed Tildie a frosty water bottle and gulped his down in three gulps. "But it was more like," his voice rose two octaves, "Dexter... do you want to lose some money?"

Tildie slapped him on the arm playfully. "I don't sound like that!" She protested. Turning back to H.P., she explained, "We're working on our cardio, so I told Dexter that if he could keep up with me all the way to my house, I'd give him all the leftover cupcakes from my birthday party."

"And he took off before you finished the sentence?" H.P. replied with amusement. "I can see why you're both out of breath!"

Both teens giggled briefly before Tildie clasped one delicate hand over her own mouth and one over Dexter's. "We shouldn't be joking around, given what we just saw."

There wasn't a single route to Boog R. Noseinair High School that passed by Lake It or Leave It State Park or the corresponding lake. For that, H.P. was eternally grateful. "I understand your curiosity, but—"

"We were turning the corner of Blackberry onto Scheddy Street," Dexter interrupted, as his hand bounced on his thigh. "That's when I saw something moving in the alley. That's when we saw... yeah." He stared at his torn sneakers, the third pair he'd destroyed this year. Somehow, Tildie's shoes, which covered the same ground, remained pristine.

Dexter's sudden seriousness concerned H.P. Normally, he reserved that emotion for an unexpected power outage while he was playing a video game.

"Was it an animal, or—" H.P. still hoped this was a game and she'd become an expert in middle school Go Fish.

"It was a person, Ms. Sweetwater," Tildie said in her calm, matter-of-fact way. "An elderly man, to be exact. Ruddy complexion, a three-inch scar on one cheek, and bushy, grey eyebrows. Oh, yeah, and a crooked nose. Like he was on the wrong end of a barstool during a fight. My father taught me to observe all the details just in case I'm ever abducted."

H.P nodded. "And?"

"I realized immediately that I should put on my old sneakers, the ones I keep in my backpack for unexpected encounters. The man was unconscious when we arrived with a serious head wound. We checked for a pulse and then Dexter put his cheek next to the man's nostrils to see if he was still breathing."

"How did you know about that?"

Dex huffed and rolled his eyes. "We had to pass the first aid section in P.E. last year before we got our report cards, remember, Mother?"

She nodded, recalling mostly his insistence that only "nobs and dweebs" needed to learn about bandages and splints. It was one of his odder arguments, but one in which she stood firm.

"Once we realized he was stable, I called my father, who, in turn, called an ambulance," Tildie finished.

Was this an attempted murder by the same person who left the swollen corpse in the lake?

"Do you know if he's all right? What caused the head wound? Did you see anyone else at the scene? You two are so brave!"

"The guy didn't have any identification on him," Dex said, picking up where Tildie left off, thankfully oblivious to his mother's distress. "We checked his pockets and everything. They were covered in blood, too, so it was kinda gross."

This was the point in the conversation when H.P. wanted to reach over and hug her son, kissing the top of his head and telling him she would never let anything bad happen to him. But that boy was the little grade schooler who told her all of his secrets. This sometimes moody, sometimes funny, prone-to-unknown smells kid was a mystery to her. "I bet he came into the diner for lunch and remembered seeing me. The brain can do funny things when it's dealing with shock."

Why did her insides feel like jelly? Was it because he could've been connected to the body she found? Or could it be something else?

"You poor... you guys must be terribly upset," H.P. continued. "That's a lot to deal with and you handled it better than most adults would. I'm happy to call you in as excused absences today if you want to hang out at our place and play video games. You need time to process this."

Tildie and Dex exchanged glances.

"What? There's more?" H.P. slammed her palms on her knees. "Tell me now!"

"After they loaded him up into the ambulance, the guy kind of opened his eyes and said something to the ambulance driver," Tildie said quietly.

They both fell silent again.

"You two are acting weird. Usually, you're both talking a mile a minute. I know you've been traumatized, but—"

The sound of the doorbell made all three of them jump then pause waiting for whoever would let themselves in. The front door squeaked as it was opened . "H.P.? Tildie? Are you here?" All eyes diverted to the clean-cut figure of a well-dressed man who appeared.

"Finally! An adult who will give me the whole story!"

Abe Bunce flashed a charming smile as he slid in next to his daughter, pressing a gentle kiss on the top of her head. The air around him filled with a captivating mix of musk, pine, and that unmistakable aura of a confident, sharp-dressed lawyer. Petite and lean, his dark, curly hair framed a smooth, light caramel complexion that matched his daughter's. His high cheekbones and defined jaw, lightly dusted with stubble, gave him a rugged yet polished look. But it was his deep, warm brown eyes—brimming with emotion—

that spoke volumes, often saying so much more than his measured, soft-spoken words ever could.

"Nice to see you, H.P."

He gave her a disarming sideways smile before turning to his daughter. "What did you tell her? I couldn't go back to work after... H.P., you must be beside yourself!"

H.P. tilted her head and studied Abe, flattered he thought so much about her. "No, the kids didn't finish. Can I get you something? Tea?"

"Water is fine."

Abe took off his long, expensive coat and sat on the couch. H.P. was still admiring him when she tripped over a small end table. It was missing one leg and she recognized it right away as an antique Gram Gram kept in the attic. She polished it weekly with lemon oil so that even decades later, it was still pristine.

"Are you kidding me, Dexter Jenkins?"

Her complaint apparently falling on deaf ears, she made sure she wasn't mortally wounded before pouring a glass of water and returning to the living room.

"Dex, why on earth would you take the time to bring Gram Gram's end table into the kitchen and then remove a leg? If you have time for some crazy experiment, you have time to empty the leaky roof bucket!"

Dexter displayed a mix of hurt and defiance. He'd gotten so good at this performance art that H.P. was never quite sure when he was lying or telling the truth.

"I don't know what you're talking about, Mom. We got here the same time as you did. And why would I take a table apart? I don't even like crafts!"

"It's true, Ms. Sweetwater. Dexter hot glued his fingers together so many times in Arts and Crafts 101 that the teacher made him go to the grade school and get an unopened bottle of *their* glue."

"Do you mind if we get back to the story?" Abe asked after taking a long drink of water. "This might be an important thing for your mother to hear!"

"We told her everything, Dad. Except... the end."

Abe nodded solemnly and turned back toward H.P. He touched his tie and cleared his throat as though he were about to give a closing argument in the trial of the century. "The man said he was the victim of a robbery and recognized his attacker. I'm sure he was mistaken."

H.P. huffed, incredulous at this non-news. "Why is that so hard to tell me? Abraham Bunce, I'm not one of your high-profile clients at Fulla, Bunce and Vinegar. Spit it out!"

"The... uh... victim said he and his attacker had an altercation last night and things became violent." Abe touched his fingertips together in front of him and sighed. "He said... that YOU were the one who attacked him."

The only sound, the dishwasher going through its rinse cycle, echoed in the otherwise quiet house. Dex and Tildie, each displaying a look of concern, stared pointedly at H.P.

"Well, that's ridiculous," she said, bringing the mood of the room back to normal. "I've explained to the kids that he likely saw me earlier in the day and was confused. Don't you think?"

H.P. stood, searching for a task requiring her full attention. Abraham Bunce made her heart flutter, as much as she hated to admit it. She couldn't bear the thought of looking into his eyes and seeing distrust. She began rearranging Gram Gram's Pie Girl figurines on the mantel above the fireplace, the same ones she'd dusted yesterday. "I was deep cleaning the kitchen over at the diner. Ever since we started closing at four p.m. I got cameras installed so it's easily proven." Quickly, she searched her mind for evidence that she'd actually turned them on.

"The victim insisted that you came to his hotel room last night," Abe paused to take a deep, dramatic breath. "He said the two of you got into an argument, at which time you assaulted him."

"Dex?" she asked, searching for support. "Am I remembering it right? I was here, wasn't I?"

Dexter nodded slightly and turned his head away, causing her

stomach to lurch. Why wouldn't her son support her?

"The man said something else, H.P. He said... that he's your father."

Chapter Three

S unlight spilled across the diner's tiled floor like syrup on a waffle.

"On the afterlife side of things, we don't spend all our days floating around willy-nilly, keeping tabs on the living."

Gram Gram's quick dismissal of the news that her long-lost son was in town shocked H.P.

Sullivan Aloysius Sweetwater, the youngest child of five, was her favorite. A dark, curly-headed boy with large, green eyes and a crooked nose from diving off the swing set and onto his brother's arm, he wasn't subjected to the same strict rules as his homely siblings. Whether it was because he was engaging and ridiculously cute, or because he reminded her of herself as a boisterous child, Gram Gram allowed him to run wild.

Prone to petty theft, throwing rocks at windows, and stealing vehicles for joy rides, Sullivan's antics made police cruisers a familiar presence at The

Honeypie Diner. Gram Gram didn't care. The day Sullivan left his daughter with Gram Gram and disappeared, however, she locked herself in the basement, missing the pot roast and new potatoes she'd prepared for dinner. There were muffled sobs echoing through the heating vents for hours. By the next morning, she acted as though nothing was wrong.

Five years later, a policeman who favored Gram Gram's pies informed her that her wayward son had been arrested for robbery in another state. That was the last time the name Sullivan Sweetwater was spoken in their home.

"When I was little, you acted as though he were the only reason you got up in the morning. Why aren't you excited that your prodigal boy has returned?"

It was all coming back now: the sweet stories of his tenderness towards his mother and sisters, the fact that H.P. looked identical to him when he was young, the funny way he mispronounced, "façade" as "fay-kade." And the memory buried the deepest, the day he left for tacos and never returned. H.P.'s anger faded over the years but the scar on her heart was permanent.

"Well, Hun Bun, now that I'm on the other side, I've been able to review my mistakes. I spent six months in the Excuse Caboose. I told you about that, right?" Gram Gram sighed and her aura turned an ugly green.

"I'm sorry, what? You've never mentioned a caboose before."

Gram Gram frowned. "Didn't I? I'm sure I would

have remembered, but I'll concede it's hard to keep all the afterlife rules straight."

H.P. shook her head. "And I'm grateful you're here to inform me ahead of time."

She wasn't sure she believed Gram Gram's stories entirely: dining with Charlie Chaplin, dancing with Beethoven—her active social life with famous friends seemed endless, or so she claimed.

"When you arrive at Salvation Station, there are several options. You can choose to stay put, as I did. Or you can take the direct train, the Afterlife Express. It's risky; but if you have nothing in your earth life to atone for, you'll get a first-class ticket. If you've done some big no-nos on earth, it's the ejection seat for you. Your eternity will be spent in the Excuse Caboose. Because I went voluntarily, I sat in the front row on a cushy seat.

"Those who were ejected must sit in the back row, behind the tall woman and the screaming baby while a movie of their indiscretions plays on a loop, forcing them to watch their earthly transgressions over and over. After each one, they must explain why they did it and what they did wrong. If they refuse to answer or don't fully express their understanding, the caboose goes faster and the track becomes smaller. Lots of people get motion sickness. As they look at the screen, however, even THAT won't guarantee an eternity of joy unless they stick around for the hard stuff. That requires years, possibly decades of self-reflection."

"Mm-hmm. Right."

All this information was interesting, maybe even true, but it had no bearing on H.P.'s current situation. "Meanwhile, back on earth, the new police chief will be banging on my door any minute. Your son will have me arrested for a crime I didn't commit!"

There were rumors the new chief was a hard-nosed professional who was serious about lowering the crime rate in Misty Cove. H.P. was relieved when Gwen reported the chief questioned her about the body, and Gwen said she was on a solo walk, leaving H.P. out of it.

Gram Gram swirled down beside her, bringing a warm, comforting energy that encompassed H.P. This ethereal "hug" was a feeling H.P. craved.

"My scrumptious girl. I'm sure it's just a misunderstanding. He loved you more than life. He used to take you fishing, don't you remember? The two of you came home giggling about the good time you'd had but never carrying any fish."

H.P. turned away so Gram Gram didn't see her cheeks burning.

"The day he left you with me, he cried harder than I'd ever seen him cry. Your own father framing you? More likely, just a big misunderstanding."

H.P. thought hard. She didn't remember any tears on his part. Just a wave as he left to get tacos from Shell Yeah! Gram Gram didn't suspect anything until suppertime, when H.P. was still there. "Your judgment may be a little clouded, though."

"No, I'm sure it's not, my dear. You do remember the County Fair incident?"

H.P. shook her head, frustrated by Gram Gram's lack of support and insistence upon living in made-up stories.

"Effie Plum was always jealous of me. Her pies were grainy and gloppy and everyone knew it. If you ask me, earning second place for her Pumpkin Pleaser was a sheer gift." Gram Gram snorted with uncharacteristic disdain. "Then out of nowhere, she beat my Luscious Lemon Chiffon. If it weren't for your father, I would never have known she bribed the judges. I heard rumors she drugged them, but of course, I don't know that for sure."

H.P. searched her memory for a time Gram Gram's Lemon Chiffon pie didn't win first place. Nothing came to mind. "What happened?" she swallowed hard. "Did my father... kill her?"

"Oh, child. That imagination of yours never quits. He never hurt anyone. He followed her for two weeks before the next pie judging. Effie and the handsome, young judge were meeting at a local motel. It's no wonder the woman lost custody of her son."

"She did?"

"The woman's crust was as dry as sawdust. That's what I need to ask her. How in the world did she form fit it into her pan? Might as well have just used the dust from her countertops."

H.P. glanced up at the clock. 6:15 p.m. "I need to get home soon. Poor Cinnamon Biscuit Maker sits by her empty dish and meows every night. It's Dexter's responsibility to feed her! I don't know how he can ignore—"

"I'm going to track her down, is what I'm going to do. I'll confront her and find out once and for all if she cheated."

It was hard not to smile at Gram Gram's sense of afterlife justice. "Back to my dad? Was there anything else?"

"Oh, yes. Your father was here earlier in the week."

"What?" H.P.'s voice rose two octaves. "Why didn't you tell me? Did he steal anything?"

"Of course not!" Gram Gram replied, indignant. "He got the ladder and went straight down to the cellar."

"Wait," H.P. squeezed two fingers together on her forehead, trying in vain to make sense of this. "We have a cellar?"

"Of course! Every business in town has one. They're all connected by a long tunnel. At one time, there were bars located in the tunnels. People came from Seattle and even Canada to sit in an underground speakeasy."

H.P. stood in stunned silence.

"Bestie? Are you talking to Gram Gram?"

H.P. opened the door, relieved to see her best friend, the diminutive coroner and owner of The Final Fold Cleaners.

"Hi, Gram!" Gwen called cheerily, waving at Gram.

"Hello, my darling. How are your parents?"

It was a silly exchange between a ghost and a woman who could see, but not hear her. H.P. moved between them. "Gram was just telling me that my father was here in the diner a few nights ago! Can you believe that?"

"We'll talk more later. Mr. Lincoln is hosting a talk on FlapFlop, the celestial social media. He sure knows his stuff. And handsome? I think half the women in attendance are merely there in the hopes that he'll wink in their direction."

Gram Gram's apparition dissipated before H.P. could protest. She turned towards Gwen ."Do you believe that?" "My father was here and she never said a word!"

"We can deal with that later. I just finished the autopsy on our Jane Doe. You're going to want to hear this."

Chapter Four

The diner was unusually quiet for a Monday. It wasn't as though every booth were empty, in fact, Edna Snarlwood, the diner's oldest employee and resident grump, was taking names for a waiting list. It was the actual level of noise that was somewhere between library silence and church service, first hour. H.P. couldn't figure out why either.

"You know, I wouldn't blame you if you did give your father a whack," Edna Snarlwood mentioned in passing. She took a moment to lick cinnamon roll frosting from a finger, her third health code violation of the morning. Luckily, Inspector Heather Lookaway only showed up once every six months.

Gwen grabbed H.P.'s hand instinctively before leaning across the table and whispering, "Let it go. We have more important business."

While H.P. agreed with Edna, it was irritating that

Sullivan's attack had already reached the far corners of Misty Cove. "Okay. Tell me about this autopsy."

"Our vic drowned, but the drowning occurred after she was rendered unconscious by blunt force trauma to the back of the head."

"What do you think they used to hit her?"

"The large, jagged wound on her scalp indicates she was struck with a heavy object repeatedly, so that when she entered the water, she was unconscious. The subject drowned not long afterwards. Whoever did this was heartless and from my experience, acting out some sort of vendetta."

While Gwen's detailed reports from autopsies weren't uncommon, this was different. She'd seen the woman's bloated body floating in the lake and felt a connection.

"And here's something strange," Gwen continued. "According to my own analysis, traces of lemon oil were found in the wound, suggesting the weapon was something coated in or used with citrus."

"Your father was ALWAYS talking back to your grandmother. The only reason he came into the diner was to rifle through her purse, looking for loose bills," Edna prattled, still living in her own world of conversation as she passed by the best friends. Edna liked to talk and talk until she was the only one in the conversation.

H.P. nodded, refusing to engage in eye contact with Edna in the hopes that she would tire of trying to carry on a conversation with someone who was decidedly not interested.

"One day she showed up with a little safe and told me to put my

valuables right beside her purse." Edna reached a gnarled finger into the back of her mouth and began digging between her teeth. Satisfied that the offending chunk was gone, she added, "Didn't slow him down none. He took the whole safe! The man's probably up most o' the nights, thinking your grandma left you piles of cash."

The bell over the door jingled. A tall man with a goatee and a twinkle in his eye stood awkwardly in the doorway, refusing to move past the entryway.

Edna paused to look him over before barking, "It's your lucky day, tall dark and vertical. Things are finally slowing down." She pushed her glasses higher on her nose and inspected him like he was a piece of steak. "Up 'til today, things were so bad that even a stray raccoon in the pie case would've spiced things up. Find an empty booth and as soon as I drop off these dirties, I'll be over to take your order."

He nodded and bowed as though Edna were royalty.

"I should go clear some tables. Can you come back later? I need to hear about this autopsy," said H.P.

"Sure." Gwen slipped her arms through a mustard-colored corduroy jacket. "Should I bring my mom's pizza casserole again?"

H.P.'s stomach lurched at the thought. "We have leftovers. You know that Dex will only eat them when you come over and call them 'culinary genius.' Shall we say, seven?"

Gwen nodded and waved goodbye as she exited the diner.

H.P. smiled at the man before remembering the need to clear her name. "Edna," she began as she followed Edna into the kitchen, "I didn't attack my father. I haven't even seen him since I was a kid!"

"Says you," Edna snorted. "I've got my opinions on things just like everyone else in town."

For the first time today, it occurred to H.P. that the crowd gathered in the diner wasn't there for the daily omelet special or a giant raspberry muffin. Slamming one hand against the swinging doors that separated the kitchen from the dining room, she put one foot on the stool in front of her and used her hands to push herself onto the counter. Never mind the ketchup bottle she stepped on. Another health code violation that would go unreported.

"All eyes up here, please!" she called out.

Everyone stopped chewing in unison and looked up innocently.

"Look, let's not play games. You've all heard the rumor that my father is here in town, and that I knocked him to the ground."

"More like you pummeled him into hamburger," Five Meal Gary, a diner regular mused.

The next time he asked for an extra slice of pie "on the house," she'd give him a firm no.

"I haven't seen Sullivan Sweetwater since I was nine," H.P. continued. "Not one Christmas card..." her voice wavered, "or birthday gift. I wouldn't know that man if I ran into him, and if by some chance I recognized him, I'd happily ignore him the way he's done to me my entire life."

A few customers shifted in their seats, and more locked eyes with their table mates.

"Please go back to your breakfast, and..." H.P. paused. "...And a portion of each bill today will be used to create a fund to pay for my—for Sullivan Sweetwater's—medical bills."

Tension in the room eased. It was a rash decision and one she would surely regret later, but for now, it brought a sense of calm to her diner and that was all that mattered. Looking down, she realized her legs were shaking and getting down would not be as easy as getting up. There were numerous condiments she'd have to navigate and knowing her, not in a ladylike manner.

"May I offer my assistance?"

A tanned hand appeared at her side. Glancing down, she realized it belonged to the new customer. "Oh, thank you!"

Edna appeared from out of nowhere and edged H.P. out of the way. "Tell me your name and I'll make a gift certificate for you, tall, dark and handsome." She pulled out a thick book and opened it to a page of blank gift certificates.

He cleared his throat. "Why, Ah'm your new chef. You must be that vision in grey Ah've heard so much about. Edna, isn't it?"

Edna eyed him up and down suspiciously. "Employees don't get gift certificates. Her grandmother's rule." She slapped the book closed and shoved it under the counter.

Unfazed, he continued. "Wilford Peppermint, but everyone calls me Minty." His bright, blue eyes twinkled when he spoke. An older man with curly salt-and-pepper hair, a bushy mustache that wiggled as he talked, and a short goatee that reminded her of Father Time, H.P. observed him with satisfaction. Minty's demeanor fit the vibe of The Honeypie Diner perfectly.

Edna refused his introduction and left to take an order.

"Edna will warm up. She's like a shy kid in kindergarten. By the end of the day, she'll be your best friend." H.P. smiled, knowing the chances of Edna befriending Minty now that her position in the diner was superior to his were slim to none. "I can't believe I forgot to prepare for your first day." H.P. thunked her skull for emphasis, emitting a forced laugh. "My life is always too busy!"

"If you'll recawl," he began in the same thick-as-honey Southern drawl that captivated her during their online interview, "my old thunker is on the fritz too. Brain injury on accounta the warmin' trays taking a nosedive on my sassy skull."

He'd explained that he'd been seriously injured in a house fire, trying to rescue his mother. It wasn't until a cousin invited him to Misty Cove for a much-needed vacation that he realized this was the perfect place to hang his hat. "Ah'm a verah charmin' in-da-vid-jal, but not so much that my cousin enjoyed my presence all day long. Ah hope y'all still have the need for a slow-talkin', old Cajun."

"Yes! Of course!" H.P. said enthusiastically. "I've never worked with a Crusty Award winner before." The Crusty was issued to the top five pastry chefs in the nation every year. Minty's award four years ago was given for his creative use of herbs in his pies. "You're a welcome sight today." *And a much needed diversion from the topic of her father.* "Can I show you around?"

She glanced at his raw knuckles, remembering their discussion about his brain injury causing a loss of balance. "Did you fall? Do I need to be concerned about your balance?"

"Us old folks can injure ourselves while sippin' our coffee. Right, Ms. Snarlwood?"

Even though Edna was within earshot, she pretended not to hear. "Did I see security cameras? You can never be too careful when you're living in a tourist destination. Lots a kooks out there."

H.P. glanced at the corner where one of six cameras was placed. "I had to stop our surveillance system. We're in a bit of a money crunch right now."

Thud Punchard, owner of the newly renamed "Punchard and Duck, Home Security," offered her free protection in exchange for free breakfasts, but H.P. was ashamed to accept his offer.

There was a burst of cold air as the door to the diner swung open. The patrons uttered a uniform gasp.

Chapter Five

H.P. and Minty turned in unison, both taken aback by the human tornado appearing before them. A compact woman with rosy cheeks and a sprinkle of freckles dancing cross her nose and cheeks, there was no disputing who she was.

"You're the Biscuit Babe!" H.P. squealed, extending a hand to the first celebrity she'd ever met. "I've seen your ads —Biscuits to Behold! It's so cool to have a famous face in Misty Cove!"

"That's me! A delightful contradiction of chaos and charm, a whirlwind of flour, sugar, and a surprising amount of online fame," she recited. "Coriander Crumb, your biscuit-baking neighbor," she said as she thrust a sticky hand forward, her mass of curly, honey-blonde hair bouncing as she shook H.P.'s hand. "Or BurnTheBiscuitBroad257669, as my millions of followers call me."

Something unfamiliar welled up in H.P.'s chest. Was it... jealousy? *Not cool, Sweetwater. Not cool at all.*

"Dex—that's my son—loves watching your videos. At first I thought he and his friends were making fun of you, but now I understand it's performance art." Coriander routinely set her apron on fire or featured some other calamity. It seemed a peculiar way to attract followers.

"I sell out by noon almost every day." Coriander scanned the room. "It looks like you do a brisk business yourself. Honeypie, right?"

"Oh, I'm so sorry. Yes, I'm Honeypie, but everyone calls me H.P." She turned back towards Minty, feeling bad he'd been lost in the chaos. "And this is my new chef—"

"Just call me Minty, ma-yam." He leaned past H.P. and extended his hand. "Ah'm not familiar with your internet fall-doo-rawl, but Ah'm sure Ms. Sweetwater will enlighten me."

"I've been meaning to come over and make you a deal on my biscuits. Think of the added customers it would bring in!"

She pulled two biscuit-shaped business cards from the pocket of her flour-covered apron and handed them to H.P. and Minty. "I moved here to utilize cheap warehouse space. I'm trying to get out of the storefront business and spend my days filling commercial orders." She smiled broadly. Dimples appeared on either side of her mouth. "And I'm thinking of branching out, maybe selling pies."

H.P. remembered watching in horror as Coriander set her own hair on fire. Dexter laughed so hard, he fell over backwards in his chair. Today, her mass of curly, honey-blonde chaos appeared unsinged.

"I appreciate your offer, but for now, Mr. Peppermint here will be doing all of my baking."

Coriander shrugged, seemingly unconcerned. "Oh, well. If you ever change your mind, I'm right around the corner, in the seafoam green building." She flounced over to the door, where she promptly caught her apron and banged her head on the cash register. H.P. moved quickly to free her, but Coriander was quicker. "I'm fine, H.P.!" she assured her. "I'm sorry about your daddy! He must be a real burnt banana bread! I bet he deserved every blow!"

H.P. turned back to Minty, who was watching Coriander bounce next door. There was something sinister in the way he smoothed the upturned tips of his mustache. Almost as though he were preparing to fry her in a nice, orange-scented oil.

Knock it off, Sweetwater, you're being paranoid.

"That—she—certainly brings a new element to Misty Cove, but I need to show you around before the next wave of lookie-loos arrive."

He tilted his head quizzically but he said nothing.

"And you'll need to wear gloves until those injuries are healed." H.P. resisted the urge to ask what actually happened, although she was curious.

"A man of too many tasks is a may-un without humility," Minty said, turning his hands over and back.

"Ah told my cousin Ah'd paint his place in exchange for his kind offering of lodging. When Ah fell, Ah took the ladder with me."

It was H.P.'s turn to nod. "If you need to reach something up high, come and get Edna. She's got the arms of an octopus."

After H.P. explained how all the appliances worked, she turned to see if she'd bored him to tears yet. "Any questions?"

Minty crossed his hands over a brightly colored Hawaiian shirt. "Only one, if you please, Ms. Sweetwater. This ol' boy's creative juices flow most splendidly when Ah'm attired comfortably. A fine shirt like this, paired with a bow tie and shorts, no matter the weather—that's the way of it. Will that be agreeable with y'all?"

H.P. grinned. "I could listen to you recite the directions on the back of a bottle of bleach. I love your accent."

"You're making an ol' Southern gentleman blush, ma-yam. I'll be here at 5:00 tomorrah morning."

"Oh, we don't open until 8:00. You don't have to worry about arriving until 6:30. I've already done most of the prep—"

"Well, now, Minty and his award-winning pies are a package deal. Ah like them to be as fresh as possible. Ah noticed your pie case was looking a little empty, so Ah'll start with five pies."

H.P. blushed. If Gram Gram were listening to this

conversation, she would blow a gasket. The Honeypie Diner only served pies made using HER recipes.

More bothersome to H.P. than the hiring process was confrontation. A conversation about Gram Gram's recipes would have to wait until later. "Let me get you a key, Minty."

Edna appeared in the kitchen, grinning from ear to ear. "The fuzz is here," she said matter-of-factly. "All the customers are sitting on the edges of their seats!"

"Oh, stop it."

H.P. carefully maneuvered herself first onto the shiny, red barstool, and then to the counter top before she cupped her hands around her mouth. "I know you're all here for a show, but I can assure you, no one is going to be arrested today."

The new police chief, followed by two deputies, entered the diner. One of the deputies recognized H.P., pointing at her.

H.P. recognized him—coffee, two sugars and just enough oat milk to make the sweetener swim—as she lowered herself to the ground. "What can I do for you guys today? Here for coffee? Or pie? We're running short on honey pie, but—"

"We're not here for food, ma'am. We'd like you to join us at the station to answer a few questions."

Chapter Six

"What you're telling me is that you don't know anything about this man in the hospital? The same man who not only says you assaulted him but also claims to be your father?"

Chief Booker Danno fixed H.P. with a steely glare, her thick black-framed glasses amplifying her intensity. Misty Cove's new police chief was all business—a striking brunette in her mid-fifties with the posture of a woman who could balance a book and a grudge on her head at the same time. She stood over six feet tall, which made her all the more menacing. Booker had been a desk clerk in Piney Falls before applying for her new role. The city council figured if she could run a desk in a busier town, she'd have no problem running the entire department in sleepy Misty Cove. And since no one else applied for the position, it was a perfect match.

H.P. fidgeted in her chair. "That's exactly what I'm saying, Chief. I wouldn't know the man if I tripped over him on my way to the pie case." She adjusted her cuffs—still sore from being marched out of her diner in front of her customers like a common criminal. "These seem completely unnecessary. I told you I would answer all your questions."

Chief Danno leaned back, touching her fingertips together, her expression unflinching. "Then why does he insist you attacked him?"

H.P. squirmed. "I don't know. It's doubtful he even knows what I look like. The last time we were face-to-face, I was a nine-year-old with a perennial smear of jelly across my cheeks. Maybe a supermodel just happened to be driving through town, and—"

Booker sighed, rubbing her temples. "Ms. Sweetwater, this isn't a joke. Is Sullivan Sweetwater your father, or is this man barking up the wrong tree?"

H.P. grimaced. "That's exactly what I'm saying, Chief Danno. I wouldn't know the man if I bumped into him on the street."

She'd successfully blocked out any images of her father when her cousin, Peanut presented her with a picture she found in Gram Gram's attic. "See? Now you can remember what your dad looks like." To this day, H.P. thought of cardigan sweaters when the subject of her father came up. Later, Peanut admitted the pictures came from the B.Q. mail order catalog.

When the memories of his face seeped back in; a bulbous crooked nose, hazel eyes that matched his years and callused hands from decades of working construction, she wished she could go back to those catalog-dad days."There was no need to cuff me in front of my customers, Chief." H.P. squirmed, trying to find a comfortable position. There wasn't one.

"You didn't need to make a scene in front of my customers. It was humiliating and I'm sure I'll lose some of them over your need to put on such a theatrical production."

Truth be told, she'd probably gain customers because now, Honeypie Sweetwater was a bonafide celebrity.

"My father hasn't been in my life for years. But if you want me to sit in a lineup for this nonsense, you'll have to talk to my lawyer first."

Booker arched a brow. "Fine. Attorney Abraham Bunce, was it?"

The mention of Abe's name made H.P.'s stomach do a somersault. She liked Abe—too much—and every time she had to interact with him, her brain turned into a plate of scrambled eggs. She could already hear her inner monologue protesting:*Focus, Sweetwater. Stop picturing his smile. And his jawline. And— STOP IT!*

"I'll get back to you about the lineup," Booker continued, her tone clipped. "But let me be clear—this situation isn't going away. If your father—if this man —is telling the truth, it's about to get messy."

A knock at the doorframe startled them both. Her pale complexion and thick brown hair covering one eye gave her an air of mystery. *No, who was H.P. kidding?* The only mystery to Maeviz Dull was how she managed to find her way to a standing position.

"What is it, Maeviz?" Booker snapped.

Maeviz cleared her throat before speaking in a monotone that rivaled the town council's reading of parking ordinances. "The state police captain wants to talk to you."

"Great," Booker said. "I'll check in with the car lot when I'm done here."

But Maeviz didn't move. She lingered in the doorway, her eyes drilling a hole through Booker the way Booker's had through H.P.

"Also, the vending machine's making those sounds again."

Booker sighed heavily. "Maeviz, we talked about prioritizing. That can wait."

Maeviz sighed. "Fine. But I'm not responsible for what happens when I don't get my caffeine." As she walked away, H.P. noticed something strange— Maeviz's shoes never made a sound, despite her clumsy gait.

"Now, please remove these handcuffs. My client is not a career criminal, she's a respected business owner."

H.P. sat taller, comforted by the fact that Abe was in her corner.

Booker stood and removed the handcuffs restricting H.P.'s circulation. H.P. rubbed her wrists, trying to remedy the problem.

"I'll let Mr. Bunce know when I've made arrangements for a lineup."

H.P. blinked. "Wait. How exactly are you going to pull off a lineup in Misty Cove? Your office is the size of a broom closet."

"We've entered into an agreement with Slice Slice Baby," Booker said, completely straight-faced.

"The pizza place?"

"They have a one-way viewing window in their kitchen, so kids can watch their pizzas being made. We'll use it before they open in the morning."

H.P. burst out laughing. "I'm sorry. It's crazy, right?"

Booker stared hard. "You need to take this more seriously, Ms. Sweetwater. If you're identified, tried, and found guilty, you're looking at a stint in prison. They don't ask how you want your eggs in the pen."

H.P. returned to the diner, her temper barely held in check. Edna was waiting, grinning like she'd just heard the juiciest gossip in town—which, of course, she had.

"Well, look who's back," Edna said, struggling to contain her glee. "Misty Cove's very own outlaw."

"Not funny, Edna," H.P. muttered, tying her apron back on.

"Funny to me," Edna sniffed. "You should've seen the customers' faces when you got hauled off. Half of 'em were snapping pictures like it was prom night."

"Great," H.P. groaned. "Can't wait for THAT to hit the Misty Cove social media page."

As she moved to check the pie case, a warm burst of air in one ear was followed by, "Let's talk."

Startled, H.P. jumped.

"No time for hippie-dippy aerobics," Edna remarked.

H.P. waited until Edna was at a safe distance before whispering, "I know what you want. I'm already drowning in drama without adding Dad to the mix. And what are you doing outside the walk-in? You're always telling me how quickly it drains your energy, so you have to save it for special occasions."

Five Meal Gary wiped the mashed potatoes from the corners of his mouth before giving H.P. a stern look. "Nothing wrong with a little self-talk, but right now when folks are already buzzing about your attempted patricide, you don't want to add *crazy* to your description."

"Of course, Gary. You're always right. Can I get you a piece of Lemon Chiffon Pie? On the house?'

"If I ever turn down a slice of your grandmother's pie," he smiled, displaying the gold tooth he'd recently acquired from an unfortunate incident at the farmer's market, where he tripped on his shoelaces and went flying into Clay's Clay Pottery, "you'll know I'm not in my right mind."

After serving Gary, H.P. waited until no one was watching and slipped silently into the cooler. "Gram!" she hissed, "since when do you have the ability to whisper to me outside of the walk-in?"

"I won it in a card game with Mr. Einstein." A

shimmering silver aura preceded Gram Gram's stunning entrance. "He's not as smart as he thinks he is."

H.P. sat on the overturned pickle bucket that had become her version of an armchair in the walk-in. "I don't have much time, Gram. What did you want?"

Gram Gram frowned, her glow dimming slightly. "I've got things on my mind, namely your father. I'll just bet he's not done stirring up trouble. And that new neighbor of yours? Don't trust her either. I put my ear up to the door of the walk in when she introduced herself. Nobody is that goofy without a reason. I'd be surprised if she could tie her shoes without somersaulting down the street."

"Yeah, I don't know what to think of Coriander. But at the moment, she seems pretty harmless."

Gram nodded. "I saw her sneaking around your trash cans last night with a notebook. She's either an amateur spy or trying to steal your recipes."

"Fantastic." H.P. groaned. "Just what I need—a nosy biscuit influencer sniffing around."

Gram's aura brightened. "Focus on the good memories, Hun Bun. You and your father and your Saturday fishing trips, for one. The two of you were so secretive..."

Did Gram know more than she was telling?

"I don't want to think about him then or now," H.P. said quickly. "I'm sure he'll get bored and leave soon. Was there anything else? And why are you always protecting him? He left you with a kid to raise and all sorts of questionable activities that probably tarnished your reputation!"

"Loving your child is for life, Hun Bun. No matter the mud they walk in."

That night, as H.P. closed up the diner, she happened to notice Maeviz standing on the sidewalk across the street. The moonlight cast a strange glow on her pale face, and her hair fluttered unnaturally in the breeze.

"Maeviz?" H.P. called out.

Maeviz didn't respond. Instead, she turned and walked away, her silent steps disappearing into the shadows.

Chapter Seven

Gwen poured Rebel Riesling into two Styrofoam cups and then handed one to H.P. "I've never seen anything like it before. That woman had to have been catatonic before she was killed. Extremes of temperature can impair brain function, or it could be from hypothermia. It can induce a stuporous state, resembling catatonia, before death."

H.P. took a sip of the wine and grimaced. "Blech. Too sweet. I like their red wines better."

"Yeah," Gwen conceded, "me too. But a family gave me three bottles of this for letting them see their dearly departed post autopsy. They didn't seem to mind that I'd removed his brain. Apparently, he wasn't very smart." She giggled at her own joke.

"Back to the poor woman who was turned into a popsicle before she died, I—"

"Slow your roll, bestie. I didn't say I was certain that's what happened. There are other options."

"Like?"

"Like... heavy metals such as mercury or toxins such as botulinum. I'll have to wait for the lab results to come back to be sure. There was something really strange though. This woman had a green substance under her fingernails that I couldn't identify. Sent that off to the labs too."

"Sorry about the cuffs, Ms. Sweetwater. Since I'm new to this community and this job, I have to follow procedure to the letter. I don't want anyone thinking I'll treat them differently," Chief Danno said.

H.P. had reluctantly returned to the police station after receiving a call from Maeviz. "Chief wants to see you," she said in her trademark monotone. "An apology is what she said. And I'm allergic to roses."

Now as H.P. sat in what she'd discovered were the most uncomfortable office chairs she'd ever sat in, she tried peering around the giant vase of roses of every color.

A knock on the door frame startled them both.

"What is it, Maeviz?" Chief Danno snapped. "When I'm with someone, I don't want to be disturbed. Didn't you have to follow those rules at your last job?"

Maeviz stared at them blankly. "No," she said after

an uncomfortably long pause. "The only rule in the prison kitchen was never take candy from an inmate."

Booker sighed. "Did you have something to tell me?"

"Umm... oh, right. They found a wallet belonging to the dead lady in the water. No driver's license, just a picture of a kid and what we think was an obituary. Too soggy to know for sure. Oh, also, the name, N.N. Nora scribbled across the bottom."

Booker's shoulders tensed. "Doesn't ring a bell. Was anything else found with the wallet?"

Maeviz stared at nothing—again. "Um, dunno. I think they said it had to go to the state crime lab first. The way they described it, it was soggy and gross."

After Maeviz made her noiseless exit, H.P. leaned around the large vase again. "This is all very nice of you, but once my attorney explained everything, I understood. You want the community to think of you as a no-nonsense chief. I get it. Women in the work-place are still considered second class."

Booker stood, handing the large vase to H.P. "I'm glad we're on the same page. And I'll be contacting your attorney about the lineup."

"Thanks again for the flowers." H.P. reluctantly took possession of the unexpected gift. Edna loved flowers. Maybe even enough to bargain for an extra hour of cleaning.

"Oh, before you go, I'd like to try some of that pie I've been hearing so much about. I was told they were your grandmother's recipes?"

"They… were." She glanced around the bare room, thinking about Minty humming a tune as he rolled out the crust for his very first traitorous pie.

"Our new chef prefers to use his own recipes. For now, my grandmother's specialty pies are on hold." She took a deep breath, relieved Gram Gram was confined to the cooler for now. "You've got to come try his Lemon Chiffon. He uses a lavender curd to give it a unique flavor."

The chief's face crinkled into circle of disgust. "I'm more of a traditional pie lover. Give me a cherry or apple pie and I'll savor every bite."

"I need to get back to my diner and reassure my staff that I'm not a criminal."

It wasn't as though H.P. actually needed to hurry, but there was something odd in the air; something tense.

If Edna's legs still had any spring in them, she would have jumped up and down at the prospect of Gram Gram's famously messed up granddaughter famously messing up. H.P. could have sworn she heard a low giggle emanating from the old woman as she was paraded through her diner in handcuffs.

"Remember, you're not formally charged yet."

"Thank you, Chief. But I have nothing to say to the man. Nothing at all."

Chapter Eight

"What you're saying is understandable. You're hurt that he dropped out of your life like a bad habit, only to return with a hidden agenda." Gram Gram's aura was inexplicably golden, a color reserved for things that made her happy, NOT her good-for-nothing son.

"And your son, Gram. He's your son and he didn't make any effort to visit you. Not even once."

Gram Gram swirled around H.P. before landing beside her. "Well, that's not quite true."

H.P. jumped up to face her grandmother. "Gram, did Dad show up at our house and you never told me? How could you—"

"Shh," Gram soothed. She wrapped a warm light around H.P., a blanket of celestial comfort that made her granddaughter feel loved and secure on any other day. Today, however, H.P.'s insides remained cold and unforgiving.

"Don't 'shush' me, Gram! How could you keep this from me? If you didn't float back into my life, I never would have known!"

"I kept it from you for a good reason. Please sit back down and let me explain."

Although H.P. had much to do since Minty was spending all of his prep time making pies instead of prepping for the breakfast rush, she was still, at heart, a granddaughter. Reluctantly, she sat back down on her bucket.

"That's better. Your father showed up one day while you were away on a field trip. To a cranberry bog, if memory serves."

"Bran's Crans. The only reason we missed a day of school was because Tim Bran's dad offered to pay for new textbooks if we took our sack lunches and spent the day there. Tim was so spoiled."

"Yes, it was on that day. It was track and field season, which meant it was nothing but school bus after school bus bringing customers. Edna and I struggled to keep up. We were just about to kick up our feet and enjoy a much-needed cinnamon roll and coffee when he waltzes through the door. Same baby face but his beautiful eyes had turned hard and cold." Gram Gram shivered for emphasis. "If I didn't know my own kin, I would have assumed he was an old-time gangster."

H.P. tried to imagine the scene: Sullivan Sweetwater loping into the diner with a twinkle in his eye

49

and stories for days. That was the man she remembered. "What did he want?"

"The only thing that ever mattered to him," Gram Gram mumbled. "Money. I told him I didn't have any and he started arguing with us. Our cook at the time, Darla Danish, heard the ruckus and came out with her large, cast iron skillet ready to bean my son over the head. Meanwhile, he emptied Edna's wallet. None of us had the courage to stand up to him." Gram Gram sighed. "Wish I'd had the energy to discipline him better, but by the time your father was born, my husband had disappeared and all of my energy went into keeping food on the table. You know how much I adored Sullivan. I guess I deserved what happened."

"How did you get rid of him?"

"He said he needed things to pawn and wanted the key to my house, so I told him absolutely not! There was a coldness in his eyes I'd never seen before. Well, that worked him into a snither. He ranted and raved and threatened to burn the diner to the ground if I didn't give him what he wanted. That's when he pulled out his weapon."

H.P. gasped. "What?"

"Don't get your knickers in a knot, Hun Bun. I remembered all the family heirlooms I'd stored in the basement of the diner. Never once looked at them, but I figured there would be enough to get rid of him."

Gram rested her chin on folded arms as she floated past H.P. and then back again. "Worked like a charm. Edna called the police while he was downstairs and the cook stood over the stairs with an electric knife, ready for whatever came next. It was a lovely moment of female empowerment."

A large, gaping hole opened in H.P.'s chest, one she thought had healed over since her childhood. "He never... asked about me?"

"I'm sorry, dear heart. He was only here to rob us. Same with the other night. I'm surprised there was anything left. In all fairness, he thought I was a product of technology, not an actual ghost."

"Gram, how is it that you never saw fit to tell me before today? Any time you spoke of my dad, you called him a 'good boy,' and 'the kindest man, unlike his father.' To be honest, I never believed it, but still... I thought we were always honest with each other!"

With a sudden swoosh of hot air and a dark red aura, Gram's face appeared inches from H.P.'s. "I'd advise you to think hard. You were a normal teen, maybe a little on the rough side, who snuck out and smoked cigarettes and drank cheap alcohol. Not once did you admit those transgressions to me. Not until I was dead and tucked away in your cooler."

She had a point. "We do keep a hidden treasure chest from those we love, don't we? You wanted me to feel like my dad cared about me, didn't you? That's understandable." H.P. rubbed her hand harshly across her face, angry at the tears she wasted on a man who wasted less energy on her. "It's the same thing I do with Dex when the subject of Eliot comes up."

"Your dad never had much of a memory. That man

was able to tuck away his feelings for his mother and his daughter and forget." Gram Gram sighed. "Just about broke my heart. Let's talk about what comes next. I believe that your father is planning something, perhaps to rob the diner or even... murder someone. When he broke in the other night, there was a hardness in his eyes that I found quite alarming. My ghost tricks didn't even faze him."

"If he's that awful, why are you pushing me to make contact? Won't that just aggravate him?"

"Not if you follow my instructions. I'll dictate those to you, and tonight, I'll keep my ear to the ground and perhaps your new neighbor will spill the peas on her plans."

"The word is 'beans,' Gram. And I thought it took massive amounts of spirit energy for you to leave the cooler? Don't bother. Gwen is all over this and she'll have Coriander's personal information by the time the diner opens." H.P. chuckled. "If I know Gwennie, she got about three hours of sleep before jumping out of bed to start her research. 'Sleep is for people who aren't emotionally invested in a 14-part true crime podcast, H.P.'"

Gwen was delightfully odd, but so kind and loyal.

"The other night, Mr. Houdini came over for enchiladas and he showed me how to Spectral Snoop."

Gram Gram pulled out a giant, hollow animal horn from behind her back and placed the small end up to her ear. "Now watch this," she said with a sense of pride that pleased H.P. too.

Gram swirled gently down to the floor, placing the large end of the horn against the floor. "Uhm... oh, my!"

"What is it?" H.P. hissed.

"There's a family of raccoons living down there. They entered through a storm drain and can't get out. Hold please while I send directions to the surface."

Gram Gram closed her eyes and hummed a sharp pitch that bounced up and down like a rollercoaster. If H.P. didn't know better, she'd think it was giving her motion sickness just like the ride.

"Yes, that's all I hear now, but I'll keep an ear out. At least, when I'm not spying on Effie."

"Gram, I'm worried about you. I thought your afterlife was supposed to be fun and full of good things? Instead, you're wasting it on this senseless vendetta."

"Don't worry about me, darling. You find a way to keep yourself safe from Sullivan Sweetwater."

Chapter Nine

"I've never found myself to be a lover of pies."

Abe Bunce wiped a tiny bit of lavender curd from his never-fully grown-in-mustache as H.P. stared at him dreamily. Because Abe was the father of Dex's best friend, she considered him off limits. She'd learned that the hard way, when early in her son's life she fell for the father of Dex's basketball buddy. When Carlos and his wife reunited, their son was forbidden from ever speaking to poor Dexter again.

"Are you about to tell me that you hated that Basil Lemon Chiffon Pie with lavender curd on top? Because that shiny plate would say something very different."

H.P. smiled. It was fortuitous that Dex and Tildie found an old book about deciphering secret codes while they were supposedly cleaning the attic. She promised them access to anything in the pie case if they agreed to organize the attic. Once she had the money, the roof repairmen would need to inspect the space.

It was also lucky that Abe Bunce happened to have a real excitement for just such a hobby. "Come down and try our new pastries, Abe. We can discuss it then."

"I'd planned to take a couple of bites, and then politely go on about my new diet." Abe winked. "But I was a pawn in the hands of your new chef. This is *practically* addictive!"

H.P. practically wilted. At least on the inside. "We have a new chef. He specializes in pies. I felt guilty that we weren't using Gram Gram's recipes, but his pies have been a real hit."

"Now, I'm interested in what worried you about this book. My daughter is a voracious reader, as you know. I've never forbidden her from reading anything. Even the most offensive book can be a teaching tool. What gives, H.P.?"

"It's in the back. I'll go get it." She hesitated. "You don't think I messed up my father, do you?"

Abe smiled reassuringly. "Never occurred to me that you did. Since you weren't formally under arrest and you didn't put up a fight, the chief was way out of line. I stopped by her office this morning and told her so."

H.P. blushed. He was looking out for her and it warmed her heart. "Did she tell you she wants me to appear in a lineup?"

"No, she never mentioned it." Abe leaned one elbow on the counter, so close she could detect the smell of lemon on his breath. "I'm not sure I'd advise you to do that."

H.P. nodded in agreement. "I've had no contact with him nor will I. He abandoned me and I'll never forgive him for that." H.P. drew in a large breath and let it out slowly. "I can assure you, I never attacked anyone. At the end of a long day at the diner, it's a miracle if I can walk across the yard and up to my front door without stopping."

"I've dealt with many a hardened criminal in my line of work. You are most definitely not one of them," Abe agreed.

H.P. sighed with relief. At least one person in town didn't immediately jump to conclusions.

"May I ask about the circumstances surrounding your abandonment? You don't have to say anything if it's too painful."

Abe's intense gaze made her concentration difficult.

"He left me at my grandmother's home and said he'd be back in an hour. It was Taco Tuesday at The Tipsy Turtle. Gram Gram was beside herself with worry when he didn't return. For that alone, I'll never forgive the man."

Abe nodded in agreement. "A child deserves the unconditional love of their parent. He failed you, too. I'm afraid your emotions might get the best of you in a lineup. That would make it obvious to him that you're his daughter."

The doors to the diner swung open with such fury, the bell over the top flew off.

"Mom! Come quick! There's something wrong with Cinnie!"

Chapter Ten

H.P. trembled, her voice full of unwanted emotion as she banged on the glass separating Cinnamon Biscuit Maker from the help she so desperately needed. "If you don't come out now," she threatened, "I'm bringing her back anyway!"

The irony that she'd never actually threatened a doctor over her son's care, but was willing to resort to physical violence to get help for her cat was not lost on H.P.

They were alone in the waiting room of Purrgent Care Animal Hospital. She and Dexter joked every time they drove by the wood-shingled building as she asked, "Which body part of yours are we selling when our little babe has an emergency?" On a whim one day, H.P. bought pet insurance. She subsequently cursed herself for every extravagant purchase she'd made when the roof began to leak. But this was one purchase she could take off that list.

Cinnamon Biscuit Maker adopted them when they moved to Misty Cove. The sweet, floofy, black-and-white cat with attitude was just the medicine she and Dex needed. Not only that, Cinnie could sense when a ghost was in their home. She informed H.P. with a series of insistent meows, as if she were saying, "Follow me, Mom! This is important!"

"Hello?" H.P. fumed. No response. "That's it. I'm bringing her back myself and you'll be charged for MY time!"

H.P. was almost to the door when she heard someone clearing their throat. "What seems to be the problem?"

An attractive, strawberry-blonde woman, whose hair was pulled tightly into a bun, touched her black, square-framed glasses. Her gaze moved quickly, from the floor to the reception desk and back again.

Unable to make eye contact? Classic sign someone is hiding something. Gwen's paranoia is starting to rub off!

"I have a cat that needs emergency care is what! I demand to see a veterinarian immediately! Go get them before "I..." H.P. looked around her. A tall, green plant tickled her leg, "...before I throw this large potted thingy into the street!"

It was doubtful she'd even be able to move it out the door, let alone, an inch or two without heaving her entire body into it.

The woman made no attempt to alert a doctor, or even breathe, for that matter. H.P. studied the woman's face. It was the color of Gram Gram's home-made vanilla ice cream and as smooth and silky as whipped cream. This poor soul had less life in her eyes than H.P. and that bar was almost on the floor.

By the looks of this place, with its plastic plants and cheap bench-style seats, this woman was probably underpaid and tired of her job. But it was Cinnie so it didn't matter whether or not this receptionist had a hard life. H.P. waved a hand in front of the reception-ist's face. "Is anybody home? Honestly, where do they find you people? Hurry up!"

The woman cleared her throat again. "I'm the only vet here this evening." She tapped a nametag on her crisp, white jacket that read, "Dr. Kitties."

"Then you need to see my cat immediately! She's in the back seat of my car. Hurry!"

For a moment, it looked as if Dr. Kitties was going to continue the standoff. A car with a flatulent muffler roared down the street in front of them, bringing her back to the present.

"I'll grab a gurney and meet you out front." Her tone was lackluster and devoid of the urgency H.P. felt this situation deserved.

"Don't be long!"

Either H.P., Dex and poor Cinnie were the unwilling participants in an episode of a sci-fi show, or this was a case of H.P.'s perennial bad luck. Luckily, she and Dr. Kitties reached the car at the same time.

Throwing the door open, she found Dexter and Tildie awash in tears. Two of Gram Gram's company towels, (the ones she saved for company-use only so they were never actually used) were spread across their laps. On top of the towels lay Cinnamon Biscuit Maker, her eyes glassy and her body limp. She moaned slightly, a sound that cut through H.P.'s soul.

Dr. Kitties reached inside the car, gingerly lifting the towels and with them, their precious Cinnie. "How long has she been like this?"

Finally, this woman had a pulse.

"Tildie and me came home right after school to work on our codes." Dex wiped his eyes with the back of one hand. "I was getting us a snack when I heard a weird sound."

"She was... she was..." Tildie sputtered in an unusual display of emotion. "She was just lying there with foamy blood coming out of her mouth."

Dr. Kitties shook her head. "Sounds like your girl ate something not meant for feline consumption. I'll get her bloodwork and do some X-rays, just to make sure we don't have something else going on."

"Is she going to... will... will she be all right?" Tildie stuttered with uncharacteristic fear in her voice.

Dr. Kitties gave H.P. a worried glance saved for adults who don't want to convey bad news to children. "We'll see. In the meantime, I could use your help. The receptionist called in sick tonight and I had eight patients whose information was never properly loaded onto the computer. Dorothy had to leave for her kid's soccer game and left the program open. Do you kids think you could figure it out for me?"

Tildie and Dex exchanged looks, their distress melting away from their faces. "Yeah!" Dex replied with enthusiasm. "Kids are always better at that stuff than adults, right, Mom?"

H.P. nodded. When she turned around, Dr. Kitties was gone.

Dex and Tildie remained preoccupied with the computer. After entering the information in probably half the time it would have taken an adult, they found a game that caused eruptions of giggles and chatter. Dr. Kitties was a genius.

H.P, on the other hand, struggled to keep her mind occupied with other things, so she took a walk around the office. On the wall opposite the reception desk, H.P. studied the displayed certificates of licensing for each doctor. When her eyes came to rest on Dr. Kitties', she noticed something odd.

"It's going to be a long night."

H.P. whirled around, feeling ashamed she'd insulted the one person who was Cinnie's only hope for survival. "What's wrong with our girl?"

"She definitely ate something not meant for cats." Dr. Kitties wiped her hands on a paper towel before glancing quickly at H.P. "When I looked at her blood-work under a microscope, I didn't recognize it so I sent a sample of it off to the lab in Seattle."

The kids jumped off their chairs and scurried to H.P.'s side. "Did you give her activated charcoal?" Tildie asked. "I read a veterinarian medical book when I was four. Charcoal is the best treatment for poison."

Dr. Kitties nodded. "Of course. I'm confident it's out of her system, and now it's a wait-and-see game as to whether her little body will bounce back. There's a bed upstairs, and I plan on spending the night here, so I can check her vitals every couple of hours. When she's showing signs of hunger, I'll feel a lot better about her prognosis."

"We can't thank you enough, Dr. Kitties!" H.P. gushed. "And while you took care of our girl, you gave the kids something to take their minds off our dear pet. I'm sure you would have been able to enter the files yourself."

"Call me Lotta. And that's doubtful. My expertise resides wholly in animals."

"Well, then, Lotta, you must stop by the diner. I have a new chef and he makes incredible pies." H.P. felt guilty as soon as the words came out of her mouth. Gram Gram's pies were the best in the state. "He also makes a mean Chicken Cordon Bleu. And whatever you choose is on the house."

Tildie cleared her throat. "I have a question, Dr. Kitties. I was looking at the certificates on the wall and when I got to yours, I noticed you didn't have a date of graduation listed. Why is that?"

Lotta's cream-colored face turned blotchy and red. "Because my college made a mistake. It never bothered me too much in the past, but you're the third person to ask about it since I've been here. I've ordered a new one but it hasn't arrived yet." She glanced at the kids and shook her head. "If you kids have finished, please shut off the computer. I don't want to use any more electricity than necessary. You can come back in the morning to check on your cat. I'll call your mother if there are any changes during the evening." Her voice was robotic, and devoid of the emotion H.P. was feeling.

Tildie nodded although she didn't seem convinced. "I'll go shut down the computer."

"Thank you!" Dr. Kitties called after her. "You kids saved me tonight."

When H.P. pulled into the driveway of the imposing three-story brick home, she put the car in park. A glance in the rearview mirror confirmed her suspicions: Dexter was nodding off, just as he'd done as a child. Tildie leaned forward from the back seat. "Ms. Sweetwater? When I shut down the computer, I found an open document."

It wasn't like Tildie to be such a snoop. "I hope you closed it without looking at it, Tildie. It's none of our business."

"Mom," Dex rubbed his eyes and leaned up beside his friend. "it was a bank robbery from a newspaper article. One that took place in Misty Cove."

Chapter Eleven

S ometime between midnight and the first crow of the rooster next door, H.P. finally gave up on sleep. As much as she hated to admit it, this little floofball that adopted them had come to be an important member of their family.

"Gram Gram, pay attention! This is really important!" H.P. clapped her hands together with frustration. Her grandmother's afterlife didn't contain the urgency of her time on earth. Earth days were sometimes minutes, sometimes months. No one in the afterlife cared, Gram Gram said.

"Look at me!" Gram Gram called as she somersaulted around the ceiling. "Never once in my childhood did I have the ability to flip around like a dolphin. I should have died years ago!"

H.P. sighed. "Okay. You can be a dolphin in five minutes, okay? Just listen to what I need to say."

"I'm trying to understand why you came to the

conclusion that a pretty veterinarian would involve herself in a bank robbery," Gram Gram said mid-float. "And you're telling me that cute, little Tildie Bunce printed it off without anyone realizing? We could use her type here."

"Gram!" H.P. was horrified. "Are you suggesting she should... die?"

Gram Gram swirled down so that her face was only inches from H.P.'s. "Of course not! Good grapes, child!"

Her aura became a pea green as she perched herself on the box containing lettuce. "You have five minutes. Go."

"Okay. You'll stay put and leave the dolphin swim for later, promise?"

Gram Gram crossed one leg over the other and gestured with one hand. "I'm waiting."

"I'm going to read this article to you and then I need your opinion." H.P. cleared her throat.

"Skip over the boring parts, darling. I'm lunching with Sinatra and if you're even one minute late, his bouncer tosses you out."

H.P. rolled her eyes before beginning:

"In the early 2000s, a notorious gang calling themselves 'The Dirty Half Dozen' terrorized banks up and down the Washington Coast for eight months. It is estimated they stole millions of dollars by hacking into the security systems and disabling cameras, security features and communication information before

the holdup. As a parting gift, they left half a dozen stale donuts in the otherwise empty safe.

"Citizens demanded their savings and loan institutions install better systems or they would move their money. The Notgunnahappen 1000 security system was marketed as 'impenetrable,' after being tested by those imprisoned for technology crimes. Cents and Sensibility Savings and Loan in Misty Cove was chosen for its debut.

"The heist seemingly went off without a hitch. While the group gathered the last of their treasure, the silent alarm system had already alerted local law enforcement by sending live surveillance footage directly to the police command center. The backup system also locked every external door remotely, trapping the felons inside the bank beside the frightened staff and customers.

"Officers quickly blocked all escape routes and surrounded the bank, coordinating with SWAT and tactical units.

"Trapped and panicked, The Dirty Half Dozen took hostages to ensure their safety. Once outside, though, the plan went awry. The hostages were pulled from their grasp and the officers opened fire, immediately killing gang member, Razor McKnuckles and injuring The Sinus and Charlie Shine.

"When it appeared as though all hope was lost, Nine Nails Nora released an incendiary device, temporarily creating pandemonium. In the end, all but one of the gang were caught and sentenced to

decades in prison. The escapee, known only as 'Shaky the Shiv' remains unaccounted for.

"None of the millions in cash taken during their eight-month reign of terror has been found. It is rumored that one of the gang members hid the money, and that once they've all been released from prison, it will be a race to uncover the hidden loot."

H.P. dropped the article and stared at Gram Gram hopefully. "This article was on the Purrgent Care computer last night. Why would Dr. Kitties be interested in this old robbery? Doesn't that at least make you curious?"

"Huh?" Gram Gram's aura turned light peach, her version of a blush. "My mind was elsewhere, my darling. I believe I've tracked down that old pie prude, Effie. There are so many of us milling around, it does take time."

"Gram! You're exasperating! This lady could be a danger to Misty Cove! What if she has something to do with the body found in the lake?"

H.P. reached for the door handle. "I was hoping you'd give me some words of reassurance. I'm worried, Gram Gram. Maybe she attacked my father and he confused us?"

The only sound was the whirring of the air conditioner in the refrigerator. "Gram?"

"Heard what you said. I thought this town had put all that bank robbery nonsense behind us. I didn't raise boys who robbed banks," she sniffed. "That's what you're trying to tell me, isn't it? That my youngest was the robbery mastermind?"

"What? No, I..." Up until that moment, H.P. hadn't considered a possible connection to Sullivan Sweetwater's shocking appearance in Misty Cove. Her father always joked his crooked nose made him look like a criminal. Sully... Sullivan Aloysius Sweetwater... could he be *Sully the Sinus?*

"Well, you can put that theory to rest. My poor boy straightened up after robbing the diner. Edna told me he was a delivery driver down in Piney Falls, Oregon before leaving for parts unknown."

H.P. frowned. "She never told ME, and I'm the one accused of attacking him. How did Edna come across that information?"

"You know Edna. She's a gadabout and heard from another Snoopy Sally, who heard from another Snoopy Sally..." Her voice trailed off.

H.P. remained unconvinced. "I'm not buying this story. What aren't you telling me?"

"Your father wasn't like the other kids. He was teased because his father ran off. Nobody else in town knew how that felt."

Did Gram Gram understand the irony in her logic?

Sullivan Sweetwater walked out on his own child, and H.P. was teased mercilessly.

"Where are your tacos, H.P.? Did your dad forget the hot sauce?"

Gram Gram never accepted that as an excuse

though. She expected just as much—maybe more—from H.P. as she did from her other cousins.

"Anyway, while he was good at stealing cars and the like, my boy never mastered technology or book learning. Our little town didn't have special classes like they do now. He tried."

Gram Gram's eyes lit up as her aura turned sky blue.

"I... didn't know."

"Of course you did. Everyone in town had a story about him. Most weren't true. Don't pretend like you didn't have ears."

Gram Gram's harsh words hurt. Although now that she was grown, customers whispered stories about her father, thinking she wasn't within earshot, but never once in her childhood had she been privy to this hurtful gossip.

"Take your cat to someone else. Problem solved. Now I'm off to my luncheon. It's a good place to network and I'm real close to tracking Effie down."

"Who?"

"Child! The whirligigs in your brain having to do with memory really concern me! Effie is the woman who paid off the judges at the County Fair, just to beat me."

"Oh, right. I'd forgotten."

That single county fair was just a blip in her grandmother's prestigious life. H.P. couldn't understand how, amongst her lunches with the famous and personal journey assignments, finding Effie Plum would take center stage. But it was Gram Gram's after-life, not hers.

"Well, now, if Ah didn't know any bettah, Ah'd say the lady in charge likes to feel like an ice cube."

H.P. jumped. After such a heavy conversation, she'd temporarily forgotten she was in a working busi-ness, HER business, and the door was cracked open. "Your accent should be bottled. It gives me a boost every day. No, I like to... go in there to think. I know it sounds—"

Minty made a "stop" motion with his thin fingers in protest. "No need to convince me, ma-yam. Ah used to do my best thinking in the courtyard. Shoulda been a govunah, what with all the heavy problems Ah solved out there."

"Sounds like you lived in a very fancy home back in Louisiana. I've heard there are beautiful historic homes there. Maybe someday, Dex and I will visit."

Minty shook his head. "Not fancy by anna-one's standards. Just big. We kids lived with our father and stepmother and her three children. We were stacked up like chickens in the hen house, but we didn't know any different. You and the boy make yourself a nice vaca-tion to my home state and get you some beignets and stay in a hotel. One with lotsa stars in front of its name."

A delicious scent met her nostrils and she inhaled again, lost in the sumptuously sweet aroma. "What is that divine smell coming from my oven? I'm sure I gained at least a dress size from this week's Peanut Butter and Chocolate Pie. It gave me such an incredible feeling of euphoria that I ate four pieces!"

"Now you know Ah can't tell you that! It's my secret recipe! No secret's worth its label unless it stays quiet. What Ah can tell you is to make us a nice cinnamon whipped cream to go on top."

H.P. saluted him. "Yes, sir!"

The phone in her pocket began playing the song, "You Are My Sunshine." She always held her breath when Dexter called. *Was he hurt? Was he in trouble?*

"What's up?" She glanced down at her watch. "Wait, are you trying to get out of Economics class again? Dexter Jenkins, I won't be your excuse to skip one more exam!"

Minty chuckled behind her.

"Mom, the vet just called and said we could pick up Cinnie. You must've given her my number by mistake. I told her we'll be there after school."

"No, you kids were going to work on your project. I'll leave the diner early and let Edna close. She's asked for more hours to pay for that alien enthusiasts cruise she's planning for next year."

"Hey, friendie!"

Just as she was ready to leave that afternoon, Gwen showed up.

It was common for the two women to spend an evening together,

enjoying wine and whatever leftovers H.P. found in the walk-in. With both of their jobs taking up more of their time, they'd fallen out of their familiar and welcome rhythm.

"What brings you by? I was just about to leave so I can pick up Cinnie from the vet. Want to ride along?"

Gwen nodded. "As long as I can take a piece of pie to eat on the way. That stuff is addictive!"

Gwen wasn't normally one for sweets, making her addiction unusual. She bragged about taking home entire cakes for her parents, but she insisted she never ate one crumb. "Sure. Minty made Peach and Basil pies this morning. Like all the rest of his desserts, this one won't be around more than a day or two."

She boxed up a generous slice topped with cinnamon whipped cream. Normally, she would find that amount of basil too much for a sweet dessert, but the man had a golden touch when it came to creative desserts.

As they drove to Purrgent Care, Gwen explained her own odd interaction with Lotta Kitties. "She brought in three doctor coats to our cleaners, all covered in a green film."

"Like... from an animal shedding?" H.P. was at a loss for any other explanation.

"No. I told her I accidentally damaged one and offered to buy a new coat. I sent that one off to the crime lab in Seattle for examination. I should have some answers by tomorrow."

"That seems a little overboard, Gwennie."

Gwen licked her fingers one at a time and then went back over each one. "There's something about that gal that raises my detective hackles, especially since you told me about the robbery information on her computer. You know how rarely I'm wrong."

"True. Something you have in common with Tildie, which is why I felt comfortable sharing that. I hope that doesn't mean you have ulterior motives for coming with me."

"Bestie!" Gwen intoned. 'I'm insulted! I'm a Cinnie fan just as much as the next gal! But you're not wrong. I want to snoop around her office and see if I find any more of that green substance."

"You can come, but if you're caught snooping, you're on your own!"

Gwen saluted her and smiled. "Message received."

After catching up on Misty Cove gossip during the short ride over, they pulled up in front of the vet clinic and Gwen grabbed H.P.'s arm before she got out. "Don't share my suspicions with her."

"Now you're insulting me!"

In the waiting room, there were two humans accompanied by a lizard and a parrot, respectively. A kind-faced man greeted them. "Here to pick up Miss Cinnamon Biscuit Maker?"

"How did you know that?" H.P. and Gwen asked in unison.

"I was in the diner last week for pie and recognized you." He gestured toward the women one at a time. "Word around town is that it's among the best in the state. Euphoric, some say." He closed his eyes and leaned his head backward.

"That Marionberry Basil Pie still visits me in my dreams."

Gwen and H.P. exchanged looks, daring each other not to laugh. "Glad you enjoyed it. We're getting nothing but positive feedback from Minty's recipes."

"Heard tell that Seattle bakeries are catching wind about our little Misty Cove and its fancy diner pies. It's going to put our community on the map!"

H.P. raised one brow. "Really?" She was slowly coming to terms with the idea of shelving Gram Gram's recipes.

"Is Cinnie ready to go?"

He pushed himself away from the desk and stood. "I'll go get Dr. Kitties and your baby. She'll want to go over a few things with you."

"Where's your bathroom?" Gwen asked.

H.P. frowned, trying to remind Gwen telepathically that there wouldn't be time for much sleuthing.

"Follow me."

Gwen turned and gave H.P. the thumbs-up sign before following the receptionist. As H.P. watched them walk away, she shook her head in disgust. Gwendolyn Folds was fearless, sometimes to her own detriment.

Dr. Kitties appeared a short time later with a cardboard carrier emitting loud kitty protests. "In case you're deaf, those sounds mean your cat is feeling much better."

H.P. suppressed a giggle as she thought about how Cinnamon Biscuit Maker was so sweet and rarely meowed unless she saw an

apparition. But take her to the vet and she became very outspoken in her protests.

"Did I say something funny? Lotta lifted one brow.

"No, I'm... an habitual giggler. We appreciate your help with Cinnie."

Despite my every effort not to, I've become quite fond of this girl."

H.P. took the carrier from Dr. Kitties, accidentally brushing her cold hand.

"Don't thank me until after you've paid," the doctor replied in her deadpan style. "I've had too many patients promise me the keys to their home just to come back an hour later to threaten my life over the bill."

"Any instructions?"

"Yes. Keep her away from people food. Cats aren't meant to eat human food."

The sound of a throat clearing reminded H.P. that she didn't come alone. "You're back! Did things go well in the... bathroom?" When Gwen didn't answer, she felt obligated to fill the dead space. "Oh, Dr. Kitties? This is my friend—"

"She meant to say, BEST friend." Gwen's small hand jutted forward in between them.

"Gwendolyn B. Folds. Owner of The Final Fold Dry Cleaning and local coroner. We've met."

Gwen only used her middle name when she was trying to impress someone, and Lotta Kitties wasn't someone she needed to worry about.

"I wasn't aware that retrieving your cat involved an extra pair of hands." Lotta inspected Gwen as though she were a sick German shepherd.

"Normally, one person is all it takes to handle a cat carrier. I asked Ms. Sweetwater if I could ride along because I needed to speak with you."

Gwen cleared her throat, a sure sign she would go into "professional Gwen" mode.

"You came into my dry cleaners and dropped off three lab coats. One of them went through the machinery right after I'd changed the... garmentine."

H.P.'s eyes grew wide. "That's an... ingredient you never mentioned before, Gwennie."

"Found in the thick jungles of Peru, it's a powerful substance the natives have used for centuries," Gwen continued, as though this story had been in the back of her brain for years. "When added to the dry cleaning solvent, garmentine extract not only helps to lift stubborn stains but also disinfects them."

Dr. Kitties studied her. "Hmmph. Learn something new every day. Well, I'll let you pay your bill and move on." Dr. Kitties glanced over at the lizard licking his human's face and sighed. "I've told Hubert a million times not to let Speed Bump lick his face. Some people deserve their misery."

"Oh, shoot! H.P., we forgot to bring in that thank-you pie! I'll run out to the car and grab it while you're paying the bill."

Going along for the ride, H.P. smiled sweetly. "If you don't mind waiting for a moment, I'm sure she'll be quick."

Her credit card had barely stopped smoking when Gwen jogged in, carrying the pie she'd purchased for her parents. "Here you go, Dr. Kitties," she said through huffs and puffs. "Our sincere thanks."

After loading Cinnie in the car and closing the doors, H.P. placed her hands on the key in the ignition but paused and turned towards Gwen. "Do you mind telling me exactly what's going on? Doesn't your mother love those pies? And did you find anything green?"

Gwen nodded. "She does. They make her positively giddy, and Dad and I are grateful for a few minutes without her grumbling. But as I was snooping around Dr. Kitties' office, I found her diary, and—"

"Gwendolyn B. Folds!" H.P. gasped. "You didn't steal it, did you?"

"I believe the correct term is, 'borrowed.' And as long as she believes we're so grateful we'd give her an entire pie, she'll suspect someone else. I'll have it back before she even figures out it's missing anyway. Her last entry was three weeks ago."

"Why couldn't you just take pictures?"

"Not enough time. I didn't want to give the staff any reason to think I was being sneaky. And no, I didn't find any evidence of that green powder. It would take hours to properly search that cluttered room."

At that unfortunate moment, both H.P.'s and Gwen's phones buzzed.

H.P. pulled the visor down and checked her lipstick in the mirror before answering. "Abe?" she purred, "is everything all right? The kids are supposed to be working on their new project at my house."

"The kids are fine, H.P. You're my main concern at the moment."

She blushed for the second time today. At least this one was earned. "Oh?"

Gwen elbowed her in the side, somehow sensing what was happening.

"Yes. I've been on the phone with Chief Danno. She's set a date for the lineup."

H.P. sighed. "I'd forgotten all about that. I wasn't anywhere near that alley."

"Don't give it a second thought. It's just procedure. I'll email you the details."

She hung up and turned to face Gwen. "My lineup is going ahead. What's your news?"

"The toxicology results from the body found in the river are in."

"And?"

"And, she was poisoned *before* her death. Some herb unfamiliar to the lab. H.P., even the FBI has no answers. And there was an usual algae on her clothing. A green powder."

Chapter Twelve

"Gwen, I look like a duck."

H.P. took off the bright yellow hat Gwen found in the back of her closet and flung it onto the floor. "I'm supposed to dress like I'll fit in with the other criminals. How am I going to do that wearing your crossing guard outfit?"

She knew her best friend meant well, but finding what Abe called "the brightest, most offensive outfit to wear" in a lineup was becoming harder by the minute.

"You know my father will recognize me. How could he not?"

Abe advised her that suspects generally looked past the person who is trying to stick out, thinking they're probably a plant. This outfit wasn't going to make her into a wallflower, but she trusted Gwen because she was seldom wrong.

"Are we going to discuss the algae found on the

deceased woman? I'd bet my favorite mustard-colored socks it's the same stuff I found on Dr. Kitties' lab coat."

"Our next step should be to inform Booker Danno. When all this is over, or when I'm booked into the county jail, I'll be the first duck to be finger-printed."

Gwen rolled her eyes. "That won't happen. I'll take the evidence to the police station tomorrow though. I've been wanting to chat with our new chief anyway. You know, professional courtesy."

"Yeah," H.P. sighed. "'One crisis at a time keeps the system on the line,' Gram Gram used to say." As if it made any sense.

Gwen motioned for her to sit down. The leak in the roof had settled to an occasional drop, so H.P. maneuvered easily around the half-empty bucket. "It's okay. You feel like a wreck right now, but I interned as a mortician for Wicker Falls and if I can make Mrs. Rustonme look like Marilyn Monroe, then anything is possible." She grinned as she bounced her knees up and down. "I was nominated for a Lasting Luster award for that work. And her daughter-in-law thanked me for taking away Agnes's evil grimace and replacing it with a sultry pout."

"You did? You never told me that. I guess it makes sense, though."

"In the biz, there are two types of mortician: the serious, 'let's make your loved ones look like they're a creepy version of themselves,' or the glitz-and-glamor type who think they'll be the next Herbert Helvenoski."

When H.P. didn't respond, Gwen explained, "He's known as the best in the biz. I went to a weekend training session he gave, and now I can turn a moldy grapefruit into a perked-up pear."

"Your point being?"

Gwen pulled out a dusty, wooden case she'd brought to H.P.'s home. "That I can turn you into anyone you choose. This is like a high school performance, only leveled up. Do you have a preference, fancy pants?"

H.P. shrugged, indifferent. "Not really."

"Mom!" Dexter came galloping into the living room. "We found something cool!"

"Bring it here. Auntie Gwen is turning me into Greta Garbo."

"I didn't say that!" Gwen protested. "Now I'll be nervous and you won't turn out as good!"

Dexter returned to the living room with Tildie in tow. He handed his mother a piece of paper with crossed out letters and numbers, and at the bottom, the words, "On the eve of the final robbery, we enlisted the help of 'V.' He's been bragging about his lock-picking skills forever, so the boss decided to give him a chance. I sure hope he's not the disappointment I've made him out to be."

"We cracked the code that was in that diary!"

Dexter held a familiar green book in his hand. "Dr. Kitties must've used the same code book!"

H.P. turned in her chair, causing Gwen's eyeliner to streak across her cheek. "Hand that to me this instant, Dexter Jenkins!" She stuck out her hand and waited impatiently for her son to comply.

Sheepishly, he extended his hand.

H.P. was shocked to see the same diary Gwen helped herself to at Purrgent Care. "You gave this to the kids? Gwen! What were you thinking? Now they're implicated in this theft too!"

In unison, the three of them replied, "It's not stolen. Just borrowed!"

H.P. rolled her eyes. "Gwen, you promised this diary would find its way back to where you found it before Dr. Kitties discovered it was missing. I expect you to honor your promise."

"And I will. It's all written in code, as you can see."

H.P. glanced down at the first page, finding the date, "October 15th, 2002 and underneath, geometric shapes, letters and numbers before handing it back to her son. "So the woman likes to write in pictures. What if she's just got a fascination with cave men and women?"

"Mom," Dex huffed in protest. "You know how me and Tildie have been working on decoding the diary? Gwen asked us to look at it and then made us promise to copy the rest of the pages so she could return it to Dr. Kitties' office. No way is that stealing!"

"Okay, okay. I get it."

"We think we've decoded the first entry, Ms. Sweet-water," Tildie said with a hint of excitement in her voice. "She slightly changes her code with each entry, so the others will take more time."

H.P. shrugged, causing Gwen to thump her on the back of her head. "Ow! Gwennie, what was that for?"

"Sit still, please! You have to be at the police station in thirty minutes, so I don't have time to start over!"

"Ms. Sweetwater, let me read the entry."

H.P. nodded. Whatever the outcome, the kids were proud of themselves and she wasn't about to dampen their enthusiasm.

"There was a car accident outside of town, gumming up the job. We'd have to rethink our escape route," Tildie continued. *"Meanwhile, Sticky Pins Bowling Alley hired a comedian who was flopping harder than a fish on dry land. Why did that matter? Because we were about to make this guy's jokes a matter of police interest,"* Tildie read aloud, her voice trembling with excitement. *"Turns out, nobody laughed—until he disappeared."*

H.P.'s brow furrowed. "Wait, are you saying the comedian was *kidnapped?*"

Tildie nodded solemnly. "Vanished. Right after his set ended. One minute he was bombing on stage, the next—poof! His car was still in the lot, keys in the ignition, and his traveling teddy bears still in the green room."

Gwen froze mid-application of the eyeliner. "You're kidding."

"I wish I were," Tildie said, flipping the notebook

around so they could see the decoded scrawl. "This entry's got a timestamp from the night of the bowling alley's *Glow & Giggle Comedy Night*. I looked it up."

H.P. leaned in. "Sticky Pins... didn't that close when the owner died last year?"

"Mm-hmm. I remember his autopsy. Poor guy fell asleep while watching television and his cigarette dropped on the carpet. Then," Gwen made a dramatic gesture with her small arms. "Poof! The whole place went up like a match. The cute fire captain said they found something odd, but it was clear he died from smoke inhalation."

"Did they ever find the comedian?" H.P. asked, not daring to tilt her head to look at Tildie.

"No, unfortunately not, Ms. Sweetwater." Tildie cleared her throat and continued reading.

"People left their cars on the highway and started walking home. Just as we were making our escape, C, our lookout, shouted, 'Half the town's walking down Main Street.' We went in the back door of the bowling alley to buy us time to figure out how to get out of this mess. Might have been the best decision we ever made."

H.P.'s knee bounced as she tried to control her anger. "These people are awful!"

"P said we should take a hostage as insurance. If the cops caught us, we'd have a bargaining chip. Poor Barry D'Punchline wet his pants twice before we got to our safe house. S told him he wasn't gonna need pants where he was going."

"Oh, no! That's enough for now, Tildie. We need

something positive. Could you read some of your beautiful poetry?"

"No, Mom. Keep listening!" Dexter grumbled.

They would have to talk about his attitude. Again.

"I didn't intend for things to end the way they did. Barry begged us to drop him off at Gimmefood Grocery in Tellum, Oregon. It was his next gig. Instead, we disposed of him. I found out later that his dad owned the bowling alley and was beside himself with grief. It made me long for my own children."

A tickle ran up and down H.P.'s leg. It wasn't the kind she got when Cinnamon Biscuit Maker rubbed up against her after a hard day. It was the kind she got when Gram Gram spoke of the dead like they were standing right beside her in the cooler. "Who... killed Barry?"

Her phone rang, startling everyone in the room. "Hand it to me, son."

It took some maneuvering to get the phone up to her ear, but when she finally achieved it, a low voice with more of a growl than an actual octave spoke before she had a chance to open her mouth. "H.P.?"

"Thud?"

Thud Punchard owned a security company in Misty Cove along with his brothers. He and H.P. had formed an unlikely alliance recently, solving crimes that occurred in their little town. She found herself looking forward to his brief, yet friendly calls. "You haven't been in lately. Edna had to take the last of the pot roast tacos home to her mother!"

"I got a call from a client today."

All business. As usual. At least she'd grown used to his gruff demeanor and knew that deep down, he was a kind and giving man. "Who was—"

"Purrgent Care. Told me their surveillance equipment had been turned off and wanted me to investigate. When I looked at the footage right before, it was working well enough that I saw Gwen rifling through Dr. Kitties' things. Thought I'd give you a heads-up first, so you could ask her about it."

H.P.'s eyes narrowed as she glanced at her friend. "She's right here."

"What?" Gwen mouthed, her face and body a mixture of innocence and uneasiness.

"I did know, Thud. She was there on my behalf. We've borrowed Dr. Kitties' diary to do some research. Don't worry; it's going back today. I'll put you on speaker so you can give her a stern talking to right now." H.P. knew she was being naughty but she didn't care. Gwen glanced at her helplessly, throwing her arms out wide.

"Hi, Thud," Gwen said cheerily. "I'm just preparing H.P. for her next mission. You can ask HER about it!"

"I know you messed with the cameras, Gwen. Next time, come to me first so I can either shut them off for you or show you the correct way to do it!"

Gwen's face turned a blotchy red but her lips were sealed.

"Does this have something to do with your arrest,

H.P.? Heard you put the hurt on some old timer. Guess you don't need those self-defense classes I've been telling you to take."

"No!" H.P. chuckled. "It wasn't me, I promise, Thud! I'm crushed you would even entertain the idea that it could be."

"Hmmph," he snorted. "Well, I'M crushed that you didn't come to me before trying this hare-brained scheme. I could have engineered a loop so they saw an empty room while she rifled around. Instead, you've put me in an awkward position. Real awkward."

The room went silent as guilt over their mission swirled around everyone in it. "You're right, Thud," Gwen said in an uncharacteristically soft voice. "We got carried away when we figured out the doctor was hiding something big."

"Well... I s'pose I could erase all of that incriminating stuff and tell them the equipment is bad. My brother has a sample *LurkAlert 220* that he's been itching to use."

"We'll owe you, Thud! You haven't tried Minty's pies yet. More than one person said they experienced their first food coma after eating it. I'll have him whip up a Marionberry Pie tomorrow, just for you."

"And I'll dry clean your shirts for free," Gwen interjected. "I know how to get those gigantic sweat stains out and your polo shirts will look like new!"

H.P. frowned. Gwennie was many things, but tactful wasn't one of them.

"Your offers are both very generous." Thud cleared

his throat as he always did before dropping a bomb. "But they won't be necessary. I have one request from the two of you."

H.P. tensed. "What is it?"

"Just let me help."

Chapter Thirteen

A heavenly sandalwood and spice scent overpowered the lingering pizza and garlic bread odors of Slice, Slice Baby, Pizza and Ice Cream. Today, Abe Bunce wore a sleek, silver suit and a light peach tie. Honeypie Chiffon Sweetwater could drink in the sight of him all day long. He was laughing and joking with an officer when she tapped him lightly on the back.

Abe turned around and immediately his disposition changed. First was horror, then curiosity, then outright anger. "H.P." he hissed, leaning close enough to give her the chills. "What on earth is this? When I told you to wear something unlike your daily clothing, I didn't mean you should scour the thrift stores looking for scary clown clothes! Do you know how many people are traumatized by the sight of clowns?"

"I'm sorry, Abe." H.P. swallowed hard, trying not to feel hurt by his words. "I didn't want to take any chance that my father could recognize me. Gwen and I spent all day on the outfit and makeup." She stole a glimpse of herself in the mirrored tiles on the wall. *Hmm.* She did look like a celebrity. Maybe not Greta Garbo, but a solid Elizabeth Taylor.

"Oh." His voice softened, which allowed her shoulders to drop respectively. "Well, if the chief watches, she may decide you have to remove your makeup and start over. Not only that, she'll think I advised you to dress up." He stared hard at her. "I guess that part won't bother me. Are you certain you want to take that chance?"

H.P. shrugged.

"All right then. I'll tell Officer Shaker that you're ready for the lineup." He touched her back lightly, sending chills down her spine.

A gruff policemen appeared, gesturing with one beefy hand toward the kitchen. H.P. turned her back towards Abe, feeling uncertain. Even though she was innocent, she still felt like she was being led into the middle of a bullfighting arena without any weapon.

"Don't worry," Abe said softly. "I know this is scary, but it's just a formality." She nodded, grateful for his support.

When she reached the officer, there were two women and one man in front of her. One wore the uniform of a fast-food worker, another was dressed as a postal employee, and the single male subject was adorned in rumpled, brown pants and a dirty, blue shirt. The officer handed them each a large, numbered card.

H.P. walked up to Officer Shaker and cleared her throat.

"Here for the lineup, ma'am?"

"You betcha!"

Her voice held more enthusiasm than she felt. Thankfully, Gwen had relented in her support of H.P. wearing the crossing guard uniform. Instead, she rifled through a rack of unclaimed dry cleaning until she found a beige blouse with a ruffled front and high-waisted, elastic-banded jeans. Definitely not the type of person who would go around beating people up.

H.P. pushed a flaxen curl from her eyes, one that was attached to a blonde wig. Now she understood why Gram Gram was always out of sorts during her dating years. She wore wigs to the diner, hoping to attract the attention of the latest object of her attention. It must've have been torture.

The oversized nose Gwen spent over an hour perfecting like a child's science project itched and felt like it was starting to slide down her face. Bright, rosy cheeks shone with a hint of theatrical blush, and heavily accentuated eyebrows arched dramatically. Her eyes were made to pop with oversized, false eyelashes that fluttered with every blink. The final touch was blue contacts.

"You're kinda pretty, Mom," Dexter told her unexpectedly. So much for years of lotions and potions to keep herself looking youthful.

As they walked in, H.P. realized the fast-food worker came in three times every day for another piece of Minty's pies. They were instructed to stand against a white backdrop, one that was borrowed from Cheesey's Fine Photography especially for the occasion. Numbers written in blue marker dotted the sides of the cloth on either side to show the height of all eight participants.

Officer Shaker brought a hand to his ear and nodded his head. "Okay, we're ready to go. I'm going to ask each one of you to step out of line and say the words, "I've been waiting my whole life to get my revenge, Daddy!"

H.P. willed her mouth to stay in the same position and not display the shock she felt. If she'd learned one thing from Gram Gram, it was that revenge was about making yourself feel better and making the other person feel worse.

"Number One, go ahead, please."

The dark-haired fast-food worker was at least ten years older than H.P. and a foot taller. She stepped forward and, with the flair of a television detective, pointed her finger guns at the window and shouted, "This is for dumping me with that crazy, old bat, Daddy!"

H.P. suppressed a laugh. The woman stood frozen in place as if waiting for the director to yell, "Cut!"

"You may step back. Number Two!"

The next woman, who sported faded, blue shorts and a crisp, button-up, blue shirt was not in fact a postal employee. Actually, she was a lifeguard at the beach in the summer, a lunch lady during the school year, and a delivery person in the winter. "This is for DUMPING me, Daddy!" she said in a breathy voice. "You left me with that crazed, old woman, and I'll never forgive you!"

Tears formed in the corners of her big, brown eyes and she bit her bottom lip. Gwen hadn't been far off in her assessment that this would be a theatrical performance.

"Okay, step back. Number Three!"

H.P. took a deep breath and moved up. "I've been waiting my whole life to get my revenge...!"

A disconnected voice called out, "Number Three, let's do that again, saying the entire line. Take a deep breath and say every word. Slowly."

Peering through the glass, she could almost make out her father's figure. He was a short man with dark curls, the complete opposite of his brother, Bash who always towered over the rest of the family. She could make out his silhouette; Sullivan Sweetwater stood with his hands on his hips. He was a little chunkier than she remembered, but probably still reeked of alcohol and cigarettes. There was a time in her life when she found that smell comforting.

The only noise in the kitchen was the sound of H.P.'s pants crinkling as her legs shook. What if, despite all this makeup, her father had indeed recognized his only child? What if he were preparing to have her thrown in prison for the rest of her life before selling the diner? What if his plan was to visit her once a week, just to gloat that he'd won some sick game that only he knew the rules to? What if...

"Just do it!" the only man, who was dressed in all black hissed. "I wanna get outta here before the game's on!"

"Number Three, you can step back!"

A rush of air left her lungs as she willed her body to move.

"You're all dismissed. Thank you for your time and commitment to the safety of Misty Cove. Collect your coupon for a free medium-sized pepperoni pizza, not to be used in conjunction with any other offer or on Tuesdays, from Officer Shaker on your way out."

Although relief swept over her body, she thought she was dreaming until the man shoved her in the back. "Move, lady! Game's on, remember?"

Officer Shaker greeted each of them at the door with a terse nod. As H.P. passed him, she tensed up once more, certain she would be detained.

"I was told there would be drinks included with my coupon!" the mailwoman griped, her breathy voice and sultry demeanor gone. "That's what my neighbor said after he was in a lineup."

H.P. nudged her way past the two of them, tossing her oversized number card at Officer Shaker. The first order of business: the ladies' room. Fear always made her have to go. She paused briefly when she saw her reflection in the mirror. What stared back at her was a defeated woman. A sad, pathetic, defeated woman.

That face wasn't the safety barrier from her father she thought it would be.

Angrily, she tore off the fake nose, the wig, and the clothing until she was scraped and bruised. She stared in the mirror once more, pleased that as imperfect as she looked, her reflection belonged to Honeypie Sweetwater: mother, business owner and kick-butt crime solver.

She held her head higher as she exited the restroom carrying Gwen's costume, or what was left of it. H.P. was clothed only in her pajama shorts and a t-shirt but she didn't care.

"Well, what d'ya know? It's my little Honey Bear!"

Her legs began shaking at the sound of his voice. "Why didn't you choose me in the lineup... um... Sullivan? You might as well play this out all the way. Heck, you and I could share a jail cell. Like father, like daughter."

A strange mix of longing and hatred filled her as she studied his face: a ruddier, more wrinkled version than she remembered. His nose was bulbous and still crooked. Sullivan's chin was covered with a salt-and-pepper beard, a small, angry scar peeking through.

She and her cousins once found hidden family photos when they were supposed to be hauling bags to a local charity. A framed photo fell out of one of the bags. There was Gram Gram as a young mother, looking regal as usual. Her five children knelt in front of her and off to the side was a hollow-eyed Gramps Sweetwater. She swore she'd never forget his face and today she didn't have to. Sullivan Sweetwater looked exactly like his father.

"I had second thoughts about that. Our plans changed and I didn't need that fay-kade anymore."

His smile revealed three missing teeth. Somehow, that misfortune made him appear even more sinister.

"That's not how you use that wor—"

"Did you forget about our date?"

She felt a welcome hand squeezing her shoulder. *Abe.* Always her knight in shining armor."No, I was just freshening up, but I'm ready to go now."

He guided her towards the door. "You were really playing with fire, H.P.!" he whispered. "If you'd said something to upset him, Mr. Sweetwater could have decided to press charges again!"

When they reached the door of Slice, Slice Baby, H.P. paused, turning back to see his face one last time. He was already gone.

Chapter Fourteen

H.P. rubbed her inflamed face with one hand as she loaded straws into a container with the other. Gwen admitted to using an industrial-strength, coroner's glue to attach H.P.'s prosthetic nose and chin to her face when she saw her friend's bright red skin.

"Geez, friendie, why would you yank this stuff off without my help? It's glue used on dead bodies, not the living!"

Someone who came into the diner occasionally was offering her services as an esthetician. Was it Lulu? Or Jessie Lou?

"No, but thanks for your con—"

"Are you on the weed? Your grandmother would be none too happy to know you're running her diner while being high as a kite."

H.P.'s head snapped around. Edna Snarlwood's arm was in the air, likely preparing to deliver one of her loss-of-breath-inducing thwacks to the back to her boss's head.

"I heard you perfectly fine!" H.P.'s cheeks felt hot, and for once, it had nothing to do with embarrassment. At least her face still had circulation. Abe lectured her all the way home about the dangers of both cloaking herself in disguise and trying to have a conversation with her father. When he'd parked, his serious face dissolved and he grinned. "That getup, though. Wow, H.P."

She laughed too, feeling relieved the day was over.

Orders for Minty's pies doubled every week. H.P. joked they should close the diner down and convert the entire space into a kitchen area for him to work his magic. "Mah, oh mah, ma'yam," he began in his laid-back, lyrical Southern drawl. You don't wanna do that. Soonah or laytah, folks in these parts is gonna get tired of old Minty's pies and move on to a new obsession."

She knew he was right; Misty Covians flitted from one "latest rage" to another. She was relieved she didn't have to purchase a macramé kit before the sandal craze finished.

"Don't recall saying anything about the pie orders." Edna huffed in disgust, an act that brought H.P. to tears in her first few months of ownership. Now, she realized it was just part of Edna's charm, if she possessed such a thing.

"I was asking if you ever called that veterinarian lady back."

"Huh?" H.P.'s ears perked up. "Dr. Lotta Kitties?

When did she call? Why? Did she think we took anything? Why haven't you said anything sooner?"

Edna's usual scowl changed into one of... amusement? "Butter biscuits and lard gravy! The days folks ask if you're losing your noodle I tell 'em no. But now I'm starting to wonder." Edna thrust an arm backward and pointed toward the back of the house. "I left the notes beside your office door." A grin, sandwiched between her large, droopy cheeks, looked unnatural.

H.P. opened her mouth to protest but thought better of it.

"You told me your office was your private place and I shouldn't go in. I used a steak knife to attach the pie orders to your door and you said..." Edna's large chest heaved as she took in a deep breath and brought her hands to either hip. "'Edna, are you trying to kill me?' Well, you don't have to say that twice."

"We don't need anymore repair issues. I can't imagine you'd use a steak knife for anything other than a steak while my grandmother was alive." H.P. rolled her eyes. "And I believe I told you that bills belong in the letter box *outside* my door."

H.P. was proud when she came up with that system. Tildie painted dainty, purple flowers on an old schoolbag she'd found in Gram Gram's attic. Dex found hooks to attach it to the wall. After two months in use, the bag remained empty.

Edna emitted a low growl, which meant anything from getting ready to toss an unruly customer out on his ear to running out of chocolate sauce while making her own personal sundae. "Like I'm your office assistant?"

There wasn't any point in arguing. Instead, she walked to her office and paused to scan the floor. Dex's chocolate bar wrappers, H.P.'s old bills, no notes. She formulated excuses in her head before calling Dr. Kitties back. "Oh, I'm so sorry. Gwen found that information under a stack of magazines? *Too cheesy.* "Oh, I'm sorry, Dr. Kitties. One of the kids went into a private space they shouldn't have and I've already lectured them. They'll be returning it today." Was she really going to throw them under the bus? Those two kids had a moral compass that far surpassed hers.

She took a deep breath before dialing the number for Purrgent Care Emergency Animal Clinic.

"This is Lotta speaking."

"Dr. Kitties? This is H.P. Sweetwater. I just wanted to apologize. I... don't have a very exciting life and I thought if I—"

H.P. paused as her eyes fell on a crumpled paper on the floor. The

handwriting, large and loopy, was Edna's. *Call that Dr. Kitkat, for the love of all things! Second time she's called wanting to know how Cinnamon Biscuit Maker is doing.*

"H.P.? You're apologizing for something?"

"I wanted to apologize for giving your clinic the wrong pie. My delivery team sent over an Alibi Apple when the order clearly said you'd ordered a Key Lime Killer."

It was Minty's idea to give his pies spicy names, providing a clear separation from Gram Gram's pies.

"The way the office staff devours those, I'm sure they didn't mind."

A short pause in conversation made H.P. nervous. What if Dr. Kitties asked about the journal? Surely she'd discovered it was missing by now. "You were wondering how Cinnie is doing?"

"Ahh. Yes. I try and check in on all my emergency patients. Is she eating and using the litterbox?"

"Back to her adorable self." Just this morning, she'd jumped into H.P.'s lap and purred while she made her morning biscuits on H.P.'s work dress. H.P. never minded that her uniform was covered in snags.

"Glad to hear it. Make sure you bring her back for her vaccinations next month. Oh, there was one other thing."

H.P. felt her pulse quicken.

"I was wondering if you'd like to meet me for lunch some day?"

This was the second-to-last thing H.P. was expecting to come from her mouth. The last being Lotta's connection to The Dirty Half Dozen Gang. "I... um..."

"No, it's fine," Lotta said firmly. "You don't have to make excuses if you'd rather not. I'm new in town and terrible at making friends. I asked Berniece, who works our front desk, out to lunch, and she left halfway through. She told me later that she needs to be around more upbeat people instead of soul suckers."

"Wow, that's harsh. I'm sorry." H.P. immediately felt sad for this woman whose dark secrets kept her from making real friendships. "I'd be happy to meet you for lunch. Shall we say, Thursday? That's usually a slow day and as long as we go after two p.m., Edna can handle the crowd. Or lack therof."

Lotta giggled. "Okay, it's a date. I've been wanting to try the new Thai place, if that doesn't offend you?"

"No, not at all. We're a small community and we have to support each other. My friend, Thud Punchard and his brothers helped to finance Thai Hard with a Vengeance. See you on Thursday at two!"

As she hung up the phone, a thought struck her: Gwen could return the diary while they were at lunch! It was almost too perfect, she thought giddily.

The smell of baking pies wafted through the diner and up to her nostrils. "That poor man," she commented to herself. "Between making all day scrambles and pie orders, he barely gets to rest."

Minty's eyes were closed, as though he were lost in another time and space. One hand covered his chest and the other bent outward at the elbow, as if he were dancing with an invisible partner. He was humming a tune unfamiliar to H.P. She hated to interrupt. The way he swayed to his music made her wonder who his magical partner could be?

As he danced around the kitchen, his tempo sped up and H.P. wasn't able to step out of the way quick enough before he landed on one of her feet. His eyes snapped open and his magical partner disappeared.

"Oh, ma-yam, Ah'm so, so, sorry!" Minty yanked earbuds from ears partially covered in grey hair. He placed a hand on her arm.

"No, nothing to be sorry for. I should have made my presence known.

You're quite the dancer! Was that a waltz?"

He nodded. "Used to dance with my gal every Saturday at the Twinkle Toes Academy. We won the local dance competition. She was also the love o' my life." His chin dropped. "Least she was 'til she left and old Minty forgot to look at the road sign."

"Huh? Were you hurt in an accident?"

"In a mannah o' speakin.' The road sign said, "Turnah 'round, boy! Nothing good down heyah. Instead, Ah found men who were more lost than me and we created our own gang of sad sacks."

H.P. chuckled. "The Dirty Half Dozen?"

Minty looked at her with distrust, causing a chill to travel down H.P.'s spine.

"No ma-yam. Best not to talk 'bout it in polite comp'knee. We didn't have a name, other 'n bad news. Spent some time in the state prison." He wiped his eyes on his sleeve. "But that was Old Minty. New Minty's as shiny as a brand new penny."

She resisted the urge to hug him. "I'm sorry for your troubles. I don't think any of us get out of this life unscathed." The reason for their conversation popped into her head. "I'm going into the walk-in. To think."

He nodded. It was wonderful that he never questioned her peculiar need to find solace in the walk-in refrigerator. "Oh, Ah can see how hard you and Miz Edna work. All these pie sales are such a burden. From now on, Ah'll take care of them. Everybody will need to pick up their orders either before or after the diner is open. Does that sound awl-right?"

"Yes! Thank you for being so observant. I know Edna especially will be pleased that she doesn't have to miss her favorite podcast, 'Pickled, Pinched and Pricked.' I've never had the courage to ask what that's about."

As soon as H.P. was seated on the overturned pickle bucket, she called to Gram Gram. "Are you here?"

The scent of pies, Gram Gram's pies, and vanilla filled the air. Gram Gram's aura was a dull beige today. That was never a good sign. She floated gently down to face her granddaughter with tears in her eyes. They spritzed H.P. like the light mist from an overhead sprinkler in a greenhouse.

"Hey! That's not nice! And how did you do that?"

"Little trick I learned from Queen Elizabeth the First. Oh, she's a naughty one. She used to tickle the servants she didn't like. Made them think they were going crazy when they felt her invisible fingers on them.

And by the way, I'm mad at you." She crossed her arms and glared at her granddaughter. "Where have you been?"

H.P. thought about the lineup and all that had occurred. "Busy with pie sales is all. I've been helping

Minty because we have so many orders..." Her hand flew up to cover her mouth before she said anything else, but it was too late. Gram Gram had the gist of the conversation.

"I'm sure there's no difference from the way I made them," Gram Gram sniffed. "If folks are suddenly flocking to buy the interloper's pies, then, something's off. I smell curdled milk on this one, Hun Bun."

In order to side-step her grandmother's feelings, she changed the subject. "Did you find Effie?"

"Yes and no. She's currently in the Big Boo Boo Room. I haven't been able to ascertain why, though. I went to the information desk to ask, but Cleopatra and Harry Truman were ankle-deep in their usual argument about how to kill a rattler, and I didn't want to hear THAT again." Gram Gram nodded knowingly at H.P. "Not to worry though. I can use a favor to find her."

"Favor?"

"You know, I used one when I helped you regain the use of your tongue."

Shortly after her arrival in Misty Cove, H.P. bit her tongue and required stitches. Gram Gram used one of her favors and healed it instantly. At the time, she told H.P. she was only given a few lifetime favors so she had to use them with care. "You can't have many left, Gram. I hate for you to waste one."

"Hon, I was able to buy a few from Julia Childs. I think I've mentioned what a suckup she is."

H.P. didn't want to stop the flow of information, so she nodded instead of admitting she had no idea.

"She's been bringing management tarts for decades now," Gram Gram continued. "The big shots are like clarified butter in her hands. I bought a dozen. Well, a baker's dozen. That's thirteen in case you were wondering."

"Gram, I saw my dad. I appeared in a lineup so he could identify his attacker. Luckily, Gwen had me looking like an elderly clown."

"Oh, darling! I'm so sorry! What that must've been like for you!" Gram Gram spread a warmth that encompassed H.P.'s body, almost as good as one of her patented hugs. "At least he didn't recognize you. Not surprising given his lack of interest in anyone in the family when he was around. He's a shell of the bubbly kid I raised."

"How did you know that?"

"Didn't I tell you? Must've slipped my mind. He was here two nights ago. Took the key from my secret spot and let himself in."

The only secret about the location of the spare key was that H.P. put it on a keyring with Cinnie's picture attached.

"He was?" H.P. stood. "Why didn't you tell me sooner?"

"You never asked. Besides, you're under so much pressure right now, it didn't seem wise."

Chapter Fifteen

H.P. was dumbfounded. "My father broke into the diner? Are you positive it was him?"

Gram Gram floated around the walk-in, her long, grey hair waving as though it were under water. "He didn't break in, child. He used the key. And don't you think I'd know my own son?"

H.P. couldn't imagine a day when Dexter's face was unfamiliar to her. "Sorry, Gram. Of course you knew it was him. I wonder why he didn't show up on the cameras? Thud Punchard would have been here in an instant!"

She allowed herself to fantasize: her father, drunk, as usual, and fumbling to get the hidden key in the door. For a guy of his size, Thud was light on his feet. In an instant, he'd be up behind her father, clothes-lining him before he knew what happened.

"You're here to bother H.P.? I don't think so, pal."

"Darling, as much as you'd like the world to take your father to the ground, he appears to be functioning quite well."

H.P. knitted her brows together. "How did you know what I was thinking?"

"Just a little trick I picked up at my dinner party. Houdini gives a class on mind-melding two Thursdays a month, but he agreed to show my dinner guests some tricks of the trade. He's visited a number of livings and enjoyed the chaotic states of their brains."

"Well, I don't like it. Do you remember when I snuck into your bedroom and went through your dresser?"

Gram Gram's aura changed to a blue green. "I got home from work and you'd emptied my fancy perfume bottle all over the floor!"

"You told me that everyone needs a place where they feel safe being themselves. That's when you bought me that gorgeous used wardrobe. I guess it wasn't your fault that Cousin Pepper found the key and locked me inside."

H.P. was half joking. She'd enjoyed being by herself that day. Having so many cousins around her all the time made her feel anxious and, as crazy as it might have sounded to others, she felt comforted by her solitude.

"I'm deeply sorry, my darling. Now, let me tell you about your father." Gram Gram swirled around H.P.'s head before sitting beside her. "He went directly to the storage room, then into the basement."

"We don't have a basement, Gram Gram."

"Yes, we do! I bought this place from a retired Army general, who built a bomb shelter for his family. He'd seen too much tragedy in World War II and wanted to ensure he could keep them safe."

Gram Gram was forever finding new things she'd "forgotten" to tell H.P. Instead of starting an argument, one that was futile with a ghost who didn't have a life, H.P. cut to the chase. "So he went into the basement... and then what?"

"Hun Bun, you know how much energy it takes for me to leave the walk-in, even with a pass. I've been putting everything into plotting my revenge against Effie Plum."

H.P.'s face fell. How was she going to tell the police chief that her father broke in with a key and didn't do anything?

"But I can hang out in the kitchen," Gram Gram continued, as if reading H.P.'s mind. "So I waited. When he came out, he had a bag with him, the type we use to take money to the bank."

H.P.'s mind raced. Had she forgotten to make a deposit? Of course he would steal from her now, when she needed cash to fix her roof. "Do you think that's why he tried to frame me for his attack?"

"Possibly. Lawyers, judges, trials—those aren't really his thing. He'd have you thrown in jail just long enough to clean out his stash, and then say it was all a mistake."

H.P. nodded in agreement. "I still don't understand why he went to the trouble of showing up for a lineup if he didn't intend to accuse me of a crime." Her anxiety eased as she remembered bumping into Booker when she'd made a deposit that night. "And where did the money come from?"

She hated to bring it up, but Gram Gram's denial of her son's criminal history had to end. "Remember when the police chief came to our door? He said the liquor store was robbed and one of the robbers matched the description of your son."

"Humph," Gram Gram snorted. "Everyone in Misty Cove matched that description. My next-door neighbor, Father Foul was a dead ringer."

Another topic that would need clarification... on another day. "Was there anything else that happened while my dad was here?"

"No. Other 'n scaring the living daylights out of him when he walked through the kitchen."

H.P. felt sick. "Oh, Gram. Tell me! Don't leave anything out!"

Gram Gram drew her body up to its full height, twice the size of her living body, and raised her arms dramatically overhead. "Sull-i-van Aloysius Sweet-water!" Her other-worldly voice echoed in the small cooler. "What are you doing in my diner?"

Silver streaks of lightning crackled over Gram Gram's head. Her eyes hardened into dark, shiny marbles as her face appeared taut and old. Her fingers lengthened into wrinkled branches with pointed nails. If H.P. didn't know her grandmother was just as loving in death as she'd been in life, she would have run for her life right about now. It was an impressive display and well worth what it cost Gram Gram to obtain Julia Childs' pass.

"SULL-I–VAN ALOYSIUS SWEET-WATER! DON'T IGNORE ME!"

A strong wind swirled up from the floor of the walk-in, continuing to rise up to the crown of Gram Gram's head. H.P.'s hair danced around her head as the wind changed directions with each pass around Gram Gram's body.

"You're up to no good, son. Drop what you stole and don't come back!"

Lacking a better show of approval, H.P. stood and clapped. "That was magnificent!"

In an instant, Gram Gram was back at her side, looking normal, a friendly apparition surrounded by a pink aura. "Do you think so? I was worried I overdid it. You know, I was quite theatrical in my day."

"You were in one dinner theater season, Gram Gram." H.P. rolled her eyes. "And yes, you were marvelous, but I think just appearing as a ghost is pretty dramatic in and of itself. What happened after that? Did he run scared and take the money with him?"

Gram Gram took one regular-sized finger and made a "Z" in the air. "If he was still the good boy I raised, that's exactly what he would have done. Instead, he laughed at me." Gram Gram placed her hands on her knees and bent down, hovering at the height of

H.P.'s head. The smell of honey pie and vanilla filled H.P.'s nostrils.

Gram Gram lowered her chin and her voice changed from soothing soft tones to... sounding exactly like her father. "'Well, hey there, Honey Bear!' That's when he waved like he was talking to a small child. He thought you'd made some elaborate plan to catch him."

Gram Gram swirled around H.P., her aura becoming a deep purple. "Leave it to MY kid to think this cheesy setup could catch a burglar."

H.P. gasped, unaware of that particular talent of her grandmother and also a little spooked to hear her father's voice for a second time.

"What a creep! What an awful, evil..." H.P. could feel the bile rising up from her stomach. "... And to think I used to daydream about my father coming back for me!"

"All children want to feel loved, my darling. Don't beat yourself up over that. After he said his piece, my son sauntered out the door with his bag of cash. I doubt he even replaced the key. You might want to check on that."

"He didn't take any cash, Gram. I made a deposit. He must've taken something else."

Gram Gram shrugged. "I gave him a burst of hot air before I said, "I know you inside and out. You've always been afraid of ghosts and right now you're as scared as a mouse in a pit full of hungry cats."

"And how did he respond? But please, just tell me

in your normal voice. The other one gives me the willies."

Gram Gram's face displayed a look of rejection. "He said he would always be two steps ahead of you. And there were derogatory comments about the disrespect you were showing me by attempting this farce."

In recalling the few memories H.P. had of her father, one stood out now. It was her first day of kindergarten and the teacher was impressed that the smallest kid in class was already reading, tying her own shoes, and counting to one hundred. All of it was owing to Gram Gram and some ambitious older cousins who liked to play school.

H.P. came home with her chest pumped up, full of pride. When she told her father, expecting him to be pleased by his only child's success, he laughed in her face.

"Oh, kiddo." He ruffled her head harshly with no concern for the tightly woven, tiny braids interspersed with colorful beads that lined her scalp. The next-door neighbor spent an hour creating the intricate braids. "It's all right that the other kids were smarter than you. No need to be making up stories. Leave that to your old dad."

Chapter Sixteen

Traipsing across the green space between the diner and her home, H.P. could barely lift her feet off the ground. The diner was packed all day with tourists, people picking up pie orders, and vacationers who heard about the pies and wanted to take some home with them. The strict, "before or after business hours" instructions fell entirely on deaf ears.

Minty cheerfully greeted each customer, nevertheless.

He'd been great for business. Maybe this year they could take a vacation? Dexter had been bugging her to see the World's Largest Ball of Twine. "Dexie? Dex? Are you home?"

H.P. kicked off her shoes and pulled off her socks before standing on the cool tile floor. An insistent meow that went on far too long alerted H.P. that she wasn't alone. Their sweet, white cat with black splotches rounded the corner, rubbing the wall with her body before greeting H.P. "At least someone is happy to see me! How are you, girl?"

H.P. reached down to rub Cinnamon Biscuit Maker on the head as Cinnie stretched up to meet her hand. After a few satisfying moments for both of them, Cinnie began her meowing again.

"Yes, yes. I know you're hungry and chances are pretty good that Dex didn't feed you."

Cinnie stared up at her with woeful, green eyes before chirping softly. "If it's food you want, our little princess, than food you shall have."

She padded into the kitchen, grumbling about her son's lack of accountability. Soon, though, she was forced to eat her words. The cat food dish was heaped full of a mixture of crunchy squares and fishy-smelling wet food. The water dish was also filled to the rim. "Are you playing games with me, Cinnie?" What was all the fuss—"

H.P. turned around, expecting to see her cat sitting behind her. Instead, she was sitting in the hallway, still meowing. "You're not sick again, are you? Oh, sweetie!"

As she moved towards Cinnie, reaching down to scoop her up, the cat took off in a dead run. "Cinnie! C'mon, girl. Take pity on me! I've been on my feet for twelve hours solid!"

H.P. stepped gingerly into Dex's room, hoping she wouldn't have to dig through the large pile of clothing to find the cat. "Cinnie!" she called. "Let's just snuggle for now, okay?"

A distant meow both relieved and distressed her. Where was she? It wasn't like Cinnie to play these games. She was either hungry, needing a litterbox change or ready for a snuggle: there was no in between.

"Cinnie! Talk to me, pretty girl!" H.P. soothed, hoping to keep the cat engaged. As she entered the guest bedroom, H.P. was surprised to find Cinnie, alternately meowing at her and pacing back and forth in front of the large wardrobe. It had been in the same spot for as long as H.P. could remember.

The rich, oak wardrobe was Gram Gram's pride and joy. She found it at a yard sale when it was scratched up and dented. Every Sunday for two months, she worked to restore it to its original luster. After the last coat of varnish dried, she insisted the wardrobe be placed in the guest bedroom. "Mom," one of her daughters protested, "you worked your fingers to the bone restoring this. Why don't you want it in your own bedroom?"

"Because I want my guests to see that I have talents beyond cooking."

The wardrobe became a favorite hiding spot for the grandchildren. When they played hide-and-seek, the little ones could easily hide behind last season's clothing.

"Peculiar that you'd bring me here, girl."

Her hands shook as she opened the doors. *Why?* Too many years of one cousin or another jumping out and shouting, "Boo!" she guessed. Instinctively, she crawled inside and sat down, shutting her eyes. She drank in the smell of fabric softener and wood finish that still remained after all these decades. That's when another memory hit her.

For days, H.P. sat in front of the big picture window, waiting for her father's return. One day, Gram Gram whispered, "We have to live our lives, child," before taking her hand to lead her to dinner. She crawled into the wardrobe that smelled of Gram Gram's lemon-scented laundry soap. It soothed the ache in her like nothing else.

"You don't have to be afraid, Honeypie," a voice said that day. Thinking it was one of her cousins playing a cruel trick, she snapped, "I'm not afraid of you. Now please leave me alone!"

The sound of a small sneeze jolted H.P. into the present-day world.

"S'cuse me."

H.P. turned the handle, but the door to the wardrobe didn't open. "Hello? Dex? Tildie? Can someone get me out of here?"

"Oh, they're not coming. I learned that the hard way. Achoo!"

H.P. jumped. It all made sense now. Cinnie was alerting her that they weren't alone. Who are you, spirit?"

"My name is Heather."

H.P. spread the clothing apart, trying to see a face

or an aura. "I can't see you. How do I know you're real?"

"I've been calling out to you ever since you were little, Honeypie. You don't see spirits until you're ready to listen."

"Uh-huh." Ghost sightings had become so commonplace that H.P. found them mostly a nuisance. Well, except for Gram Gram. "What is it you want?"

A chirping sound, like a persistent baby bird, filled the air. "You're mad at me. I can tell because you sound just like my mother. 'Don't play in there, Heather. One day you'll get stuck and miss dinner.'"

H.P. pushed the button on her watch, causing it to light up. 8:30. She was more concerned about the location of her son than this whiny child's story.

"And you got stuck one day and died waiting for them to find you. Can you work your magic and get me out of here? I need to check on my son."

Heather chirped again. "You aren't listening." Dex's two-sizes-too-small funeral suit slid to the side before the image of a young girl, probably five or six, appeared.

H.P. gasped when she saw her, this poor child with a purple face and dead eyes. "What happened to you, sweetie? Did you suffocate?"

"No, Honeypie Sweetwater, it was a terrible accident. I liked to hide in here to read, see?"

Heather held up a book entitled, "Birds, Bees and Lots of Trees."

"And?" H.P. asked impatiently.

"I was just about to finish the book when I overheard two people, a man and a woman, come into the room and shut the door. At first, they were whispering, so I had to lean forward to hear. It was a robbery they discussed. When I leaned too hard against the door..." Heather demonstrated by pushing her ghost body on the door. There was no way for her to touch the wood, therefore her demonstration was worthless. "Look up, Honeypie Sweetwater."

Obediently, H.P. tilted her head back. For the first time, she noticed a large box containing a heavy slide projector, teetering precariously on the top shelf. "Oh, no! It didn't—"

"I'm afraid so." Heather pulled back her hair to reveal a nasty wound.

"Did the people in the room try and get you help?"

"No. Sadly, they were more concerned about drawing attention to themselves. They just... left."

H.P. often wished she could hug ghosts, to comfort them when the subject of their deaths came up. This was one of those times. "You poor thing. Do you remember who they were?"

Heather nodded grimly. "You won't like it."

Chapter Seventeen

"Mom, not even my weirdest friends sit inside their closet."

Dexter heard his mother's startled voice just as she was asking Heather for more details about her death. As soon as she heard the front door close, H.P. ended the conversation quickly and was in the process of climbing out of the wardrobe when Dexter found her.

As H.P. brushed slivers of wood from her uniform, Dex stared at her in disbelief. "Do I need to call Auntie G and ask her to run one of her mad scientist tests on your brain?"

"I know, it seemed like a comfy place to gather my thoughts and I just fell asleep." She forced a laugh. "Guess I learned my lesson. Next time, I'll make sure I sleep somewhere without a lock."

He tilted his head and viewed her with skepticism.

"Whatever. I came home from Tildie's to tell you we've cracked the rest of the code!"

"Oh, really?" She took one last glance inside for any lingering evidence of Heather.

"Tell me what you found!" she said, only pretending to listen. Her mind was stuck, reliving Heather's revelation, one that would take time to process. No one else needed to know in the meantime.

"Oh, man. There were detailed blueprints of future bank heists, including dates, times, and the names of her accomplices."

"Who were her accomplices?"

Dex punched her playfully in the shoulder, causing H.P. to wince in pain. His early morning trips to the gym with Tildie were really paying off. "Mom, get this. Dr. Kitties was in a gang called, The Dirty Half Dozen. They robbed thirteen banks and supposedly gave all the money to poor people."

The hairs on the back of H.P.'s neck stood straight up. "Supposedly?"

"Well, she didn't mentioned any specifics about giving the money away. At least, not that we found."

"Oh." H.P. didn't try hiding the disappointment in her voice. "I was rooting for her to be a good person."

"There's way more. She gave away all the safehouse locations where they hid after the robberies."

H.P. took the grease-stained paper from Dex and made a face as she held it at arm's length. "That's the last time I buy Greasy Grady's barbecue chips. You might as well eat handfuls of lard, son. It would be cheaper for me."

"Mom!" he protested. "Can't you stop being a... mother... for a minute and look at what we uncovered?"

"Dex, this is so—"

"Cool, right? I can't believe we did this! Well, mostly Tildie. But I made no-bake bars and helped decode some of the last entry. And guess what? Dr. Kitties was planning another heist!"

"I was going to say this is so invasive. The diary is Dr. Kitties' private property. But now that you've told me she's planning another robbery, you've got my interest. When is this going to take place?"

She brushed the dust from her uniform and motioned for Dex to follow her to her bedroom. Lying on her bed, she feared she was so tired she couldn't get back up, but she was willing to take the risk.

They flopped on her light green comforter with a pink daisy pattern simultaneously.

"Okay, go. I can't guarantee I'll be alert much longer."

"The only evidence Dr. Kitties included is a nursing home in Tellum, Oregon. And an anonymous donation of $10,000 for a new air conditioning system. The gang went to prison, those that survived, and the loot is hidden somewhere here in Misty Cove. Isn't that cool? Misty Cove is way more exciting than San Francisco. We never found cool stuff like this!"

The excitement in Dex's voice made H.P. happy

for him. Other than video games, very little captured his undivided attention. She didn't have the heart to tell him he'd already shared this evidence. "And which part was Dr. Kitties'? Was she in prison, or is she back in town to find the hidden money?"

Lotta Kitties looked like she was H.P.'s age, making her a child when the robberies took place. It didn't make any sense. Especially the part about donating money to the nursing home.

"It didn't say in the diary. It's written in third person."

H.P. stared at him quizzically.

"That's what Tildie said," he replied, as if reading her mind.

"Was there any description of the robberies? Did they hurt anyone?" Her voice wavered as she remembered poor Heather's swollen face. "I mean, it would be terrible if she were describing something like that."

"I don't think so, but Tildie is still trying to finish decoding the last entry."

H.P breathed a sigh of relief. "Well, that's good. I'd hate to think my own father—" She stopped short of telling her son about her suspicions. Dexter was just a kid and as such, didn't need to burden himself with that ugliness. He'd only asked a few questions about his grandfather and H.P. told him she'd only known him when she was a toddler. She claimed she didn't have any real memories of him.

"What I meant to say was that if any of this gang

that got away with it had family members, I'm sure they'd know something. Were any names given?"

Dex rolled over and rested his chin on his hands. "These guys used code names and they were just hilarious. Let's see if I can remember... Nine Nails Nora, Phat Wallet Phyllis, Shady the Shiv," Dex stopped to laugh. "Who comes up with these names?"

"They didn't have the convenience of the internet then, son."

"Tildie's dad is going to the police with this information tomorrow," Dexter continued with pride in his voice. "Mr. Bunce trusts our deciphering skills. He wants you to meet him there at 1:30."

H.P. propped herself up on her elbows and stared at Dex, wide-eyed and incredulous. "And when were you going to tell me that? Son, we have to work on your burying the lead every time there's something I need to know. Besides, the lunch rush isn't over until closer to two. Abe will have to handle this on his own."

Dex turned and jumped up with little effort, smacking the top of the door frame. "I'm going to take my shower now."

"Really?" Her voice rose. "I mean... of course you are... without my telling you..."

"You finish reading," he gestured toward the greasy page in her hand. "You're gonna be real surprised."

Chapter Eighteen

H.P. glanced up to find her son standing in the doorway with wet hair dripping on the floor. "We do have towels, right? I know I washed some on Sunday."

Dexter huffed and turned to leave.

"Wait!" The older he got, the less time he offered her without complaint. Ever since she'd accused him of dismantling Gram Gram's antique table, things had been cold between them. "I was reading your decoded pages. I'm so impressed!"

"Really?" He moved to the table and sat down beside her. She didn't even mind that his hair was making a puddle on Gram Gram's oak table.

She pointed to the paragraph she was reading. "Lotta spends a lot of time talking about guilt. It's hard to imagine she's old enough to have taken part in the robberies, but as often as she mentions a young girl, I have to wonder if she was a child who was watching a parent?"

Although H.P. had absolute faith in Tildie's deciphering skills, this could all be a product of two kids' fervent imaginations. Lotta may have robbed some banks and used The Dirty Half Dozen as a sort of how-to guide or at least witnessed them as a child, but she was no murderer.She continued reading:

> *Misty Cove Briberies:*
>
> *Chief Environmental Inspector Walter Moose*
> *Position: Head of the Environmental Compliance Division*
>
> *Reason to Bribe: Chief Moose makes frequent visits to towns up and down the Washington Coast. His main focus is protecting wildlife living next to financial institutions but contacted B.S. after a robbery and said he had a clear shot of his plates. Agreed to delete the photo in exchange for monthly payments.*

The next one took H.P.'s breath away. She blinked twice and then looked again. "Gram Gram?"

"Gram, you'd better start at the beginning!"

H.P. bounced her fuzzy, blue slipper nervously as

she perched on the overturned pickle barrel. Her soft, pink robe was belted tightly at her waist and she hadn't bothered combing her hair. That was a mess better left for daylight. "Why were you listed as a business bribed by The Dirty

Half Dozen Gang? And why haven't you told me about this before?"

When she'd read Gram Gram's name on the bottom of the greasy page her son handed her, H.P. knew it would be a sleepless night if she didn't confront her grandmother immediately. "Well? I'm waiting!"

Tonight, Gram Gram's aura was a fitting midnight blue. H.P. had come to recognize this color for the mystery and darkness that followed. Gram Gram swirled slowly and deliberately around the cooler like a wisp of heavy smoke before settling beside H.P.

"There was a time when The Honeypie Diner served as an unofficial information hub, where local gossip flowed more freely than the coffee."

"That's still the case." H.P. prided herself on providing a service to the community—where Read It and Weep Book Club met on Thursdays; Stitch, Please! Knitting Group met on Saturday afternoons; and Good Deeds & Good Feeds Rotary Group always requested she order extra hamburger meat for their once-a-month meetings.

"I'm proud of what I created," Gram Gram said. "I can't count the number of times I overheard secrets being shared over a cup of coffee and an Edna Special."

It wasn't the right time, but just like the news that Gram Gram's name was on a list of people The Dirty Half Dozen could bribe, H.P. knew she wouldn't sleep if she didn't ask. "What was the Edna Special? I don't recall seeing that on any menu?"

Gram Gram cleared her throat before reciting: "Peppery Pulled Pork with a side of Thrice-Spiced Slaw, packed with extra hot mustard and tangy vinegar, guaranteed to make your eyes water—just like one of Edna's withering glares."

"Okay, I've got to implement that! Five Meal Gary has been asking for barbecue!"

"That man and his superhuman stomach," Gram lamented. "We just told people about it and didn't put it on the menu because we only made it when the smoker worked."

H.P. glanced up at her grandmother, who was doing dolphin flips on the ceiling. This new habit was becoming irritating. "I'm still waiting for an explanation about the bribery."

"Do you remember the year you got your braces?"

"Vaguely. I usually try to block out the taunts— metal mouth, zipper jaws, human paperclip— it wasn't a favorite time in my life. Why?"

"Because the diner was struggling at that time and my car was on the spitz. I didn't want you to feel bad about crooked teeth, but those braces, Hun Bun, they just about broke me."

"You mean the fritz."

Gram Gram's apparition swirled in a tornadic

circle, taking a downward motion until it was inches from H.P.'s face.

"Sorry!" she whispered into the tornado. It was like she was ten again and trying to apologize for putting an entire box of laundry soap in the washing machine. "No disrespect intended!"

"Neither here nor square, child."

H.P. would let that one pass. Her chest felt heavy, thinking about how much she complained about her mouth full of hardware. *I want them off, Gram Gram! You're so mean for forcing me to wear them!*

"I was in desperate need of cash," Gram Gram continued. "One evening while I was cleaning the floor, a table in the back refused to leave. A man and a woman, both with negative energy surrounding them. You know your old Gram Gram is never afraid of anything!"

"You were my hero. We cousins could always count on you to step in and support us."

"I finally got the nerve to tell them I was closing, and that's when the woman pulled a huge wad of cash out of her pocket. She wanted to meet with Mr. No Smile once-a-week, no questions asked, no time limit. Clients would come and go, and I wasn't to ask questions." Gram Gram sighed. "I thought Elvis himself had ascended from heaven to help me."

H.P. swallowed hard. She'd had some lean years when she couldn't seem to keep a chef's job. Dex's father only sent child support when he felt like it, which wasn't often. She knew exactly how her grand-mother felt and she wished she could still hug her.

"I'm not judging you, Gram Gram," H.P. whispered as a tear rolled down her cheek. "I just wanted to know why. And how did that evolve into a robbery?"

Gram Gram's kind face became clouded and stern. "For another day. Tonight is a dinner party and bridge at Mr. Hendrix's home. Betsy Ross, and..." Gram Gram attempted to snap her fingers, but instead a puff of air hit H.P.'s forehead. "Fiddlesticks. I forgot to find a fourth. We'll talk tomorrow, my darling girl."

H.P. stood and adjusted the fuzzy tie on her purple robe. "I'm sorry you were in that position. My father should have sent money for my care. I know you still think of him fondly, but after he said I hurt him and now hearing this, I don't ever want to see him again."

Chapter Nineteen

The next day seemed to drag on longer than the Sea What's Up text chain discussing the best place for a second stoplight in Misty Cove. H.P. didn't want to get lost in a mindless conversation with a customer and forget, so she glanced up at the fork and knife arms of the big clock as often as she remembered.

"You gonna make a run for it, or is a certain lawyer waiting at your place for a mattress mambo?"

As Edna purposely pushed past H.P., an egg yolk slid over the side of the breakfast plate she was holding. It narrowly missed H.P.'s uniform before sliding gently back to the center of the plate.

"Hey! Be careful with that!" H.P. snapped. "The price of eggs has gone through the roof!" H.P. cleared her throat before she regained control of her temper. "I have an appointment. I told you that when I got here this morning, Edna."

She could never tell if Edna's memory issues stemmed from lack of interest or failing ability. Gram Gram never lost a beat in her waning years, but H.P. was well aware of others who had.

"I kinda thought you'd set an alarm on your phone like a normal person would," Edna snapped, reading her thoughts. "Or maybe you're not up on your technology as well as I am."

That jab would pass unheeded.

When it was finally 1:15, H.P. tossed her apron on the counter. "Gotta run. I have confidence in you and Minty that this place will shine like never before!"

As she walked briskly toward the police station, it occurred to her that the remains of the kale salad she'd eaten for lunch may have still been caught between her teeth. No time for beauty now.

Maeviz only glanced up from her book momentarily, a bodice ripper complete with a nearly-naked man on the cover entitled, *Roman's Romp*.

"Yeah?" she asked without sparing H.P. the courtesy of a glance in her direction.

"I'm here to see Chief Danno."

H.P. was out of breath and that was okay. She wasn't used to a serious jog, not since college when she took up running as a way to impress Eliot Jenkins, Dex's absentee father. While he appeared interested in the sport, the fact remained he hadn't ever managed anything speedier than a brisk walk to the keg of beer at their parties.

"She's busy." Maeviz licked one finger before

turning the page. When H.P. didn't move, Maeviz expelled a loud sigh with such force it sounded like a wounded dog.

"I'd like to report a crime. Several crimes, actually."

"Oh, yeah? We've got a process for that." Maeviz stuck one arm out sideways and pointed randomly, her eyes still trained on her book. "Down the hall and to the left. You might have to wait until Sargent Pen comes back from lunch. He tends to linger over his soup. We're still working on improving his work ethic."

The irony of her statement was lost on lazy Maeviz. "No, this is something big," H.P. insisted, determined to get this woman's attention even if she had to spice up her story to do so. "This might possibly even involve the FBI."

Finally!

Maeviz glanced up, her face showing a mixture of amusement and annoyance. "I hear that at least ten times every week. Everybody thinks they've uncovered the crime of the century. If I had a twenty dollar bill for every time I heard, 'My neighbor's garage has—'"

"Bank robberies. Thirteen of them. I have proof of everything."

As though she'd been listening through the crack, Chief Danno's door flew open so fast it created a rush of warm air. "Ms. Sweetwater? Come in."

Chapter Twenty

"Please sit down," Chief Booker Danno said in a deep, velvety voice that could have been used in a sleeping aid commercial. She leaned back in her brand-new, plump, blue office chair and gestured to H.P. to sit in the other.

"Thank you. I'm not in the habit of saying things like this because I know how difficult it is to find help, but your secretary needs more instruction in proper communication. Her skills are... somewhat lacking."

Booker nodded vigorously in agreement. "I made the unfortunate decision to imbibe in too much Sassy Lasses Rebel Riesling one night at a party. I made an even worse decision to challenge a friend to a bow and arrow shooting contest. With far too much bravado, I agreed to employ my friend's difficult niece if I lost."

H.P. tried to picture Booker losing control. If anything, this woman needed to loosen up a bit and show the world she had a personality.

Shaking her head, Booker continued, "Obviously, I lost. Maeviz has since told me she's an expert with the bow and arrow, and that her parents own the country club where I made my mistakes."

"You were totally set up!" H.P. said. "That's not right. You aren't bound by any laws to keep her." H.P. didn't know that for sure, but it sounded right.

"I still hang out with my friend—sober these days —and I guess I value her friendship too much to boot Maeviz out of a job."

H.P. nodded sympathetically. "When I lived in San Francisco, I worked at a restaurant called Spit. We roasted all our meats, thus the strange name. The boss lived half the year in Hawaii, so he installed his nephew as manager while he was away, thinking this kid would be his eyes and ears. Instead, he hosted parties every weekend after we closed. When we arrived the next morning, the place looked like it'd been looted. There was garbage everywhere and bottles of alcohol, broken and empty. There was nothing we could do."

"What brings you in today, Ms. Sweetwater? Did I overhear you say you had personal knowledge of a bank robbery?"

Her keen interest felt odd, especially given Maeviz's easy dismissal. "You'll probably think I'm crazy, but please, bear with me."

Booker chuckled. "Almost every case begins with that sentence.

Please, tell me everything." She leaned back in her chair, touching her fingertips together.

Booker's intense gaze made all the air in the room disappear. H.P. felt the heat rising up from her neck and filling her cheeks.

As she recited the story of the diary, a strange thing happened. The tenseness she felt got heavier instead of lighter. Booker didn't try to help, but leaned forward and stared intently at H.P. If this was the usual way she interrogated people, H.P. could see how easily they'd crack.

"My... um... friend was looking for the restroom at Purrgent Care and found a diary on the ground, outside Dr. Kitties' office. 'Ben' loves deciphering codes in his spare time and..." H.P. opened her purse and slid the information across the desk.

Chief Danno picked it up and read it over quickly. The corners of her mouth rose slightly. "I can understand why you'd be concerned." Booker opened up the top drawer of her desk and pulled out a small recording device. "This is just between us, Ms. Sweetwater. I feel like I can trust you."

H.P. suppressed the urge to ask why and merely nodded.

"I'd like you to record any further conversations with Ms. Kitties. Just clip it to the inside of your shirt, like this."

She demonstrated what to do on her own top button, as though it were a small microphone she were connecting. "You see? It sends recorded information to an app I have that I download periodically."

Not only was the chief taking her seriously, but she

also respected H.P. enough to ask for her help. It was much more than H.P. expected and made her a little embarrassed to have doubted her. "Thank you for your understanding, Chief! I was worried you wouldn't believe me!"

"I take all reports of crime very seriously. Was there anything else?"

H.P. thought back to the child ghost in the wardrobe. "Yes. I can probably research this for myself, but would you have access to any information about the murder of a child? It happened at least thirty years ago."

Booker nodded as she crossed her arms over her chest. "I can look. That seems like a big deal and if I can't find anything, you most certainly will find it in the newspaper archives at the library." She stood and opened her door. "It's admirable when citizens come in with this kind of information at the risk of their own safety." She smiled, a reaction that creased her normally stoic face in an odd way. "Was there anything else?"

This conversation, while going well—too well, perhaps—was ending far too soon. Didn't she want to know how they decoded the diary? Didn't she want the diary so the lab could confirm their translation? And where was Abe? He was the only reason she came there. "If you need more information from me, I'm happy to—"

Booker touched H.P.'s back lightly. "I know where to find you, Ms. Sweetwater. I'll be very interested in listening to any further conversations with Dr. Kitties.

Of course the child you're speaking of is important as well."

They both stepped out of the office, H.P. feeling a little guilty at the thought of secretly recording Lotta Kitties.

Maeviz emitted another loud, long sigh. Maybe she had a digestive issue?

It was a relief to know that Chief Danno's intense gaze was trained on someone else.

"Maeviz Dull, how many times have I asked you to put your books away? This is a place of business!" Chief Danno's tone was icy, barely above a whisper, but severe enough to make H.P. glad it wasn't she who deserved the scolding.

Instead of apologizing to her boss, Maeviz kept the book in her hands, tilting her chin upward in a clear act of defiance. H.P. was almost impressed. It took guts, or maybe ignorance to speak to the police chief like that, even if Maeviz was only there because the chief lost a bet.

"There's no one here."

"This is your last warning, Maeviz. If I catch you reading on my time again, you're out."

Without a moment of hesitation, Maeviz continued, "Oh, and you have a call on line one. Something about the body found in the lake."

H.P. paused.

Booker turned and slammed her door shut, causing both H.P. and Maeviz to jump.

When H.P. turned to Maeviz looking for a reaction, the young woman raised one brow slightly. "What?" Maeviz asked innocently. "She was in a meeting and I'm not supposed to bother her when she's in a meeting."

"What did they say, Maeviz? Spill it!"

Maeviz stuck her tongue in the side of her cheek. "How much is this information worth to you?"

Letting out her own sigh of frustration, H.P. dug into her pocket. She slammed everything she had on Maeviz's desk, knocking her next read, *Wind on the Planes, a Story of a Real Blow Hard*, onto the ground. "Fourteen dollars and twenty-three cents."

"I want a free lemon pie. With plenty of that fluffy topping."

"Deal. Come in tomorrow after you're done here and it will be waiting. Now tell me everything."

Maeviz leaned forward as though she were gossiping with a friend. "Well, the body in the lake was finally identified. It was a woman wanted for bank robbery from like, before I was even born. She was part of a donut gang or something."

"The Dirty Half Dozen?" H.P.'s voice rose unnaturally high. "What was her name? Tell me!"

Maeviz shrugged, reverting back to her noncommittal self. "Dunno. Nine Nails Nora, maybe? The FBI lab in Seattle said she was the only member of the gang to escape."

"Why would she return to Misty Cove after all these years?"

"Dunno. Probably has something to do with the hidden money everyone talks about."

Before H.P. could question her further, a loud sound was heard. It was... the sound of crying—sobbing, actually—and it was coming from behind Booker's door. Knowing this woman's stern demeanor, it seemed out of character for her to break down at her job. Was Nora someone close to her?

H.P. turned back to Maeviz. "What else did they say? Think!"

"Maeviz!"

H.P. whipped around. Booker stood in her doorway, completely composed. Maybe H.P. had been wrong to assume she was crying. Except the sound of pain was one she knew well. Too well.

"We're going to have a discussion about what is appropriate for work."

Maeviz slammed her book on her desk. "Last week, you told me I could read when I was done for the day."

"I told you that you could go and read AT HOME. That's different from reading at work."

Chief Danno picked up one of the books and stared at the image of two half-clad people with disgust. "I'll keep these in my locked drawer until the end of your workday."

She gave H.P. a knowing look. "Thank you for coming, Ms. Sweetwater."

Something was off. She'd have to investigate Chief Danno further, but for now, she needed to talk to

Gwen. And Abe. H.P. was slightly hurt that Gwen didn't come to her first when the body was positively identified.

The Final Fold Dry Cleaners was full to the brim with customers. She waved to Gwen from the rear of the tiny lobby. Gwen pushed a dark chunk of her hair out of her eyes and waved back to her friend. She motioned for H.P. to come to the counter.

"Hey! I've been here for thirty minutes! Why does the diner lady get to cut in front of me?"

H.P. ignored the unhappy customers and pushed her way up to the counter. Gwen leaned over and whispered in her ear, "I know why you're here, bestie. Nora Danopolis was positively identified last night. Cause of death wasn't drowning, but a knife in the back. I had to wait until the toxicology report came back, but now I can say with confidence that she died from two stab wounds, one in the back of the neck and one between her shoulder blades. Bled out. I'll be over tonight and we can discuss it further."

"Sassy Lasses Rebel Riesling?" H.P. asked.

"I'll pick up the wine, you call in pepperoni and pineapple," Gwen agreed.

H.P. turned to leave.

"Oh, and bestie?" Gwen asked, irritating the customer closest to H.P. He responded by uttering, "Save your girl talk for after hours!"

"Yes?" H.P. asked, using every ounce of self control to keep from rolling her eyes.

"I've never seen a knife that can make wounds like that. Whoever killed her either butchers their own meat or has a really sick hobby."

Chapter Twenty-One

Wilma, the receptionist at Fulla, Bunce and Vinegar greeted H.P. warmly. "Ms. Sweetwater! How nice to see you! Mr. Bunce is finishing up with a client. I'm sure he'll be out momentarily." Wilma gestured toward a plush, brown chair. "If you'd like to have a seat while you wait, I can get you some coffee or tea. Of course, nothing holds a candle to The Honeypie Diner though."

H.P. blushed as the warmth of Wilma's words washed over her. "Thank you, Wilma. I appreciate hearing that. We just changed coffee providers."

Wilma nodded. "Mr. Bunce told me all about the documents that were decoded. Your son and Tildie are really making waves at the high school! When I was their age, the only code I cracked was on the back of a cereal box."

"Oh?" H.P. took a small sip of the coffee Wilma

had poured. Ooh. *It was wonderful.* Far superior to the coffee at The Honeypie Diner. Edna would throw a hissy fit if she suggested changing vendors again so soon. The most recent vendor was her nephew. He displayed the same permanent look of disgust as his aunt, something H.P. could do without.

"Yes! It's all anyone can talk about in our breakroom."

H.P. didn't feel comfortable to have this news spread all over a breakroom or Boog R. Noseinair High School. Misty Cove was a small town, and eventually, it would get back to Dr. Kitties.

"Those two would make great explorers, wouldn't they?" Wilma continued, "I heard they found a diary that might lead to—"

"Ms. Sweetwater?"

H.P. had been thinking about how she would pay to bail Gwen out of jail when the news hit the police station. "How long have you been standing there, Abe?"

"Long enough to hear that my daughter is brilliant," he chuckled. "But I already knew that. Would you step into my office?"

Gladly.

Just as he always did, Abraham Bunce exuded a delicious smell, a combination of the deep woods and citrus. Tildie said it was called "Man-Lee" and she'd chosen it for him when she was four. "It's supposed to attract the babes," she'd said innocently.

H.P. slid back in the smooth leather chair, her bare

legs screeching as they moved against the surface. She explained everything she'd told the chief and ended by showing him the recording device. Abe furrowed his brow as he turned it over and over in his smooth hands. "Hmm. Looks to me like a child's toy. I've had my doubts about this new chief ever since she got to town."

H.P. swallowed hard. How could she have been so stupid? The chief didn't take her seriously at all. Instead, she'd pacified a worried woman with a toy. Booker Danno must be laughing hard. She might even have told Maeviz, and the two women finally found something to bond over.

"Don't feel bad," Abe said as if he were reading her thoughts. "The only reason I know is because I had a case last month where my client was accused of using toy guns, explosives and recording devices to pretend he was law enforcement. It was hard for me to appear in court with a straight face."

"That woman made a fool out of me. Booker didn't believe a word I said. I was... hoping you'd have been there to make sure I didn't do something dumb."

H.P. crossed her legs and hugged her body. She felt like she was back in grade school and her father had just abandoned her. Instead of being supportive, the kids in her class called her Sour Honey. Gram Gram insisted there was no such thing, but she talked to the principal all the same.

Abe glanced up at a large, gold-faced clock on the wall behind H.P.'s head. "Oh, boy. I'm so sorry, H.P. I completely lost track of time. I had a client who stayed an hour longer than I anticipated. She's suing her ex-husband for theft after he took all of her nana's casserole recipes." Abe sighed. "She had to discuss every single recipe and its meaning to her family. Tuna Casserole Supreme wouldn't seem like a reason to go through my entire box of tissues, would it?"

H.P. giggled like a schoolgirl and quickly brought her hand to her mouth. "I shouldn't laugh. I'm sure they're important to her, just like Gram Gram's pie recipes are to me."

"That goes without saying, H.P."

He leaned against his desk, clasping his hands together. "I'll be honest, I had my reservations about going to see Booker with you. I asked to be on the hiring team for our new police chief and I was summarily dismissed. No one would tell me why. I made the mistake of telling my daughter, and one afternoon while she was waiting for me, she accessed Wilma's computer and got on the city's website. She found Booker's application, or rather, what it should have been."

"I don't understand, Abe."

"The application contained her name and phone number. That's it! An extensive background check and three pages of questions are contained with all the other applications. I've been trying to find answers ever since."

H.P. realized that despite recent developments, she was beginning to like Booker Danno. Knowing that she was not only a liar but also a crooked police chief hurt H.P.'s heart.

"At the very least, she should have asked you for the diary," Abe continued. "The fact that she didn't, means—"

"That she's got another copy?"

"I was going to say that she's aware of its existence. But two can play at this game."

He dug inside the top drawer of his desk and pulled out a tiny microphone. "One of my clients used this for, let's say *creative purposes*." He winked at H.P. "How about you record the veterinarian with an actual recording device? Let's see what she has to say that Chief Danno is so afraid of. Not to pressure you, but we'll need all the ammunition you can gather."

"Abe, do you think... they're both connected to these robberies in some way?"

Chapter Twenty-Two

"I'm always fascinated by what brings people to Misty Cove," H.P. remarked while sipping blackberry iced tea slowly through a green-striped straw. She and Abe had gone through a list of questions she could ask the veterinarian without sounding suspicious. However, if she were being totally honest, she wasn't concentrating so much on the questions as she was on Abe Bunce.

One thing she did remember: it was important to draw out their lunch as long as possible, not only to figure out why Chief Danno wanted a recording of Lotta Kitties but also to give Gwen time to return the diary.

"Just the usual. I found a job here and I took it." Lotta mirrored her actions. The poor woman was just as nervous as H.P. obviously. Neither looked the other in the eye.

"I don't see you out and about much. You must be

in hiding," H.P. said without thinking. She added a nervous laugh to soften the blow.

Lotta frowned as her gaze shifted to H.P. "What is that supposed to mean?"

"Oh... I didn't mean... it's just that Misty Cove is so small, we run into each other all the time whether we want to or not."

Nice save, Sweetwater. H.P. felt a lone drop of sweat trickling down the center of her back.

"Oh." Lotta's shoulders relaxed. "I get my groceries early in the morning or late at night in order to avoid my patients' angry owners. I'm not one for socializing, but I felt an instant connection to you the other day." She shook her head. "I decided to take a chance and see if we could form a friendship. That's how it's done, right?"

H.P. studied Lotta's face. It was tense, perhaps because she didn't want to divulge her criminal past. But H.P. didn't get that vibe from Lotta. Poor woman. She must feel so alone. Even if she were a criminal, she was still a human being.

"That's *exactly* how it works, Lotta. Once you know one of us, the others will follow suit. And now we have to get through the perfunctory stuff. First, tell me about your family. Any siblings?"

Two steaming bowls arrived as Lotta opened her mouth to speak. They ordered the same Revenge of the Drunken Noodles, thick noodles drenched in a rich, brown sauce with crispy vegetables, which H.P. took as a good sign.

"Hey, I know you!" the waitress grinned, squeezing H.P.'s shoulder.

"You own The Honeypie Diner! We went there every Saturday for breakfast when I was a kid. Good memories."

"It's a Misty Cove tradition!" H.P. replied cheerily. She waited for the waitress to leave before she leaned across her salad and whispered, "See what I mean?"

Lotta broke into an easy smile. This woman she'd assumed was a devious bank robber plotting to take down their community was really just horribly, painfully shy.

"You were preparing to tell me about your family. You know—siblings, that one aunt you hope never shows up when you have friends over, et cetera..."

Lotta smiled for a second time, this time nodding with enthusiasm. "More like a crazy father and a sister who never liked me."

She stared down at her salad as she brought one tiny bite to her mouth. "I shouldn't say anything about my family. It's a complicated—"

H.P. began to choke on a frozen blackberry hidden in her iced tea and Lotta immediately jumped to her aid, thrusting H.P.'s arms in the air. Eventually, the blackberry popped out and landed on the floor. Everyone in the restaurant clapped as though they'd just witnessed performance art at its finest.

"Thanks!" H.P. whispered when her voice allowed. "It helps having a doctor nearby."

"All mammals have the same basic parts," Lotta

said as she shrugged with nonchalance. "You asked about my family and I'm scared to tell you. Why ruin the beginning of a friendship?"

"No, Lotta. Every family has its skeletons." H.P. insisted. "My own father forced me to appear in a lineup because he wanted to humiliate me. The man was attacked, but I wasn't the one who attacked him. There are more skeletons in my closet than clothes. You don't have to tell me anything, though, not if it makes you uncomfortable."

H.P. reached into her purse and pulled out her wallet. Time to leave before things got tense. As much as she hated disappointing Abe, she didn't want to pressure Lotta. They could meet again and things would be less strained.

"Are you familiar with the Bucksa Cheapskate Savings and Loan?"

H.P. didn't want to share that her grandfather waited in the bank parking lot and stole from cars with unlocked doors. Her cousins wore it as a badge of honor that he was never caught. Gram Gram refused to talk about it. "I think I've heard of them. There's one in Tellum, right?"

"Yes. We went from not having enough to eat to my father owning banks in one year. He brought us to a mansion that would become my prison for the remainder of my childhood."

"Reminds me of those bank robbers, The Dirty Half Dozen. Have you ever heard of them?"

Lotta's eyes darted back and forth. "No."

"Your father kept you as a prisoner? That's awful. How did you escape?"

H.P. lifted her fork and began picking at the remnants of her noodles. Her stomach was full to the point of exploding, but she didn't want Lotta to stop talking. It also occurred to her that Abe's recording device was picking up her not-so-ladylike slurping sounds.

"Forgive me, but why were you kept inside the gates?" she asked when Lotta didn't reply. "And how did you go to school?"

"Tutors. Mostly experts in their subjects. My sister and I got the best education money could buy. Unfortunately, that led us to believe there was something beyond the wrought iron gates surrounding our home." Lotta clucked her tongue.

"On the rare occasions he agreed to let us leave for an afternoon, the guards came with us. One day, as we finished our rocky road ice cream cones, my sister asked why we had a guard when none of the other kids around us did. He told us that our dad was a loan shark, and that meant people were always looking for ways to hurt us." She shook her head. "And they say animals are wild. At least they understand how to treat each other."

"How did you escape? Is that the right way to ask?"

"Yes, I *did* escape. I'd researched the college of my dreams online and after I achieved a perfect score on the entrance exam, the advisor gave me detailed instructions on how to escape. We planned for a Saturday night when the security detail were all playing poker. Just as I'd reached the window to climb out, my sister caught me."

"Was she mad?" H.P. asked.

"At first she was. She always asked a million questions and this night was no different. She was questioning me when my father overheard us and yelled up the stairs, telling us he was going to come up and discipline us if we didn't pipe down. My sister told me to leave quickly. So I did."

Lotta took a long drink "My advisor was waiting for me exactly a mile from our home. And that was when my REAL education began."

H.P.'s phone buzzed and she glanced down and read quickly before Lotta became curious:

> Book returned to library. Pie may exit.

> She smiled, remembering the silly way Gwen insisted they communicate. I know you'll be anxious to get out of this lunch situation, given all that you know about that woman now. I'll send you a text when I'm out and it's safe to leave. Don't worry, it won't take long. 😉

H.P. slid her phone into the pocket of her dress. "Sorry. I get these weird wrong number texts all the time. Why do you think your sister didn't like you? She saved your life that night, didn't she?"

Lotta nodded. "I tried staying in touch with her over the years, but she never responded. I gave up when I realized she didn't want to be in my life. I can understand why."

H.P. leaned forward and touched Lotta's cold and clammy hand. "Don't beat yourself up for taking care of yourself. I'm sure that by now she's forgiven you and moved on."

"For the first time in my life, I saw things through a different lens," Lotta continued." My father dealt not just with gangsters but also people drowning in the interest he charged them. Families ended up homeless when they were unable to pay his exorbitant fees." She clucked her tongue again. "I tracked down one family where both parents worked two jobs. The husband became ill and lost his jobs, and my father didn't care. My advisor, the one who saved me, found them living on the streets, so we started a fundraiser to help them. That's where I got my last name, you know."

Lotta scooped up the last of the thick noodles and somehow placed them delicately into her mouth. "I'm proud to say, along with business donations, we raised enough money to get them a house. I legally changed my last name from Cheapskate to Kitties, after Stray, Darling and their daughter, Manx."

Lotta really WAS a modern-day Robin Hood. "There's so much more I'd like to ask you, Lotta."

They both looked up at the big clock hanging above the entrance to Thai Hard with a Vengeance.

"Shoot," Lotta said. "I've got a full afternoon—three spays and an eye removal." She stood abruptly, causing her purse and its contents to spill on the floor.

H.P. jumped up and began scooping up lipstick, gum, two protein bars, and said, "Who's Frances Fudge?" A driver's license with the picture of a red-headed woman wearing very large, square, black-rimmed glasses stared back at her. It was issued in the state of Idaho and she was just about to memorize the address when Lotta snatched it from her hands.

"That's a silly game I play with my boyfriend. We make these fake IDs to use once a year. We meet up at a hotel and... like I said, it's all for fun."

Both women stood in awkward silence.

"I've got to go," they finally spoke in unison, followed by a polite laugh.

"This has been fun, Lotta. I'd love to hear more about your life. I'm sure it's much more exciting than my childhood growing up here in Misty Cove. I do have one question, though. You never mentioned your mother. Did she pass away when you were young?"

Lotta's face quickly turned blotchy. "No, it's nothing like that. She didn't like my father's dirty business dealings, so she left. I haven't seen her since I was four. I have to go now."

Chapter Twenty-Three

After a dinner of cold leftover pizza and salad, H.P. asked Dex to feed Cinnie while she went to the diner to make sure Edna hadn't left anything out of place. H.P. was surprised when her son didn't think that odd. Edna had been opening and closing the diner for longer than she'd been alive.

H.P. hoped she could entice Gram Gram to leave whatever social event she was attending by sharing Lotta's story. She was disappointed that Abe hadn't contacted her. He had to be curious about what had transpired during their lunch and why she hadn't reported back.

She knew he had a strict nighttime routine with Tildie: dinner, world affairs discussion, reading to each other, and bed, and there was no way H.P. wanted to disrupt that.

"Gram Gram?" she hissed, and then felt silly for whispering when she was the only living being.

Almost immediately she smelled Gram Gram's scent, a mixture of vanilla and one of her honey pies baking. "Kind of late for you, isn't it, Hun Bun?"

As she raised her arms expectantly, Gram Gram's warm and comforting golden aura encompassed her. She closed her eyes and allowed her body to relax. There was no feeling on this side of existence like it.

When the aura dissipated much too soon, H.P. opened her eyes. Gram Gram was wearing a short, black dress with a V-neck and oversized diamond earrings. Completely out of character for the woman who wore a pale blue house dress with two large pockets every day of her life on this side.

"Did I catch you in the middle of a date, Gram Gram?" H.P. asked innocently.

"In a manner of speaking, yes. I've always told all my grandkids, kill 'em with kindness, haven't I? Since we're already dead, that statement takes on an entirely different meaning."

H.P. pulled up the comfy chair she used only when no one else was around to question its use inside a refrigerator. "What are you plotting, Gram Gram? Is this about Effie Plum? Is she out of whatever torture chamber she was in?"

Gram nodded. "Fancies herself a hostess now. She's been courting Mr. Gable to come to her parties. Can you believe the gall of that woman? When I found out, I invited him to a showing of my favorite movie."

"Oh, I know this one! It's *Gone With*..."

"*Invasion of the Body Snatchers*," Gram Gram

replied matter-of-factly. "The man knows every single line and even does impressions of the actors. Pretty good too."

"And what was the purpose of your movie night? I don't see how any of this pertains to Effie Plum."

"That woman needs to learn the rules of etiquette up here. You don't jump into hosting parties; it's a position that must be earned."

"So?"

There was an uncharacteristic silence in their conversation, when the only sound was the motor of the air conditioner.

"I'm trying to get her goat. Once she figures out I'm here to make her afterlife as miserable as possible, she'll make a beeline to my doorstep. That's when I can confront her about stealing my pie recipes."

H.P. resisted the urge to remind her grandmother of her adage, "Be kind to others, above all else."

"It was quite the sacrifice on my part. That man and his salty jokes. Not my cup of tea."

"Gram, did you ever stop to consider that she may have forgotten all about the County Fair? It's been decades and she probably let that guilt go. You did say she spent some time coming to terms with her earthly faults, right?"

H.P. held her breath, waiting for the hurricane that might come her way. Instead, Gram's face remained uncharacteristically stoic.

"I'm short on time. What did you want to tell me?"

"It'll keep." H.P. stood, wanting to be the first to leave. There was something about her grandmother floating away angry that scared her. Gram Gram could decide she'd never return and then H.P. would spend the rest of her days feeling guilty over some silly spat that drove her grandmother to leave the living world for good.

"I'm here now, darling. Don't waste your visit."

H.P. shrugged. "You're right, Gram Gram. As usual." After she'd described every detail of her lunch with Lotta, including not telling Abe about Lotta's horrid childhood, she waited patiently for Gram Gram's approval.

"Oh, dear me." Gram Gram's aura changed to a bright orange, the color of the reflective jackets highway repairmen wore at night. "That woman is definitely a danger to you. Why would she confess all that the first time you met?" she asked.

"No one does that unless they want people to believe their fictitious story," Gram Gram continued. She swirled down next to H.P.'s face. "Stay away from that Kitties woman, my dear."

Now H.P. felt stupid. "I'm sorry, I—"

"Oh, there's Mr. Gable. We'll have to chat more tomorrow, Hun Bun."

A loud clunk startled H.P. "What was that?"

She turned around to find Gram was already gone.

Chapter Twenty-Four

Eliot Jenkins, Dexter's father, left when Dexter was four. After living with Gram Gram, an ever-evolving rotation of cousins, a college roommate, and finally Eliot, H.P.'s worst fear was living by herself and now she had a child to worry about too.

Little by little, she learned how to fix a clogged sink, catch a wily mouse, and change the oil in her car. She grew to enjoy her independence, but hearing bumps in the darkness of night reminded her that no matter how old she got, she still felt like a little girl without a real home.

"Hello?" H.P. called timidly. Gram Gram was gone and no one else was around, at least that's what she thought.

She heard the sound once more. "Dex? Edna? This isn't funny. You know how much I hate the dark."

After watching one too many horror movies, H.P.

ran around the diner turning on every single light. No one was going to pop out of the shadows on her watch.

Tonight, however, it was time to call in reinforcements. "Gwennie? I hope I didn't wake you," she whispered. Gwen never went to sleep before 1:00 a.m., but it seemed polite to ask, just the same.

"Huh?" Gwen answered sleepily. "I wasn't sleeping. I was listening to a true crime podcast about a group of bank robbers who were never caught. What do you need?"

"Could you come to the diner?"

"Now? Are we making something? I could use a triple scoop sundae with extra whipped cream. That's all I could think about through two autopsies."

"There's someone here, in the diner. It's not my Gram Gram because she left. I'm... scared."

Gwen knew about the secret ghost in the walk-in and rarely brought it up. H.P. paused. "I'm sorry. I'm acting like a big baby. Never mind."

"Wait!"

Gwen must've sensed the severity of the situation as her voice rose. "Don't move! I'll be there in ten minutes. And friendie? Stay on the phone with me and tell me everything. Just... hum your favorite song while I'm in the little girls' room."

Normally, H.P. would argue that even amongst close friends, bathroom time was private, but these were indigent circumstances. "Okay. I came over here to tell Gram about my day and then all of sudden, there was this thumping sound. Oh, Gwennie, hurry, please!"

"I'm on it. Bathroom can wait. My keys are in my hand and I'll grab a weapon."

H.P.'s phone buzzed and she pulled it out, wondering how Gwen could text her and talk to her at the same time.

> Mom? Tildie just cracked the last page of code in the diary. 😊

> "If you're reading this, it means the game isn't over. You thought we got away clean, but some debts don't stay buried. Meet me where we swore we'd never go back—Misty Cove, April 17, twenty-five years from now. No cops, no excuses. Just us. Or else the truth comes out."

Chapter Twenty-Five

G wen Folds' father, only known to H.P. as "Mr. Folds" had an obnoxiously huge pickup truck he'd used when he worked for the Forestry Service. He washed and waxed the truck every Saturday and Gwen often wondered if he loved his truck more than her. Upon his retirement, the Forestry Department gifted the truck to him. Gwen said she thought the truth was that they needed to get rid of the old gas guzzler and that was an easy way to do it. He called the truck "Winnie" and spoke of it as though it were a living, breathing person. "Winnie and I are going for a drive today." Or "Winnie is feeling a little under the weather. I'm going to change her oil and see if that perks her up."

When he wasn't waxing, vacuuming or changing Winnie's oil, he drove her to the Dairy Wheeze drive-thru for a small twist cone. Winnie was so long, she had to park bumper to bumper with Gwen's small car, leaving Gwen at her father's mercy.

The diner was so quiet now, every drip of the kitchen faucet echoed like a gunshot. H.P. glanced at the clock: twenty agonizing minutes had ticked by since she called Gwen.

H.P. finally heard the *glug, glug, glug* of Winnie from her hiding spot under the counter and felt immediate relief.

H.P. rose, glancing out the window. It looked as though Winnie was driving herself. Only Gwen's knuckles grasping the steering wheel were visible. She ran out to greet them, not one bit concerned that her fuzzy slippers were getting muddy from a recent rain.

Gwen chugged around the semi-circle in front of the diner. When the truck lurched to a halt in front of H.P., the driver's side door opened and two striped feet slid to the ground.

Gwen's hair was pulled up and away from her face by the use of pin curls and her dark-framed glasses were fogged over from the late-night humidity. She was dressed in footed, baby blue-striped pajamas with a red cape sewn on the back. Not the professional known to the community, but there was no mistaking Gwen Folds.

"Gwennie, you got new pajamas! Did you mother sew the cape on the back?"

Gwen nodded. "You know my rule: go to bed a Superhero, wake up a Superhero."

"With or without a cape, you're my hero," H.P.

said with admiration. Holding each other's hands to steady themselves, they made their way over the soft, uneven ground and up to the diner's front door.

"I went over every inch of the diner, Gwennie. I didn't see anyone. But I know what I heard."

It was ironic to think about her life in the condo, when she was the one all the neighbors sought out to find the source of noises. "It's just your old pipes, Mrs. Shellbottom." Or, "I'm afraid you have invaders, Mr. Busby. It's time you call an exterminator."

These days though, after seeing more than one ghost and enough villains to fill a lifetime, she'd become more cautious.

As they reached the top of the steps, Gwen pulled something from the trapdoor pocket on the back of her pajamas. "I brought this, just in case," she said, brandishing a bright pink gun.

H.P. pushed it away from her face in disgust. "Where did you get that? And who are we really going to shoot?"

Gwen stared at her with eyes barely open. "Well, it sure beats hitting them over the head with a waffle maker. I'm not making that mistake twice!"

She rubbed her palms together and winced slightly. Gwen bravely intercepted a would-be killer using that appliance and ended up with sprains in both of her hands.

"I guess," H.P. answered without conviction. "It's probably a raccoon, now that I think about it." She opened the door and allowed Gwen to enter first.

As H.P. entered behind her and shut the door slow enough the bell over the top didn't jingle, the thumping sound began again. "That's it, Gwen!" She clutched her friend's shoulder tightly. "I'm not crazy!"

Gwen pulled the pink gun once more from the back of her pajamas.

"Put that thing away!" H.P. hissed. "If we need a weapon, we'll call the police and run for my house, got it?"

"Okay," Gwen sighed. "Suit yourself." She set the gun on the counter and grabbed a tall glass pitcher instead. "But if something happens to both of us, your boy will be on his own. And then you'll spend eternity watching him wear the same socks and underwear while he plays video games."

H.P. shuddered at the thought. "We'll be careful." She touched Gwen's back, urging her forward.

As they searched each booth for signs of a hidden thief, the thumping began again.

Gwen's eyes widened. "It's definitely coming from the basement. If we're going to find out who—or what —that is, we're going to need to protect ourselves. Should I..."

H.P. walked behind the counter and found a pitcher of her own. "No guns," she reiterated. "I just finished repainting the place and I don't want to start all over because there are bullet holes in the walls."

Together, they crept through the kitchen. Although the door to the walk-in was closed, H.P.

glanced that direction, hoping Gram Gram was watching.

Thump. Thump. Thump.

"It's not in the cellar!" Gwen whispered. "It's coming from somewhere else."

She shone the light from her phone around until it landed on a rubber mat. "What's this?"

"Oh, just a mat to cover the hatch that used to go to the coal room. Gram Gram had it sealed and the old lid was raised up, so she glued the mat there to keep us from tripping on it."

Gwen knelt down beside it, easily pulling the rubber mat away to reveal a trap door.

"What in the..." H.P. gasped. It was louder this time, and definitely coming from whatever was underneath the trap door. The two women stared at each other, willing the other to offer to go first.

"I'll go," Gwen said after an uncomfortable pause. She swallowed hard, pulled her shoulders back and held her head high. "Technically, I don't get scared. It's in the genes of coroners. My reaction was to mimic yours."

"I do appreciate that, Gwen."

She shone her light at the floor as Gwen pried the hatch open. There was light coming from the hole, illuminating a metal ladder.

"Jeepers! That makes it easy!"

Gwen hiked up her footed pajamas as best she could and lowered herself down the first rung. "If you don't hear from me in ten minutes, just assume I've been gutted like a deer."

"I'm coming with you!" H.P. said with disgust. "Just take your time and let me know when you've reached the bottom." She kicked off her muddy slippers in order to grip the ladder better. H.P. didn't want to think about how easily Gwen could fall.

"I'm down, bestie!" Gwen called in a loud whisper. "You won't believe what I found!"

H.P. moved quickly and when she was close to the ground, Gwen grabbed her by the waist to help her the rest of the way.

They stood frozen for a long beat, only the flickering overhead lights keeping them company. Dust floated lazily in the tunnel's stale air, and somewhere deeper in the shadows, something skittered.

"Turn around," Gwen said.

It was a room filled with shelves, each holding... *was that food?*

"Gwen, it's almost as if someone has been living down here!" H.P. touched the jars of peaches, beans, carrots and pears. None of them appeared dusty or forgotten. On another shelf were books, old appliances and neatly stacked plates. Each shelf was well-lit with a small light illuminating its contents.

"I've been paying for electricity in this room the whole time? I wonder how much that cost me?"

"That's not all!" Gwen pointed to a darkened tunnel. "Someone is making regular trips through here." She reached her hand up as high as it would go and waved it back and forth. "See?" she said. "No cobwebs." Just as Gwen was about to march into the darkened tunnel, something struck H.P. Something she couldn't believe she'd forgotten.

H.P. grabbed Gwen's arm. "Wait! I know who's hiding down here and I don't want them to hurt you."

Gwen's face scrunched up tight, the way it always did when she either ate something with hidden onions or was feeling irritated. "Didn't I tell you a few minutes ago that I don't get scared?"

The thumping began again. This time, it was so close it made H.P.'s teeth rattle.

"I know it's you, Dad," H.P. called out. "Just be man enough to show yourself and admit it."

The thumping stopped and for a moment, the only sound she heard was her own heart practically beating through her chest. "C'mon, Dad. It's late and we both have to work in the morning. We're not going to call the police, just come out and—"

"Well, hello there, lil' neighbor gals! Ain't you a sight to behold!"

They turned in unison to discover a woman with frizzy red-hair barely contained underneath a baseball cap reading, "In Rust We Trust."

She was dressed in faded blue jean overalls and a bright blue shirt

and holding a very familiar object in one hand.

"Wha... where did you come from?" H.P. stammered.

"More a question I should be askin'. What are you

two doing, skulking 'round like raccoons before trash day? Don't particularly care for trespassers."

The woman removed her red ball cap and ran her fingers through her curls, making absolutely no progress in taming them.

"Where did you get that table leg? My grandmother's antique table is missing its leg and that looks very familiar."

The woman's beady eyes narrowed. "Whatever I find is mine by rights. You'll have to get yourself another one."

This woman was simply mad. Poor thing. Gwen would know where to find resources to help her. "No, my diner has been in this location for over thirty years. You must be confused. We're happy to take you home, dear."

She cleared her throat of its unsavory contents and spat them on the ground. "I bought the empty shop directly behind you. Only reason I bought it was the scrawny, little realtor said this whole underground tunnel came with it. Technically, y'all only own what's above ground."

She smiled, displaying a large silver tooth front and center.Despite her anger at being forced to drag Gwen out of bed and the fact that both of them had been scared out of their wits by this mentally ill woman, H.P. remembered how Gram Gram would search for the good in everyone, almost like a game. "Five Meal Gary has a file cabinet full of jokes, H.P.! He's going to bring one every day!"

H.P. scrunched her face and studied the woman's face. She looked hardened by life, unwilling or unable to show kindness. Nevertheless, H.P. wouldn't be her grandmother's namesake if she didn't try.

"I'm H.P. Sweetwater. This is my friend—"

Gwen shoved herself in front of H.P. and held out her hand with no shame attached to her current attire. "Gwendolyn Folds. Dry cleaner and coroner."

"Now ain't that somethin'."

he woman took Gwen's delicate hand in her considerably larger one, bouncing it up and down so hard, Gwen had to stand on her tiptoes. "Ain't never seen a dry cleaner owner after dark." She used a grubby finger to point from the top of Gwen's head to the floor and back up again. "Guessing your getup comes with pockets for snacks and regrets." She chuckled at her own joke.

"I'm Charlotte Shine, 'cept everyone but the bill collectors call me Charlie. I'm doing a bit of remodeling work so's I can open up a magic antique shop."

Charlie seemed more suited to the role of circus clown.

"Nice to meet you, Charlie. I don't think we've ever had a magic shop here in Misty Cove before."

H.P. scoured her brain for any memory of a magic shop. Nope. It never seemed like a business that would thrive in their tourist-driven economy. "What made you choose Misty Cove? It seems like magic would be a hard way to earn a living here, unless you know how to make refrigerator magnets appear."

Charlie's pleasant expression tensed. "I s'pect you can let me worry 'bout that. You ladies can go on 'bout your business. I won't come to the surface and bother you none."

"Mother? Where did you run off to now?"

The voice sounded familiar but H.P. couldn't place it until she saw the face dusted in flour. "Coriander? You're part of this too?"

Coriander's face was a mixture of embarrassment and anger. "This is my mother, but it looks like you've already met. She's opening a magic shop next door to me."

Charlie turned to her daughter and yelled, "These gals think this here tunnel is *their* property. The little one wants me to believe she's a coroner too! Them are all men, right?"

Coriander huffed, causing a large chunk of bangs to flutter before falling back into her eyes. "No, she was telling you the truth, Mom. These are my new neighbors and we need to treat them with respect."

"In MY tunnel?" Charlie snickered. "Ya always was too kind, Corrie."

"Well, you may own the tunnel, but there's a city ordinance that doesn't allow this kind of noise after 9:00 p.m.," Gwen retorted, using her official voice.

Charlie paused as though she were unsure whether to challenge Gwen or not before bowing. "Apologies, darlin'. I'm a real night owl, but I'll keep my racket down. Least 'til I can throw together some colorful charts on the advantages o' workin' after dark."

H.P. had given this woman the benefit of the doubt, but now she was sure of it: Charlie Shine was both infuriating and completely off her rocker. "May I ask what it is you hope to find down here? My grandmother owned this restaurant since I was a child, and I never knew anything about it. I'm sure there isn't anything in here worth all of this digging."

Charlie smiled broadly. "One lady's trash is another lady's treasure.

Ain't that right, Corrie? Surely, I didn't just make it up."

"Mom thought she'd build herself a little apartment under our shops. She likes to stay hidden most of the time." Coriander's face was a shade of crimson usually reserved for ripe raspberries.

"There's no sense in arguing tonight." H.P. yawned as loud as she could to reinforce her point. "Just tell your mom to keep the noise down during business hours, okay?"

She directed her comments to Coriander since she seemed to be the one in control.

"Sorry, gals. It won't happen again. Mom's just excited to get her own place. Right, Mom?"

Coriander gave Charlie an elbow in the ribs, causing Charlie to grunt by way of a response.

H.P. walked briskly to the ladder, trying to get out of the small room without losing her temper.

Once she and Gwen reached the restaurant level, she slammed the

lid shut with satisfaction.

"Yes, but how do you really feel?" Gwen joked.

There was something comforting about her footie pajamas that made. H.P. take Gwen's small body in her arms and squeeze her.

"Okay," Gwen whispered in a hoarse voice as she hit H.P. with one balled up fist. "I'm amazing and the best friend you could ask for. Now put me down!"

"That woman... is ridiculous!" H.P. said as she lowered Gwen carefully to the ground. "Is this real? Or am I in my bed, having a weird dream like I did the last time I ate extra-spicy Chinese food?" She hated that her hands were shaking. H.P. Sweetwater wasn't going to let Charlie Shine best her.

As H.P. slammed the trap door shut, she pressed her forehead against the cold kitchen floor and simply breathed for a moment.

Above ground, the world hadn't changed—the diner still smelled like cinnamon and fresh-brewed coffee—but inside her chest, something had shifted.

"Okay," Gwen said after a long beat. "We need emergency sugar. Stat."

The two friends clung to normalcy the way shipwreck survivors clung to driftwood, raiding the walk-in for pie slices and pretending for a little while that nothing had changed.

"It's real. And all of this sleuthing has given me a huge appetite."

"I owe you, Gwennie. How about a piece of Minty's pie? There are three different kinds in the walk-in."

"I'm embarrassed for your grandmother to see me in my pajamas."

They looked at each other and released the tension they were feeling in laughter. "I don't think a ghost will care what you're wearing, Gwen. And besides, Gram Gram has this weird vendetta against Effie Plum, so she's not around as often as she used to be."

Once she'd said it out loud, H.P. realized how much it hurt. She'd come to rely on Gram Gram as though she were living. It hurt her to be relegated to second place for a silly vendetta from years ago.

She opened the door to the walk-in, still hopeful Gram Gram would be there. When no apparition appeared, she stood on her tiptoes to view the pies. "Let's see... Lemon Chiffon, Apple or Peach?"

"One of each, please," Gwen replied without an ounce of embarrassment. "I'll need something for my 3:00 a.m. snack too."

H.P. shook her head as she placed the pies on the stainless-steel counter. "I wish I had your metabolism."

"People say it's part of my quirky charm."

Gwen found Styrofoam containers and handed them to H.P. "What are we going to do about your horrid new neighbor?"

"The timing of her arrival seems mighty convenient, doesn't it?"

Gwen stared at her, blinking slowly. "I guess the low blood sugar issue is getting to me. I don't follow."

"Well, the kids just finished decoding Lotta's diary and she mentioned that the money from their heists had never been found. Makes me wonder if Charlie is involved somehow. It would be a giant coincidence, but..."

"I don't believe in coincidences, H.P. In my profession, there's always a reason things happen." Gwen covered a yawn. "Tomorrow we'll take a fresh look at everything and I'm sure it'll all fall into place."

"I could be completely wrong." H.P. shrugged. "But I know someone who may be able to help."

Chapter Twenty-Six

"I understand your ingredients are pricey, Ms. Sweetwater. But raising the price two weeks in a row? It seems a little greedy."

Minty's flat tire turned into a trainwreck for H.P. She was still trying to figure out his confusing ordering system while waiting on hungry customers. This was the second person to complain about the price. Although she trusted Minty's business sense, she hadn't approved another price increase. "I'll look into it, Mr. Pennyhugger. If I find you're owed a refund, I'll give you a call."

As she closed the hatch of his car, she lost her balance, landing on her rear end.

"What's the deal with the mud all over the place?" Edna stuck her head out the door of the diner and yelled. "Looks like hog wrestling took place last night. I know you're needing money for that leaky roof, but there're easier ways to—"

"Thanks, Edna! I'm fine!" H.P. snapped as she stood and brushed off her uniform. Not only did she find a gaping hole on the lapel, but the pin Gram Gram gave her when she started working at the diner was gone. It was in the shape of a slice of pie. H.P. cherished the pin and immediately dropped to the ground to search for it.

She looked underneath Mr. Pennyhugger's car first. When she made out its unique shape, she stretched as far as she could. No luck.

"What's got you crawlin' around on the ground, neighbor?"

She recognized Charlie's voice, a gravelly, irritated sound that didn't make her want to stand up anytime soon. "Looking for something I lost, Charlie. Nothing for you to worry about."

Ignoring her dismissal, Charlie bent down so that she was eye level with H.P. "Oh! You need a stretcher-madoodle. Why didn't ya say so?"

"A what?" H.P. forgot momentarily that she was under a car and tried lifting her head. "Ouch! This morning isn't going at all the way I planned it!"

"Just hang tight, little lady. I'll be back soon."

H.P. wasn't ready to give up. Her uniform was already a casualty of the morning, so it didn't bother her to Army crawl forward. Only when she reached what she thought was her pin, she discovered a completely different object. It was gold—most likely, real gold—and circular. In the center were the letters, "DHD."

Just as she was about to grab it, she felt something tugging at her feet. "No need to worry, darlin.' Your pin is safe and sound. All's left is gettin' its owner upright."

Realizing she was in no place to argue, H.P. allowed her new annoying neighbor to pull her out with a nylon rope. Charlie offered her hand to H.P.

"No, thank you," she replied curtly. "And I don't appreciate your 'rescue.' I'm fully capable of getting myself out of trouble."

She brushed herself off, then held her hand out expectantly. Charlie hesitated. "I'll settle for a thank you. And maybe a slice o' that pie I've been hearin' about."

"Thank you. Now give me my pin."

Charlie handed the pin to her and turned to walk away.

Although H.P. would have liked to wait for Mr. Pennyhugger to leave so she could pick up the gold object, there was a crowd gathering and the last thing she wanted was to be the center of attention just because she'd crawled under a car.

"Free coffee for as long as it lasts!" she yelled with an enthusiasm she didn't feel.

"Now why'd you go and do that?" Edna was standing outside the diner with her arms folded across her chest.

"Don't you have customers needing attention?" H.P. snapped. "I'm going home to change and I'll be back in ten minutes."

She was secretly relieved she didn't have to wear her uniform today. Abe was meeting her for breakfast to discuss her lunch with Lotta Kitties and she wanted to look professional, not like she'd been playing in the mud.

After a quick change into her forest green sweater and black slacks, she ran a layer of Burnt Blossoms lipstick over her lips and looked in the mirror. "Not bad, Sweetwater. Not bad."

She felt Cinnie rubbing back and forth against her leg. "Sorry, sweetie. I'm glad you're feeling better, but I don't have time to pet you right now."

Cinnie continued to meow insistently until H.P. realized why. "A ghost?" She looked up at the ceiling, although she'd had no indication the ghost was within her sight line. "I'm not doing this now, Heather!" she said to the empty space. With everything else going on, she'd forgotten to follow through with the research on Heather's death. Booker hadn't called either. "I'll check in with you later!"

H.P. scurried out of the house before she changed her mind. Gram

Gram told her that she could control when and where she interacted with spirits, but H.P. still felt as though it were a gift and she couldn't refuse to acknowledge their presence.

"Thanks for meeting me for breakfast, Abe."

H.P. rubbed her rough hands on her knees. An hour later, she couldn't be sure if it were physical pain or an ego bruising.

"Are you sure I can't send you home with one of Minty's Basil and Lemon pies? We sell at least thirty every week! I've already saved enough for a new roof, and..."

H.P. paused when she realized she was oversharing. "Sorry," she apologized sheepishly. "Dex always tells me to stop after the first twenty words."

Abe shook his head and laughed before taking a sip of his tea. "No need to apologize. As an attorney, people confess all sorts of things to me; most of them not relevant to their case." He wiped the corners of his luscious mouth with a napkin. "I appreciate the offer for pie, but Tildie and I have undertaken a strict diet, no sugar for two months."

Setting his cup down, he took a small bite of his egg white omelet. "Now, what was important enough for you to give up valuable booth space at 8:00 in the morning? I'm feeling a little guilty, seeing all the people lined up." He gestured toward the line of puffy jackets and unruly children still waiting for pies in front of the building.

Edna had taken to calling them cattle to the feed. "We ought to round them up with a cattle prod."

H.P. leaned over the table, feeling relieved that she had a reason to be so close. "Did you listen to the recording?" she whispered. "It's clear she's hiding something, don't you think?"

Before he could answer, she continued, "And something happened last night in my basement. Or

Charlie's basement. It's a little confusing who owns what."

"First things first, H.P. I did listen to the recording and I agree with you; Lotta's keeping things hidden. People don't tell elaborate stories, especially to total strangers when they're being truthful, and that story about her father being a gangster and imprisoning her sounded far-fetched." Abe shook his head. "How did she manage to arrange for her transcripts to be sent to get admission into the college? If her father was so protective, why didn't he send someone to retrieve her when he discovered her location?"

"That's what I thought too." She hadn't.

"I wouldn't mind if you wore a wire again. Now that she's comfortable around you, let's see what accidentally pops out."

For a moment, her loyalty was torn between the gorgeous-and-always-right Abraham Bunce and this stranger who wanted to be her friend. Outside of Gwen and Thud, she came up short in that category.

"I'll call her today and set something up."

Abe glanced at his fancy-schmancy gold watch. "I've only got a few more minutes before my secretary will assume I'm dead in the gutter somewhere. Was there anything else? Something about a basement?"

She was almost ashamed to tell him now. It seemed ludicrous, like a dream she'd have after consuming one of Gram Gram's triple chocolate, banana, whipped cream pies. Maybe it was just a rumor that would only whip everyone into a frenzy if they started selling portions of the tunnel to anyone who wanted to keep their families "safe."

"I met a woman who claimed there was a city ordinance declaring the underground space ownership separate from above the ground and I wanted to know if that was true." Abe merely nodded.

H.P.'s mouth dropped open. "So there's nothing I can do about that woman?"

"Correct." Abe pulled his raincoat over his suit, shaking the shoulders until they fell into place. "I'm on next month's agenda with the city council. I'll ask them to abolish that old ordinance. But for now, you'll have to tolerate her, I'm afraid. Oh, as I was walking over, I found this gold symbol." He pulled it out of his pocket to show her. "It's got the letters, DHD etched on it. I read an article with a picture of a medallion just like this. It belongs to one of the members of The Dirty Half Dozen."

H.P.'s phone rang, giving her no time to digest Abe's information. "Booker? This isn't a great—"

"I looked into the girl's death as you asked me to. Heather DeCeased, aged six. She was found on the floor of her parents' wardrobe. Looks like it was just an accident, after something fell on her head. There's no connection between Heather and anyone in that gang."

H.P. swallowed hard. "Are you positive there isn't any other information? Like something about her brother?"

"What are you trying to tell me without telling me, H.P.? Out with it."

There was no way H.P. could share information about Heather's death without sounding crazy. "The kids have been decoding things for school. They've looked up old newspaper articles to create a code of their own." She was proud of herself for coming up with that on the fly.

"That body you found in the lake is just the tip of the iceberg," Booker continued. "I have an uneasy feeling about what's going on in Misty Cove."

Chapter Twenty-Seven

The moment Edna removed her thin jacket the next morning, H.P. practically sprinted to the door. "I'm going to run an errand. I'll be back soon."

"Do you actually work here or is this just a minor inconvenience in your day?" Edna yelled after her.

"I have complete faith in you, Edna!"

There was no winning an argument with that woman. How she and Gram Gram had remained friends their entire lives was something of a mystery.

After an exhausting day dealing with Minty's pie customers and a full diner, H.P. barely made it up the stairs to her bed. She couldn't even muster the will to yell at Dex for forgetting to feed Cinnie.

When the phone rang at 6:00 a.m., H.P. sat up and touched her clothing. She was still wearing yesterday's outfit.

"Hello?" she said in the most awake voice she could muster.

"Ms. Sweetwater? This is Booker Danno. I'd like to discuss the Heather DeCeased case further with you. I know your schedule at the diner is challenging, but I'd only need ten minutes of your time."

"I'll be there this morning, after Edna arrives. We don't get busy until at least 8:00 a.m."

As she slid out of bed and headed to the bathroom, she heard a thumping on the ceiling. Looking out her window, she realized it was raining and the wind was blowing the large drops sideways. Was the roof going to cave in?

She did her best to ignore the noise and go about her morning routine.

"Mom?" a bleary-eyed Dexter appeared in her doorway. "I don't have school today."

H.P. stared in the mirror as she applied her lipstick. "Yes, son. I'm aware of that." She'd completely forgotten.

"Yeah, well, why do you have someone working on the roof? Tell them to come back at a decent hour, like after lunch or something. This is my day to sleep in."

She turned to face him. "You're hearing that noise too?"

"Yeah. It's been going on for an hour. The cat's all freaked out too."

Heather.

H.P. forgot all about her promise to visit Heather

the day before. She had more questions to ask the little girl. "Go back to bed, baby. I'll take care of it."

She waited patiently for her son to go to his bedroom and close the door. It was fortunate that he valued sleep above everything else. He'd even skip video games and an extra-large pepperoni pizza for a few extra hours.

H.P. took a deep breath before walking down the hall to the wardrobe. "Heather! What's so urgent?"

The pounding ceased in an instant. "You never came! I have very important news!"

H.P. waited.

"Now I'm not sure I want to tell you."

Without even seeing her, H.P. envisioned a small child with her arms crossed, refusing to comply. She'd had plenty of experience with master pouter, Dexter Jenkins.

"Fine. I'll just close these doors and leave—"

"There were two people here, while you and your son were out. I recognized them."

H.P. scanned her memory. She was positive she'd locked the doors.

Too many years in a big city taught her that an unlocked door was an open invitation to a criminal. "When, Heather?"

"Oh, I don't know what time!"

"Well? My day in the living world is booked solid. Just tell me—who was here?"

"Your father. He was looking for something and I

heard him using bad words. I used to get my mouth washed out with soap for saying them."

"Did you hear what he was looking for?"

"Money. He thinks you moved it or spent it. Either way, your daddy is so mad, he's spitting nails."

Chapter Twenty-Eight

All the way over to the police station, H.P. replayed her conversation with Heather. What was Sullivan Sweetwater looking for? And why did he believe H.P. knew anything about the money? Didn't he already find it when he searched the diner? How terrible to think that her father was associated with someone who killed a child!

H.P. hurried up the steps to the police station and was surprised to find Booker's secretary, Maeviz Dull sitting up tall in her chair and smiling without an off-color book in sight.

The closer she got, the more evident it became that Maeviz was putting on a performance, either for her boss, or H.P., or both. Her mouth was pressed backward as though she'd been frozen by a superhero's ice gun.

"Hello, Maeviz, I'm here to—"

"H.P.!" Booker exclaimed with an enthusiasm that

seemed to stumble out of her mouth. "Thank you for taking time out of your busy day! Please come in!"

After they were inside and the door closed, H.P. whispered, "Is Maeviz okay? The expression on her face looks like it got stuck there somehow."

"I gave her an ultimatum. Either start acting friendly and accommodating or I'd have no choice but to bring in every member of her book club."

H.P. frowned. "And why would you bring them in? Have they done something criminal?"

Booker leaned in closer to H.P.'s ear and whispered, "They check out one book from the library and then pass it on to the whole group. Never to be returned."

H.P. resisted the urge to ask how Booker came to be in possession of that information.

"Today, I came in to find a note of apology on my desk with a P.S.—'I'm leaving early tonight to teach the You Can Lose An Eye Beginner Bow and Arrow class.'" Booker's face displayed a mixture of puzzlement and humor. "She said something about a pie, and how it gave her a clarity she'd never experienced before." Booker chuckled. "This frozen face has to be some kind of a record. She's been like that since I arrived."

"Good luck." H.P. gulped hard. At least Maeviz wasn't displaying the same signs as Dexter and the Pennyhugger family.

"Did Abe Bunce bring the medallion from The Dirty Half Dozen to you?"

Booker shook her head. "I don't recall seeing him."

"Peculiar."

After showing it to H.P., he said he was turning it over to the authorities. Maybe he'd just forgotten. "What was it you wanted? Edna gives me a thirty-minute grace period before she sends Five Meal Gary after me. You don't want to be on the wrong side of Gary—he bench presses double my weight."

Booker leaned forward and H.P. wasn't sure if she were about to vomit or cry. She was hoping for the latter.

"Your neighbor phoned me yesterday. I don't know how she got my personal number and I told her never to contact me by that method again." She leaned back, thus relieving H.P. of her concern exactly how far vomit could travel. Dex was something of a pro during his first three years of life. There wasn't a surface in their small apartment that hadn't been covered at some point by nasty projectile chunks.

"My reservations aside, she said you trespassed on her property. Now she's concerned you may use her passage to help yourself to her personal effects. I assured her that you wouldn't."

H.P.'s mouth dropped open. "I... she..." she stammered. "Charlie Shine? I didn't even KNOW about the tunnel or that it was hers exclusively until a few nights ago."

H.P. thought back twenty-four hours, when Charlie pulled her out from underneath the car like she was a benevolent helper. The more she thought about it, the angrier she became. "Why is this woman so upset? I was minding my own business, doing some cleaning when I heard banging. Believe me, Booker, there's no way I'd descend that ladder without a good reason."

"Why's that?"

H.P.'s face reddened. Despite wanting her father put away for whatever he was planning, she didn't want to implicate him... YET. "Oh, my Gram Gram kept some family heirlooms down there and Gwen's a bit of a paranormal expert. She said the spirits of my dead relatives have attached themselves to lamps and newspapers, that sort of thing."

Booker seemed unconvinced, so H.P. continued her ruse. "We were in there one time, trying to find an antique sugar canister Gram Gram left me in the will. It was copper, I believe." Now she was completely off book. The only copper she was given in the will was Gram's large copper pot with a mysterious dark stain that wouldn't come out. "It had the stamp of a rooster on the side. It was important to my family. My... great uncle made it for her. It was from a set of six, and—"

"Okay, okay, I get it." Booker put one hand in the air. "You didn't land on her property on purpose. She said you were argumentative when she explained. Ms. Shine wanted me to make it clear that she will call the authorities the next time it happens."

H.P. bit her lip and nodded. "Oh, I was just wondering about something. You can tell me it's none of my business, but the last time I was here, you were crying. It was right after you got the call about the identity of the body found in Lake It or Leave It lake. I was concerned it might be someone close to you."

Booker's pale face took on a dark hue that H.P. thought was only reserved for Pouty Princess Pink lipstick.

"I... It's all right if you don't want to tell me. I'll just go." H.P. thought about Dex and Tildie's confession, that they'd spied on her and overheard a conversation with Lotta Kitties. Now wasn't the time to ask, but—

"No, wait! I want to be transparent. Nora was a distant family member. I'd heard rumors of her involvement in The Dirty Half Dozen but didn't ever have concrete proof. Imagine my shock when her body ended up in a lake, in my territory."

H.P. wasn't convinced. "You must be very empathetic to be so upset over a relative you didn't even know."

"I try to hide it. In this job, there isn't any room for tears. It just happened to come on a day when I had too much on my mind."

"I should be getting back. Edna's probably sticking all sorts of pins in the Honeypie voodoo doll. Did you find any information about Heather DeCeased?"

"Yes." Booker shuffled papers nervously. "Let me see... oh, here it is." She pulled one page out of the pile and handed it to H.P. "This is the official police report. We don't usually give them to civilians, but I feel I owe you a favor for the lineup."

H.P. practically snatched it from her hands. "Thank you!"

"Oh, H.P.?"

H.P. didn't move. "What?" She snapped.

"If you do happen to find your copper sugar canister, be sure and let me know."

Chapter Twenty-Nine

"Take that gal some pie. At least she'll have to stop while she's shoving it down her gullet."

Edna's frustration with Charlie Shine was evident in her words. H.P. understood. It was becoming so annoying that customers complained.

During the morning rush, she banged on the ceiling of the tunnel while yelling something indecipherable. H.P. decided to confront Charlie Shine, even though there was something eerie about her, like she wasn't afraid of anything or anyone. An evening stroll past brown paper covered windows only led to more frustration. This lady didn't want casual snooping, and it was unlikely she would open the door for H.P. after their uncomfortable encounter. It was an odd mixture: Coriander's quirky-but-upbeat persona and her mother's grating nastiness.

Even Gram Gram had no suggestions.

"It was probably for the best. I don't know if I

could control my temper. The sound of electric tools underfoot unnerves the diners too. It will take more than a simple pie to fix this, Gram Gram."

"Lawdy, lawdy... what am Ah gonna do?"

H.P. jumped when she heard Minty's mournful voice at the door. She gave Gram Gram a quick wave and hopped up, opening the door in one swift motion. "What's going on, Minty?"

"The locals can't stand someone coming into town and stealing their thunder," Edna, who was leaning around Minty's lithe body, growled. "Jealousy, pure and simple."

H.P. studied their faces for some sign they were joking. The twinkle in Minty's eyes was missing, and Edna, well, she only had one expression—something between indigestion and underwear that was two sizes too small.

"Someone had better fill me in before we open for business. I've never been good at games."

"The Pennyhugger family all have the stomach flu," Edna replied quickly before Minty had the chance to open his mouth. "And now they want to blame it on our pies. Just when you think you've seen it all..."

H.P. glanced over at Minty, hoping for clarification. "And?"

"And the mister says he's gonna get a lawyer and sue us. Lawdy lawdy! There's nothing worse for a chef than to have their work put undah the microscope. Littrally."

H.P.'s face felt warm and flushed. "Unbelievable."

She remembered her conversation with Mr. Pennyhugger. Things had been so busy and strange, she'd forgotten to mention it to Minty. "Minty, I think there's been some confusion over the price of the pies."

He raised one brow. "Oh?"

The bell over the door jingled and they all stared at each other. Edna was the first to crack. "Sure, force the frail, old lady to do it. You two don't move a muscle, just stay here and wait a few minutes. If you hear me slip and fall, don't worry. I'm sure my organs will make some pale kid very happy."

Although the morning rush ended at 10:00, there were still people lined up to purchase pies they'd ordered. Minty bought velvet ropes to zigzag across the front of the building. As H.P. left the building, she didn't have the heart to communicate with anyone today.

"Ms. Sweetwater?"

Booker was back to acting like they didn't know each other. It was... weird.

"Hi, Booker. Can I get you something? A slice of Lemon Basil Pie?"

Booker scratched the back of her neck, staring at the floor. "That's why I'm here, actually. We've had a report that you have been poisoning your customers."

Luckily, there were only four customers in the booths. Five Meal Gary, a diner staple, dropped his fork dramatically and stood, wiping his egg white omelet from his chin. "Lemme tell you something, Sheriff." He stuck a crooked finger in Booker's chest and H.P. held her breath, hoping she wasn't about to see their best customer on the ground and in handcuffs.

"It's Chief, not Sheriff," Booker corrected him in an even tone. "And I'll thank you to remove your finger from my face before I arrest you for threatening an officer of the law."

Five Meal Gary wasn't one to admit defeat. "Well, if I didn't have a pilates class in ten minutes, I'd stick around and challenge you on that."

He dug into his pocket, the price of his meals now committed to memory.

"Forget it, Gary. It's on the house." H.P. needed everyone out before Booker dissed The Honeypie Diner's food. "Everybody!" she called. "It's your lucky day. Due to unforeseen circumstances, we're closing early today. Let Edna know if you want the rest of your meal boxed up before you go. Come visit us again soon!"

While Edna dealt with the remaining customers, H.P. ushered Booker into her office.

"There isn't a restaurant in the world that hasn't caused someone to get sick. It's just part of the business. And how do we know it came from here anyway? It could be a virus going round. Heck, Five Meal Gary has never once been sick!"

His recent health kick aside, he'd eaten everything on the menu at least three times.

Booker shook her head. "The entire family is in the hospital being treated for food poisoning. They believe it came from a Lemon Basil Chiffon Pie, which they consumed the night prior to their illness. For now, I need you to allow the county health inspector to come in and make sure there's nothing here causing illness."

H.P. opened her mouth to speak.

"Give me a minute," Booker cautioned before continuing. "If the health inspector finds there are no violations, the Pennyhugger family will have to search further for the source of their illness. I've already called and they are pretty backed up, so it could be a couple of weeks. In the meantime, I'm asking, informally, for you to stop selling pies."

H.P. already felt better. The entire place was spotless. But the more she thought about all the time she'd been spending in the walk-in, it might not be at the proper temperature.

"It would go a long way if you got them a bright bouquet of flowers and signed it, 'Your community friends,' or something similar," Booker advised her.

Chapter Thirty

Instead of going directly to the flower shop, H.P. paused to run a tube of Peachy Perfect Pucker lipstick across her lips before entering Fulla, Bunce and Vinegar law firm. She was staring at her reflection in the glass, hoping there weren't any spinach remnants from her morning smoothie still lurking around in her mouth when she smelled that delicious scent. Abe's scent!

"Well, hello there, Ms. Sweetwater! I didn't expect to see you this morning! Did we have an appointment? I haven't been sleeping well, so if we did and I forgot, I must apologize."

She stood quickly, embarrassed to have been caught staring at her reflection. Abe told his daughter he didn't have any respect for men or women who thought more about their smiles than their actions. "No, something came up this morning and I wanted your opinion. Now that I think about it, it was foolish of me to expect you to drop everything for me."

H.P. was turning to leave when she felt the electricity of his hand on her arm.

"I always have time for Dexter's mother." His large brown eyes glanced from side to side. "Please make yourself comfortable in my office and I'll get us coffee."

If she didn't know better, she'd think he was flustered. Abe Bunce was never flustered though. He was pure, polished perfection.

He set two steaming blue mugs on his desk and pulled up his plush lawyer chair. Before bringing her mug to her lips, she read what was written on it, "Instant lawyer, just add coffee" and chuckled.

"Our founder's granddaughter sold them for a school project." Abe rolled his eyes. "I didn't realize she'd cleaned out the appropriate mugs when she brought them. In any case, you're taking time away from the diner, so there must be a serious matter before me."

She meant to explain the threat of legal action over Minty's pies and stop there, but what came out amounted to an entire therapy session. Their creepy new neighbor, the police chief's disinterest, and her concern about bumping into her father. "It's such a small town," she finished, bringing her napkin to her teary eyes.

"Well." Abe studied her with an intensity that made her blush. "That's an incredible load on your shoulders, H.P."

She nodded. "But as a single mom, it's kinda my thing. What should I do about the pies?"

Abe pondered her words as he spun around in his chair. She'd never seen him exhibit this behavior before, almost as if he were reverting back to his childhood days. Tildie said her dad had a rough childhood, growing up poor and alone as an only child.

"I'm going to work backward through your mountains and see if we can't get them shaved down to mere bumps in the road."

She felt better already. If Abe Bunce was taking charge, her worries were practically over.

"First, I want you to bring me a piece of the pie. I'll have it sent to a lab, where—"

"Oh, Gwen can do that. I never thought about it this morning!"

"No, that wouldn't be prudent." Abe shook his head. "The less people who know, the better. At least until we have a better idea of what's going on. Bring me a piece of the pie in a discreet brown paper bag and I'll take care of it. Try and make it the same flavor they bought."

"Of course."

"Next is the matter of your new neighbor. I can do some snooping and find out if this Charlie Shine person filed the proper paperwork to open a business. If so, I'll have access to information like her previous address and we'll be able to suss out anything fishy."

H.P. let out a long sigh. She already felt like an enormous weight had been lifted from her shoulders.

"And about your father... I don't quite understand how you know he was in your home. To my knowledge, you don't have a security system, right? We can't go hunting him down until we have more evidence that he trespassed. But..." Abe leaned forward again, this time clasping his hands together in front of him. "You know how lawyers talk. There's more gossip going round this office than in all three beauty shops combined!" He chuckled to himself. "This morning, I heard through the grapevine that your father is suspected of robbing a liquor store in Tellum."

"Doesn't surprise me one bit!" H.P. felt vindicated. Her father was as much the loser as she'd thought for all of her adult life. "Is he in jail then? And what about the person who was arrested for beating him up?"

"I have to caution you that this is all still in the preliminary stages. He hasn't been arrested, nor does anyone really know where he's staying. An anonymous tip about the robbery is all we have to go on."

"If my father knew it wasn't me all along, why did he put me through the discomfort of appearing in a lineup? What kind of a father puts his daughter through all that?"

She thought back to her silly attempt at disguising herself the day of the lineup and how her father recognized her anyway.

"After the lineup, Booker Danno called to let me know they'd arrested someone. I couldn't tell you because it still wasn't clear you were off the hook."

H.P. cleared her throat, steadying herself before

staring into those beautiful, brown eyes. "I'm a little upset, Abe. I really thought we had a better relationship than that."

Abe lowered his dark, curly-haired head. "I do owe you an apology for that. I'm terribly sorry I treated you like an average client, and not an incredible mother and business owner."

His apology felt as nice as the warm light from one of Gram Gram's ethereal "hugs."

"Well, thank..." unlike Gram Gram's hugs, Abe's compliment stuck in her throat, preventing any further educated conversation.

"Bring the pie over as soon as you can," he continued. "Let's get ahead of this before it becomes a bigger problem. This family could destroy everything you and your grandmother have built."

All the way back to the diner, H.P. chided herself for acting so silly and forgetting that yes, once word got around, which took a total of one day in this town, her reputation would be permanently damaged.

Two days later, during the mid-morning rush, the phone rang and she answered it. "H.P.? Abe Bunce."

"What now, Abe?"

"Come by my office tomorrow when you can."

That night, sleep evaded her. Even with Cinnamon Biscuit Maker curled stubbornly against her hip, H.P. kept replaying the day's disasters in her mind like a bad movie. Two previous nights passed in the same manner.

She was starting to feel like a zombie from one of the movies she watched as a kid.

She'd been drooling when her alarm blared, "Wakey, wakey, time to bakey!" Bleary-eyed and low on energy, she decided to forego her usual five-minute makeup job. It was a good thing, too, because the first real spring storm rolled in just as she stepped out the door. It wasn't far to the diner—right across the street —but the rain was coming down in sheets.

She was slicing lemons in the empty kitchen when her phone buzzed, displaying Abe Bunce's name.

"H.P.? We've got a problem," Abe said grimly. Outside, thunder rumbled low, a warning growl from the sky.

Chapter Thirty-One

"Your herb specialist must be mistaken, Abe. Don't you think I'd KNOW if there were drugs in my pies?"

H.P. caught Edna's glare as she walked by with dirty plates. "Didn't know we were back to official breaks. Don't mind me; the oldest woman in the joint can handle everything by herself."

H.P. put one hand over her phone and called, "I'll be done in a minute, Edna. This is important!"

Although she knew her words fell on deaf ears, as they always did, H.P. continued to feel the need to defend herself. She walked outside, into the alley where the protests of a stray tabby cat expecting scraps was the only noise.

"Sorry, Abe. I missed the last thing you said. Could you repeat it, please?"

"I was telling you that the two pies you brought over both contained high levels of mysteria. It's a hybrid strain of marijuana that also contains an addictive agent. Very new to the market and lethal for those who ingest too much."

"Why would Minty do that? And if it's such a deadly herb, why haven't others gotten sick or... died?" Her insides felt cold just saying it. Gram Gram put all of her staff—grandchildren included—through rigorous training before they were allowed to work in the diner. They had to know how to cleanse and sanitize everything, and after that, how to ensure food preparation was conducted properly. She even invited the county health inspector to quiz them, grading them on their knowledge.

Every single grandchild grumbled about their perceived mistreatment, but when she became a chef as an adult, H.P. was more than grateful to have that knowledge. Gram would roll over in her grave, or inside the walk-in, if she knew.

"What should I do now, Abe?"

"Nothing."

"What? I can't take the chance of anyone else getting sick!"

"Of course not. You also can't leave your diner open to a lawsuit. I'm going to come over and have a conversation with your chef at the end of the day. I'll grill him using my fancy lawyer talk and see what I can get from him. For now, find a way to fake an accident in your walk-in cooler. It will have to be a catastrophic accident that causes all the pies to fall to the ground. Do you think you can manage that?"

H.P. let out a loud snort. "Clumsy is my middle name, Abe. I've broken more glassware than any person I know."

"Good. I'll see you this afternoon."

Although she'd assured him she knew how to create a catastrophe, the actual implementation was something else. She stepped inside the cooler and began moving things around, trying to stage such a scene.

"If you're trying out for the community theater, this grandma's heart may explode."

H.P. turned abruptly, knocking one of Minty's signature Lemon Chiffon pies to the ground. She stared at the broken meringue with a mixture of sadness and humor. "Well, there's one down."

Gram Gram swirled around until she was nose-to-nose with H.P. "Tell me, darling. Tell me, RIGHT THIS INSTANT!"

She explained the whole story, taking note of Gram Gram's glee. "That's a darn shame. Poor man and his pies," Gram said, sarcasm dripping from her voice.

"You're as transparent as a... ghost, Gram. I know you were upset he wasn't using your recipes. I'll give you all the gloating time you want, once this deed is done. I was thinking this morning about the kitchen prep lectures you gave. And inviting the county health inspector was gen—"

H.P. paused and snapped her fingers. "What was that guy's name? The one who said you reminded him of his grandmother and then proceeded to ask you out?"

"You don't mean Sal, do you? It was bad enough I had to endure his bad breath during our dinner theater performances, but he asked me out again and again. Thank the heavens he didn't hold a good report over my head. It took threats of violence to get Mr. Monella to slither back under his rock."

"Sounds like the perfect person for this job. Thanks, Gram!"

H.P. stared at the wreckage of pies oozing across the walk-in floor, the lemon basil filling already starting to congeal under the cooler's fluorescent lights. Then she practically skipped out of the cooler, forgetting about the mess on the floor. After a discreet call, she returned to work.

A mere fifteen minutes later, a shiny-headed man in his late fifties with a bushy mustache and hard, green eyes appeared in their lobby.

"Oh, SHOOT!" H.P. oversold his entrance, but this was her performance day.

"Now what's got your pretty mah-nd in a tizzy, Ms. Sweetwater?"

Minty drawled.

"That's the county health inspector. Always showing up at the most inconvenient time."

"You keep this place cleaner than a shiny penny, ma-yam. Don't you worry 'bout a thing. Ah'll charm him up one side and down t'other."

"NO! You can't!" she blurted. "He and I have a

special... repertoire. Would you help Edna while I shadow Sal? It shouldn't take long."

Minty studied H.P.'s face for an interminably long sixty seconds before looking underneath the counter for an extra apron. H.P. breathed a sigh of relief while catching her reflection in the antique Babble Cola she'd just acquired.

Since Sal tripped over his tongue every time he saw Gram Gram, it stood to reason that he'd find her granddaughter a feast for the eyes as well. "Mr. Monella!" H.P. took his arm and guided him toward the kitchen, hoping to avoid any suspicions.

"Sal? What's got you out of retirement? Guess your phone IS working, eh?" Edna said snidely.

Shoot. It was the worst possible trainwreck and one she could have avoided with another convenient lie. "Edna, he's helping us out. You heard about the legionnaire's disease outbreak in Tellum?"

She didn't pause to wait for Edna's answer. "Well, Sal, here, heard about it and jumped right in to help, didn't you, Sal?" H.P. squeezed his arm as tightly as she felt was safe without cutting off the circulation. She'd explained in detail how she didn't want her staff to know the truth, and that she'd pay him handsomely. "Gram Gram said you played her love interest when you performed the musical, 'Cello, Dali.' That must've been an interesting musical."

"Oh, yes. I played Salvadore Dali, the famous artist and your grandmother played Trusilla, the lovesick cellist. A full two minutes the audience were on their feet, after they finished their five-layer pie, that is."

"Yes, Edna. I'm helping out this week. And I do apologize for my poor manners. I promised I'd phone you after our date and I didn't. Please accept my sincerest apologies."

Ooh. He was good. *Had he done this before in his years as health inspector?*

"Hmmph!" Edna snorted before returning to her customers.

H.P. took his arm again and moved them toward the kitchen.

"It's quite unusual for a business to actively seek out an inspection.

Especially one that gets such excellent marks for every inspection."

"Well, as I mentioned on the phone, I've got a sticky situation. With all the pies we've been selling, we're thinking of expanding our operation. It won't look good if we have a questionable report. I called and asked for your replacement, but she's running months behind."

Sal rolled his eyes. "Yes, so I've heard. I trained the woman myself, but she hasn't figured out how to properly budget her time. Calling me was the right thing to do, although I'm sure..."

H.P. held her breath as he looked at the mess of pie filling dripping down the shelves and meringue and crust spattered on the floor. It was her first time as an adult creating that kind of a mess. She was proud of the chaos she'd produced.

Sal turned around and stared at her, his beady eyes becoming hard. "Am I the subject of a prank?"

"What? Why?" she asked innocently. Tilting her head to the side, she pretended to see the mess for the first time. "OH, NO!"

She gasped so harshly, her throat closed up and she bent over coughing and gagging. Gram Gram would have been so proud of her scene. As she attempted to regain her composure, she felt Sal's arm on her back and the hairs on the nape of her neck rose to full standing position. H.P. jerked upright, defensively, catching Mr. Monella on the chin.

"Ms. Sweetwater!" he gasped as his hand flew up to his face. It wasn't his gasp, however that concerned H.P. It was the blood spurting from his nose. Gram Gram was watching the show from the top shelf, between the mayonnaise and the peach filling for crepes.

"Couldn't have worked out any better, Hun Bun," Gram Gram mused.

"Huh?"

Sal glanced at H.P. "I didn't say anything. But I will now. I need a wet washcloth for my nose, and a phone. I'm calling your restaurant in for bodily fluids found in the cooler. You're officially shut down as of now, Ms. Sweetwater."

H.P. stood outside the darkened diner window after posting a "Closed for Repairs" sign on the front window. She crossed her arms tightly against her chest as the rain began to fall again.

Inside, Edna stacked chairs on tables with grim determination. The "Closed for Repairs" sign fluttered in the wet breeze, looking more like a tombstone than a reassurance.

The afternoon dragged by in slow, soggy misery.

By sunset, H.P. was ready to believe no good news would ever come again.

Chapter Thirty-Two

When the sun rose over Misty Cove the next morning, the smell of lemon meringue still lingered in the diner's back alley. H.P. stared at the wreckage of pies oozing across the walk-in floor, and it definitely felt like a crime scene.

H.P. glanced around the empty walk-in with satisfaction. It hadn't smelled this fresh and crisp since she was a junior in high school. H.P. and one of her cousins thought it would be funny if they stole the sign from the Heap Reaper, the local junkyard.

Gram Gram happened to be on her way to musical rehearsal and recognized Grandpa's rusted out pickup, speeding down Main Street with the large sign bouncing around in the truck bed. She phoned the police chief immediately, promising the sign would be returned. She assured him that the punishment she dealt them would be far more severe than a fine. For the next six months, the girls spent their weekends polishing the diner like it had never been polished before.

When H.P. called Abe to explain how well their plan had worked, he replied, "Never doubted you for a minute."

She felt like a giddy teenager.

Every time H.P. started to question Minty about inflating the pie prices and putting mysteria into the recipe, they were interrupted. Truthfully, confrontation was her kryptonite. She wasn't ready to confront him in front of others yet. He'd been such a nice man while Edna was happy to leave early enough to prepare for a blind date. "Gotta make this business shine!" she said, gesturing up and down her body.

Gram Gram's aura changed to a lovely lavender and silver sprinkles fell to the ground. She unfurled one long, smooth finger as she spoke. "Number one, you don't owe that creepy crawler anything. He would have found a way to keep you in his debt for months, trust me."

"That's probably true." H.P. wondered what Gram Gram had to do to get rid of Sal, but now wasn't the time to ask.

"Second, those pies are all going into the trash. Now, you've got two days to come up with a good excuse to go back to the PROVEN recipes." Gram didn't try to hide the bitterness in her voice. "The man used herbs in his pies like a child making mud pies with grass in them. He probably had no idea what he was using."

"Minty was the only person who agreed to the salary I was offering. I didn't have much choice in hiring him, and I doubt he would take it well if I told him we couldn't use his recipes anymore.

She glanced sideways at Gram before continuing, "Insulting for the livings."

Gram nodded. "Third, you've got a hefty nest egg that I left you. Use that to restock your refrigerator and pay your help. Other than poisoned pies, there's nothing more you need to worry about. There's a light in every pen full of mud, Hun Bun."

"Other than that," H.P. rolled her eyes. "That's a pretty big thing, Gram. Abe said there was an addictive hallucinogenic in the pies, and cutting everyone off is going to force them to go through withdrawals. What if they're so angry they never want to come back? What if someone decides to sue me? Even that nice stash you left me won't cover an expensive lawsuit."

Gram tapped her chin. "Hmm. I see your point. What if the issue wasn't the filling at all? What if it was bad flour?"

"That's no better. I'd still get sued for using it." H.P. wrapped her arms around her waist. "I'm afraid the diner will have to close."

"Posh pish, my darling. We Sweetwater gals are resilient. Nobody keeps us down for long." Her aura became a lovely shade of lavender.

"You know, there's an idea swirling around my ethereal brain." Gram Gram tapped her skull for emphasis. "I have an event soon. I'm closing in on Effie Plum. She's definitely avoiding me, but my sources tell me she's a special guest at the Dead and Deranged Ball."

H.P. resisted the urge to ask about the ball.

"I'll be back tomorrow morning," Gram Gram continued. "Don't worry, my love. Our little diner will keep serving the best pancakes in the entire state long after you've joined me on this side."

Gram Gram blew her a kiss, which manifested into a subtle, warm breeze.

Unsure whether or not she could trust Gram Gram to come up with a way out of this mess, H.P. locked up and walked over to The Final Fold, forcing her eyes forward. She couldn't bear to look at the paper taped to the glass front doors that read, "Closed by Order of the State Health Department."

Gwen was as busy as always, her small but firm voice could be heard over the hiss of the cleaning machines and ever-rotating racks of clean clothing. "Twenty-four? Number twenty-four?"

The patrons turned to see which one of them was lost in conversation on their phone instead of listening for their number to be called.

"Last call for twenty-four!" Gwen looked down at her pad and wiped the sweat from her brow. H.P. jumped into action.

"I'm coming around to check numbers," H.P. said

as she leaned in to examine the number Mrs. Bill Bored held.

"Got another job already? Well, bless your heart," the customer murmured. While seemingly words of comfort, H.P. learned quickly that the phrase, *Bless your heart*, was actually an underhanded slight.

"You've got number twenty-four, Mrs. Bored," she replied with a sense of satisfaction.

The woman lifted her bifocals up halfway and glanced down at the scrap of paper in her hand. "The numbers are smaller 'n they used to be," she grumbled, pushing her way up to the counter.

H.P. continued her perusal of the customers, lining them up by number to make the process quick and seamless. When every single customer was gone, Gwen lay her head on her counter. "Holy Jankers. This day has been nonstop chaos."

H.P. joined her behind the counter and began massaging Gwen's neck with two fingers. "There's a lull now. Why don't we sit down in your office and I'll make you a coffee?"

Gwen groaned. "Does that mean my neck massage stops?" She raised her head and winked at H.P. "Just kidding, bestie. Let's go sit down. My feet are killing me."

H.P. followed her friend to her office, a room decorated like some kind of jungle fairyland. It was a far cry from the sterile environment of the dry cleaners and in the other connected building, coroner's office and exam room.

After she'd made two cups of Vampy Vanilla, a pre-flavored coffee that H.P. found tasted like stale vanilla and cardboard, they both settled into their chairs.

"I don't know why, but when I make the coffee it never tastes this good. You have a knack for it." Gwen said, smacking her lips with satisfaction.

"Thanks for that. But I have to confess; I'm not here just to help. Well, I was glad to help, but I need to pick your brain."

Gwen thunked her head. "That's what this noggin lives for. Shoot."

"I need to find a way to stop Minty from using his pie recipe without sounding suspicious."

"Tell him you don't make a habit of drugging your customers? I don't see what the problem is."

"He's such a nice man. His cooking is amazing. I'm not ready to lose him, at least, not until I'm sure he did that on purpose. Maybe he just found this weed in the swamps and thought it tasted good?"

"His air-fried chicken is delicious," Gwen conceded. "But is it worth losing your reputation?"

"There's more. I have to tell my customers something that will explain why they're all going through withdrawals. Something that won't open the door to a lawsuit."

"Boy, that's a real humdinger, bestie."

Gwen's work phone rang. "I've got to take this. Coroner stuff."

H.P. nodded before showing herself to the door. While Gwen would certainly tell her everything about the conversation later, she didn't want to appear too nosy. She walked the length of the dry cleaners, wondering what Gram Gram was doing. At least dead celebrity drama and Effie Plum's evasive maneuvers didn't affect the living side.

H.P.'s phone buzzed in her pocket. She looked at the number—Boog R. Noseinair Schools— and answered quickly. "Hello? Is my son all right?"

"Yes, Ms. Sweetwater. He's come down with a migraine though. His cheeks are flushed and he says this is what usually happens right before he vomits. If that should occur, we'll have to shut down to sterilize... Not unlike your current situation, or so I'm told."

Busybodies were certainly on their game today. "I'll come and get him. Thanks!"

She tapped on Gwen's door and stuck her head in, mouthing that she had to leave. Gwen nodded and gave her the thumbs-up sign.

When H.P. arrived at the nurse's office, Dex was seated in a chair with his hoodie over his head. Not unusual for him, but since they were in school where it wasn't allowed to walk around with your hood up, she prepared to lecture him.

"Dex? Honey?" Whether she believed him or not, she had to go through the motions.

Hearing his mother's voice, Dexter sat upright and lowered his hood. His cheeks were indeed bright red. Instinctively, she placed a palm on his forehead. "You're burning up! Didn't they take your temperature?"

"I can assure you, Ms. Sweetwater, we took his temperature when he came to the nurse's office." The principal's secretary had the same judgmental voice H.P. remembered from her childhood, and it still turned her body into jelly. H.P. turned around slowly, hoping her mind was just in a tricky mood. "Ma... Ma... Mrs...."

An elderly woman with thick brows that curled menacingly upward greeted H.P. She was wearing the same outdated nurse uniform, a white, button-up dress with a pleated skirt, white stockings, and white orthopedic shoes as she rocked back and forth on her heels.

"I STRONGLY SUGGESTED to your grand-mother that you needed speech therapy. It's evident now she didn't take me seriously."

H.P. swallowed hard. "Ms. Bonebreaker—I'm surprised you're here! I would have thought you were..."

"Dead?"

She chuckled with the precision of a theatrical witch. "That's what most of my students hoped for back in the day. No, I'm filling in today for the regular nurse. Pressure's off, now that I don't have to chase hidie- hidingtons around, trying to get them on my scale."

She stared emphatically at H.P. over the top of her octagon-shaped, wire-framed glasses. Probably the same ones she wore when H.P. was in school.

"I was sensitive about my size." H.P. blushed and

turned away. *Get a hold of yourself, Sweetwater! You're a grown woman now!* "My cousins made fun of me for being short and small. When you posted everyone's height and weight on the bulletin board in front of the principal's office, it caused no end to their cruelty."

She felt her confidence growing as she turned back to face her former nemesis. "Now that I think about it, I wasn't the only one you terrorized. Poor Gertrude Fenway. She knew she wasn't the same size as the other kids. You didn't need to make her feel bad about it! Because of you, she went on a cola diet and ended up with a mouth full of false teeth. You should be ashamed—"

"Mom!" Dex pleaded as he tugged on her arm. "People are watching," he whispered. He'd moved to her side without her noticing. Now she realized with irony that she was causing her son the same amount of embarrassment she was blaming the nurse for.

The principal, secretary and three teachers who were in the teacher's lounge all looked up and glared at them. "I'd stay and tell you more about the ways you hurt us kids, but I need to get my boy home. Come on, son."

Dex flopped his hood over his curly head as they exited the building. Even in a state of misery, his reputation as a normal, "I'm only with her because she signed me out," kid was more important than his comfort. When they were finally in the car, he banged his palm on the dashboard. "Why do you have to embarrass me? Why couldn't you just keep your mouth shut?"

"Dexter E. Jenkins! Don't talk to me like that!"

Although he was often a surly teen, he never disrespected her.

"Sorry. I don't feel good. Can we go home? I think I'm gonna be sick."

Chapter Thirty-Three

"It appears your son has been poisoned, Ms. Sweetwater."

H.P. nodded through bleary eyes. She'd been up with Dex all night. The poor kid never made it out of the bathroom. At 5:00 a.m., she decided it was best to take him to the hospital. He was so weak by then, he didn't put up a fight.

"Who would do that to my baby?" she cried. "He's never hurt a fly."

"Not criminally. I'm sure no one would want to hurt him," the male nurse reassured her. "He probably ate something that wasn't properly cooked. He mentioned something about a pie?"

Oh, no! "One of Minty's pies? How did he get a hold—" He'd helped them empty out the walk-in. She thought she'd miscounted the pies they needed to destroy, but he must've taken one home. "Is he going to be okay?"

"He'll be just fine. He had an unpleasant experience with activated charcoal. We're giving him IV fluids now. I'll check his vitals later and if he's still improving, you can take him home. I've already advised him to take it easy on the pies." The doctor chuckled. "Doubt he needed to hear it."

The diner was closed until Sal could return and give it the "all-clear."

H.P. got the distinct impression a dinner date would hurry things along, but she wasn't THAT desperate. Thankfully, she didn't need to worry about leaving her son home alone. She pulled out her phone to cover her bases though. "Edna? I know you have a busy social life and whatnot."

She waited, hoping Edna would disagree. When she heard nothing, she continued. "But I was up all night with Dex. I had to take him to the emergency room." She could feel the Strong H.P. dissolving into the little girl who came to her grandmother's diner and confessed all her woes. Edna listened but never offered comfort, although H.P. still felt better afterward.

"Dex is in the hospital," she continued, sniffing hard for emphasis. "And the truck to resupply the walk-in may show up today. Would you mind going over there? I'll pay you double."

She knew Edna wasn't motivated by money... or anything else... but it was worth a try.

"Yes."

"What?? Are you pulling my leg?" H.P. blurted

out. It was unlike the crankpot to give in so easily. "I mean, thank you, Edna! You're the best!"

"Don't need syrupy words. And just because I'm unlocking the door doesn't mean I'll be unpacking those boxes. That's your job, little lady."

"Of course. Thank you again."

A wheelchair ride to the car didn't bring one word of protest to Dexter's lips. He was still sick enough he didn't take advantage of his situation. Instead, after his release, H.P. helped him upstairs and tucked his blankets around him. She left cold water on his nightstand. He rolled over and emitted a loud snore before she even left the room. Poor kid. Dexter's reprimand would have to wait.

Gently, she pushed the hair from his face and kissed his forehead. Cool as a cucumber.

H.P. crept silently into the kitchen, avoiding the loose boards that gave off a healthy moan when feet crossed over them. She opened the garbage bin on her way. Sure enough, an empty pie tin with the words, "Honeypie Diner Lemon Basil Chiffon" was displayed on a cheery sticker. Minty insisted they invest in stickers for his pies so they wouldn't be confused with less superior offerings around town. "Folks'll remember bettah. We want them to know where to get more when they're lickin' their chops."

Did Minty mean to poison her son, along with the Pennyhuggers?

AND CINNIE? Surely not. The old man spent time showing Dexter how to flip a pancake without a spatula and make the fluffiest scrambled egg. Those weren't the actions of a killer.

Or was she just shying away from confrontation one more time?

H.P. felt the warm furry body of Cinnie wrapping around her leg. She reached down and picked her up, pushing her nose into Cinnie's white-and-black fur. There was nothing like the sound of a contented cat purring.

"You're just the medicine I need. Should we sit on the couch and cuddle?"

Recently, Cinnamon Biscuit Maker learned what those words meant and raced H.P. to the couch every time she heard them. They reached the couch at the same time and Cinnie immediately began searching for the perfect spot.

As H.P. clicked through the channels searching for a mindless movie, Cinnie curled into a circle and was about to nuzzle in when her body froze.

"Oh, no."

H.P. had come to recognize this as her cat's warning single. A ghost was in her house and nine times out of ten, it was hanging out in the kitchen.

"I'm not getting up!" she called out, feeling irritated. These ghosts were going to learn some manners. Those in the living world didn't need to constantly be at their beck and call.

When she heard nothing more, she resumed channel surfing with one hand and petted Cinnie's spiked fur with the other. "It's okay, girl. Whoever was there is gone now. I guess it's too much to ask that they walk ten feet to—"

Cinnamon Biscuit Maker let out a loud screech and jumped from the comfort of H.P.'s lap onto the floor, quickly scampering underneath the couch. Instantly, the shape of Heather, the ghost she'd met in the armoire, appeared.

"Wow, you can move about freely, out of the armoire too? I'm impressed. It takes all of my Gram Gram's strength to leave the walk-in."

Heather pursed her lips. "I've been working on my talents for decades, Honeypie. Please, there isn't much time. You and your son are in grave danger!"

"What kind of danger?" H.P. smirked. "Was there a creepy crawly critter in the dresser, or was it a mouse? Either way, I can take care of them, you don't have to worry." Although she treated her dismissively, H.P. was glad to see Heather's demeanor was back to normal. The blotchy crazed look last time they met gave H.P. nightmares.

The ghost child wasn't amused. "No time for jokes. I overheard a conversation. Someone is coming to threaten your life tonight."

The pleasant expression on H.P.'s face gave way to an ashen contortion. "What? Why? And how would you know?"

"They believe you know where the treasure is buried."

"Treasure? What—"

H.P. paused. Her father had broken into the diner

looking for money that he'd likely obtained from bank robberies. According to Heather, he'd done the same in their home. "Heather, are you talking about my father? Would he really try and... kill me? Why wouldn't he know where he buried the stupid money?"

"Pack your things while I tell you a story."

Obediently, H.P. headed upstairs into her room and started removing overnight items.

"I told you I fell asleep in here, and that no one missed me. That's when I heard two people talking."

Heather took a long, dramatic breath. Her body dissolved and a familiar face appeared. "He got away, didn't he?" Her voice so perfectly mimicked her father's that H.P.'s pulse quickened.

"I told you he couldn't be trusted," Heather continued in a deep voice, decades beyond her short life. "Some folks, they put up a fay-kade and you don't see who they really are until the pedal hits the highway. Me—I'll tell you right upfront, I've got secrets."

H.P. swallowed hard.

Heather's form dissolved again. This time, she took on the appearance of a woman.

"Yeah, but we'll find him. Pretty sure I know where he stashed the loot. Wait—did you hear that? Someone's in the fancy dresser! Sinus, you said we were alone! You gonna take care of this, or am I?"

A sickening feeling overtook H.P. and the room began to spin. Grabbing onto the wall to steady herself until the feeling passed, she uttered, "It was my father who killed you. And the woman?"

Heather returned to her given form and nodded before pointing to stab wounds in her chest.

"Someone named Nora. But don't worry, I've seen her in the afterlife.

Your father was here, though, with another woman. They planned to tear the place apart, looking for a treasure they were sure you'd hidden. Instead, I scared them pretty good."

Heather giggled, the first sign H.P. had seen that this child was still, in fact, a child. "We can play games later. Now take your son and get out of here!"

"Thank you for the scrambled eggs, Gwen. You're a lifesaver."

H.P. spooned more onto her plate before shoving Dexter's feet off the table. His appetite, along with his attitude had returned with a vengeance; the child ate half a loaf of toast and H.P. lost count of the number of eggs.

"That's what friends are for." Gwen sat down next to her, wearing the same footie pajamas she wore the night they confronted Charlie.

The doorbell rang. Panicked, Gwen rose quickly and unplugged a lamp imprinted with dachshunds and held it over her head. "Take Dex and go downstairs!"

H.P. took her son's arm and pulled him down the steps.

"I'm not a baby, Mom!" he protested weakly. They had just made themselves comfortable on Gwen's old, nylon-looped, blue sofa when the door opened. Instinctively, H.P. grabbed her son's shoulders, ready to throw him to the ground and take the bullets herself.

Someone descended the stairs slowly. The footsteps didn't match an old drunk with a vendetta. Even so, H.P. could feel her knees shaking.

"Whoever you are, leave my son alone. He's done nothing wrong!"

In one swift motion, the figure jumped down the last step. *Tildie!* H.P. let out the air she'd been storing up for the last few minutes.

"Hi, Ms. Sweetwater! I brought Dexter a mixture of the things he likes when he's at my house. Kalakand, which is Indian fudge, nankhatai, Indian shortbread, and cookie dough/potato chip brownies. The last one is a Tildie-Dexter original."

Tildie handed a large basket to H.P. and smiled at Dexter. "Are you still barfing, or will you inhale your favorites in one sitting?"

Dexter chuckled. "You already know the answer to that."

Tildie giggled shyly. "My father says baking comforts the soul of both baker and recipient." She motioned to Dexter with a delicate thumb. "I tried to make enough for both of you, but I know how this guy eats."

Both preteens smiled. The bond between them was undeniable.

"That's certainly true, Tildie. Food and friends. What would we do without either?"

"Are you going to tell me what happened? Drew Defib's dad was at the hospital and heard you were poisoned."

"Who?" H.P. asked.

"Oh, sorry. Drew's dad is an ambulance driver. He's not supposed to talk about the patients, but he tells his son everything."

She could have blamed it on a sleepless night, too many pieces of Mrs. Folds' homemade raisin bread, or just plain insanity. The tears rolled down H.P.'s cheeks and she let out a sob.

Tildie cleared her throat. "Is everything okay, Ms. Sweetwater?"

Chapter Thirty-Four

Dex was back to his usual goofy, impatient, smelly self, thankfully.

"Now that you're feeling better, tell me what you ate for breakfast yesterday, son," H.P. said. "Was it an old leftover I forgot to toss? And I promise, I won't yell at you for eating junk, just this once."

"Minty gave me one of his Lemon Chiffon pies." Dexter's eyes peeked between the thick, brown curls. It was one of his tweenhood traits that bothered her the most. She'd often thought of cutting his bangs while he slept.

"So you had a piece of pie. Anything else?"

"Not exactly."

She waited for his words and lack of explanation to sink in. "Dex, you ate the... ENTIRE pie?"

He slammed his hand on the table and stood, causing his cereal bowl to flip its contents all over the table. "You said you wouldn't yell at me! I'm going to school." He grabbed his book bag from the back of the stool.

"No! Wait!" H.P. leaned over and grasped a corner of his t-shirt, the only thing within her reach. He wouldn't mind wearing it to school if it had ripped. "I'm sorry, Dex. It was shocking, that's all. You ate the whole pie, and then—"

"I AlREADY TOLD you everything!"

He slammed the front door to Gwen's place and H.P. heard loud voices outside. She hoped Dex hadn't upset Gwen's parents. They'd been so kind and generous. When H.P. could stand the suspense no longer, she rose and walked toward the door. Just as she reached it, it flung open, narrowly missing H.P.'s face.

"Ms. Sweetwater? Are you here?"

"I'm behind the door, Tildie." H.P. stepped out to see Tildie dressed in matching black-and-white plaid shorts and shirt. Dex was leaning against the railing on the outside steps, refusing to look at his mother.

"What did you need, hon?"

"I wanted to be completely transparent."

Tildie Bunce never left a word unspoken. H.P. appreciated that; when they reached high school, Tildie would report any illegal goings-on in Misty Cove before her son had the opportunity to do them.

"You must know already about the body they found in Lake It Or Leave It lake. Well, it's kind of a badge of honor if you're brave enough to go out to the spot where Nine Nails Nora was found."

"How did you know her name?" H.P. would have

expected a stunt like this from her son, but Tildie should have known better. "Don't tell me that you two..."

"We rode our bikes out there. It wasn't frightening at all. In fact, there were so many other kids doing the same thing that we barely saw the crime tape." Tildie's voice conveyed her disappointment. "But we did see one strange thing."

"What was that?"

"Dr. Kitties. She was there with the police chief and they were arguing over something. Dr. Kitties was crying."

H.P.'s heart ached. That poor woman. All she wanted was to make a few friends in Misty Cove. Booker obviously didn't understand social cues. "I'm going to take some cookies to her this evening. Thank you for telling me, Tildie."

"I'm going to the diner, Gwennie!" H.P. called out. Gwen did a morning meditation every day before going to the cleaners. Her father called it, *new-agey hocus pocus*, but Gwen swore it made her brain twice as productive.

H.P. made a bee-line for the walk-in and called to her grandmother, telling her everything.

"I don't understand your hesitation, Hun Bun." Gram Gram crossed one shapely ethereal leg over the other. "Frankly, I'm shocked that you aren't taking any action. This man and his hocus pocus pies should be out on their rears before morning."

H.P. suppressed a smile. Although the situation

was somber, it wouldn't have mattered whether Gram Gram were see-through or not. She was clearly jealous of the man whose pies were the talk of the town. "If I fire him now, then we'll never know exactly why he's been doing that in the first place. I need all the information I can gather. I want to take it to Booker while he's working, so he'll be here, unawares, when she comes in to arrest him."

"The man poisoned your son! You don't have a minute to spare! Report his misdeeds to that new policewoman, haste post."

"No, Gram, it's post haste. Believe me, I'm upset that he would offer my son poison. I need proof before I go to Booker, and I don't want him getting suspicious before that happens."

Dexter's inability to remember anything after eating the pie coupled with Tildie's description of her son as "acting like a zombie" worried H.P. the most. *Was Minty planning to control everyone in the community?* "Gram Gram, the minute I know what's going on, he'll be sitting in the city jail. Sweetwater Swear."

The oldest of Gram Gram's grandchildren were consummate liars. Gram Gram came up with an ingenious way to put them to the test. "Sweetwater Swear" meant they pledged they were telling the truth and if it was discovered they weren't, each one of their cousins were allowed to go through their possessions and pick whichever one they liked. It only took one incident each before the lying stopped.

As H.P. exited the cooler, she bumped into Minty.

"Didn't mean to disrupt y'all's confabulation," he said slyly. *Did he know? How could he?*

"I was talking to myself. It's something I've found keeps me on track." H.P. framed her head with her palms. "This head would roll right down the block if I let it."

Minty chuckled, easing the tension. "Ah didn't come in early, as you requested, but now Ah find mahself severely behind on pie orders. Ah told you my cousin lives here in town, and Ah was wondering if you'd mind terribly if Ah brought her in to help me catch up?"

"About that..." H.P. glanced sideways. Her heart was beating so hard she worried it might jump out of her chest. "We've had some... complaints about the recipes you're using."

He slapped the metal table so hard, she was sure Charlie would voice her displeasure.

"MAH recipes? Well, if that don't burn mah crust! Never, ever heard that before! Did you get the name of the person who complained?"

"It's not you!" H.P. said quickly, unable to keep herself from comforting him. "It's these small-town folks. I had the same frustration when I moved here from San Francisco. I worked for three of the top four restaurants there. I naturally expected I'd be doing these folks a favor by sharing the recipes I'd learned. Instead, I had veal that went bad and sauces the soured. It was a hard lesson."

She wasn't lying, exactly. No one in town would

touch her carpaccio, a dish made with raw, thinly-sliced meat. "For now, I need you to follow my grandmother's recipes. We'll ease the community into your style gently."

No, Sweetwater. He poisoned your son. Your Dexter.

"Maybe it's just a matter of using different herbs. But we don't want to take any chances that someone might get sick."

There was a harsh knock at the back door, startling them both. Outside of deliveries, no one came to the back door, ever.

H.P. felt embarrassed to show fear in front of Minty, so against her better judgment, she opened the door without a heavy skillet in her other hand.

"Ms. Sweetwater?"

Her shoulders tensed further. "Charlie Shine? What are you doing here? I haven't been in the basement since our uncomfortable meeting, so don't worry that I'm stealing from you," she snapped. Her sleep had been less-than-wonderful lately, what with the semi-nightly visits from Heather.

Charlie fumbled with a "Luv Me, Luv My Truck" cap.

Before she could reply, H.P. felt Minty's hot breath on her neck. "Well, if it idn't my cousin now! Are your ears burnin' darlin'?"

H.P. whipped around. "Your cousin? Why didn't you tell me before?"

His face was as empty as the four over-priced billboards on the outskirts of Misty Cove. "Before what, ma-yam? Didn't know it was anyone's business."

Charlie Shine pushed her way through the door and went into the kitchen before H.P. had the chance to block her.

"Nice setup you got here," Charlie said as she turned in a circle. She ran one rough hand across the shiny, stainless-steel counter. "Musta cost a bundle."

"That is none of YOUR business!" H.P. felt violated. She wanted nothing more than to throw this pair out and never see them again. Instead, H.P. took a towel and buffed an oversized handprint off the counter. "I'll thank you to leave now, Ms. Shine. Cousin or not, only my employees are allowed in the kitchen area."

"Ah invited her to help with the pies, ma-yam. Didn't mean to ruffle your feathers."

No. Absolutely not, Hun Bun. Not in my kitchen.

H.P. steeled herself before answering sweetly, "That's kind of your cousin, but it's best that Minty and I handle the pies ourselves. If you cut yourself or worse, my insurance agent will blow his stack."

Minty and Charlie Shine exchanged glances, giving H.P. the distinct impression they weren't telling her everything. "And now, Ms. Shine, I would like you to leave." She opened the door and held it while Charlie did what could only be described as a "mosey" toward her. Charlie paused when she was directly in front of H.P. Her breath was scented with lime and hot sauce.

"Didn't mean to upset you, Ms. Sweetwater, but I

can understand how you'd be uncomfortable, given my conversation with the nice police chief." One side of Charlie's mouth rose. "'Til we meet again." She touched the brim of her hat and stepped outside. "See you at home, Minty," she called.

Once she was sure the woman had left her property, H.P. turned to Minty. "I'll help you with pies. We've suspended orders for a week, so there is plenty of time to catch up. If need be, I'll pull an all-nighter." H.P. found the hook where her rain jacket hung and pulled it on over her arms. "Go ahead and start prepping. At least we know everything is fresh. I've got an errand to run."

For possibly the first time, H.P. was relieved when Edna chose that moment to walk in. "What?" she barked when the weight of the room hit her. "Do I have pickles in my teeth?" She closed her lips and ran her tongue across her teeth, then poked one index finger in her mouth and did the same. "Can't feel any."

"No. You're just fine, Edna."

Minty waved before turning to the walk-in. "Edna," H.P. whispered, "I'm leaving you in charge. I have to run an errand. Something big happened..." She paused to build suspense, knowing how much Edna loved good gossip. "It turns out, our new neighbor is Minty's cousin!"

Edna brought all the fingers on one hand to her lips. As though that meek measure could keep a new version of this story off her lips. "Shoulda figured.

Nutty chefs must have their own employment site. We're number one on that list."

"Just make sure Charlie Shine doesn't come back while I'm gone. If she does, you have my permission to kick her out."

Edna stood taller with the gift of her new responsibility. "You want me to go after her with the broom, or maybe something sharper?"

"No. Call Booker Danno."

H.P. practically ran to her next destination. She was dismayed to find the door to Punchard Security locked up tight. Taking a page from Charlie Shine's book, she knocked vigorously until the door finally swung opened.

"H.P.?" Thud Punchard asked. "What's wrong?"

"Can I come in? I need your help."

Over coffee and the most delicious cinnamon rolls she'd ever tasted, H.P. told him the whole story, including Dex's mystery ailment. When she'd finished, she looked up hopefully at him, waiting for his response. When none came, she continued, "I'd like to hire you to follow Dex. I don't want my father, my chef, or that creepy lady, Charlie anywhere near him."

"On it," Thud said matter-of-factly. "If necessary, I can let myself into their place when nobody's home."

"I... don't have a lot of money, but maybe if I pay you in installments?"

"No. You're a friend, H.P. And if this turns out to be something big, the entire town will be in your debt."

She stood and glanced at her watch, shocked to see an hour had gone by. "Shoot. I need to get back before Edna decides to clobber Minty with my expensive pots and pans." H.P. giggled. "My guilty pleasure for today: picturing that scenario!"

Thud walked her to the door of his empty office. It was unusual for his brothers not to be typing away on their computers, working on security for some big business on the other side of the world.

"Where did you get those rolls? They're divine!"

"I like to bake," he said without emotion. "My favorite thing to bake is Lemon Chiffon pies."

Chapter Thirty-Five

"I'm so glad I didn't start you on fire! That'd be so bad!"

Coriander Crumb stood upright, her apron covered in flour and burnt biscuit crumbs. Her hair had a dusting of powdered sugar for some inexplicable reason.

"Yeah, me too. Where are you off to in such a hurry?" H.P. smoothed the front of her dress, now hopelessly stained with burnt biscuit crumbs. The second one she'd lost in a month. She'd thought about crossing the street to avoid the human tornado, but at the last minute, she convinced herself that would be rude.

"To see you, silly! I have very important information for you!"

"Oh?" H.P. somehow doubted Coriander had a complete thought in her brain.

"Yes, yes. I'm concerned about your well-being. I

heard all about the threats on your life. Your father believes you're hiding money?"

"I don't know how or why you have that information." H.P. stared hard at Coriander's messy hair. "Whatever is going on in my life isn't your concern. Nor your mother's."

She'd had just about enough of Charlie Shine. Her daughter couldn't be trusted either.

Coriander glanced up the street one way, then down the other. She motioned for H.P. to come in closer, whispering in her ear, "The Dirty Half Dozen Gang believes you have intel on their hidden money."

H.P. pulled away. "I already know that. And I've hired protection. I don't understand why they'd think I know where it is. Wouldn't I have used it by now if I did?"

Coriander took a deep breath and attempted to run her fingers through the ratty mess on her head. When they became hopelessly entangled, H.P. moved to her side reluctantly. "Here. Let me."

After she'd freed Coriander's fingers, H.P. stood back. "How do you have this information? Did they come in for biscuits and confess their evil plans?"

Coriander's face became cherry red. "I can't tell you."

"I'm concerned for my son's safety, Coriander. What if they come for me and he gets caught in the crossfire? If you don't care about the life of a young boy, then—"

"Burnt butter! I'm no good with secrets. I've been working with the

FBI."

H.P. burst out laughing. "What? Did you bump your head too hard when we clashed?"

"They contacted me when Nine Nails Nora went missing. They said the last few members of The Dirty Half Dozen Gang were about to be released from prison and I was told to follow them closely, to find the money they hid."

"Why on earth would the FBI think I had any information?"

She scoured her brain for anything to help make sense of this mixed-up mess.

"Your dad never had much of a memory. That man was able to tuck away his feelings for his mother and his daughter and forget."

"He forgot where he stashed the money!" H.P. stared at Coriander, trying to absorb the words that just spilled out of her mouth. "My father forgot where he stashed the money while he was locked up, so he came back here, hoping I'd found it."

Coriander let out a puff of air, causing one unruly curl to float up and return to the same spot on her dirty forehead.

"Can't you just contact your FBI people and tell them that there's been a mix-up? I have no idea where the money is hidden and I'm getting tired of people suspecting me. And what about your mother? Wouldn't she know?"

"H.P.!" Coriander gasped. "Mama said someone tried to break into my shop yesterday. I wonder if they're trying to access the top-secret tunnel under my place!"

"I'm going to Booker now."

"Can I come too?"

The poor woman was a pathetic mess. How the FBI ever thought she was capable of pulling off something this big was hard to fathom.

"Okay. But let me do the talking!"

"Are you sure it's okay to eavesdrop?" Coriander hissed.

H.P. kept her head pressed against Booker's door, ignoring the weight of Coriander's body against hers. It was a stroke of good luck that Maeviz was out sick.

When the door opened abruptly, both women toppled to the floor, H.P. falling on top of Coriander.

"Were you eavesdropping? That's dangerous territory when the victim is in law enforcement!" Booker offered one hand to H.P. and the other to Coriander, pulling until both were back on their feet.

"I heard you talking to Lotta Kitties," Coriander blurted out. "Last week I saw the two of you together at Lake It or Leave It lake. You were talking about The Dirty Half Dozen Gang and how many people lost their lives. Are you two involved with them?"

Tildie and Dex and every kid looking to prove their bravery spent time at the lake. "How did you manage to go there unseen, Coriander?"

H.P. felt hot breath on her neck. She was afraid to turn around, afraid of whoever snuck in behind them. A body pushed past Coriander and H.P. and H.P. was relieved to see it was Lotta.

"I thought we were friends, H.P.! How could you accuse me of that?"

H.P.'s cheeks were burning. "We ARE friends, Lotta. Coriander has crazy ideas."

"They deserve an explanation, sis," Booker said quietly.

The room felt cold as H.P. tried absorbing that news. Lotta wasn't lonely at all. She'd been plotting with her sister to find the money, just like everyone else!

"Sis? You two are... sisters?" Coriander asked. "That wasn't in the brief!"

Booker knitted her brows together and frowned. "What do you mean by that?" she asked.

H.P. squeezed Coriander's arm and shook her head. "It's a long story," she said. "What's more important is what's going on with the two of you. How do you know about The Dirty Half Dozen Gang? My kids found articles about them on your computer."

"I told you the story of my leaving home," Lotta began, "what I didn't tell you was that our mother was in The Dirty Half Dozen Gang. She only admitted it when I found her diary, which she'd written in code."

"The one in your office!" When H.P. realized she'd blurted that out, she clapped her hands over her mouth.

"Yes, that one. I've been reading books that explain decoding to try and make sense of it. Six months ago, I received an anonymous letter stating that the gang would be reconvening here in Misty Cove. I knew I had to be here on the off-chance Mom would come." She took her thumb and wiped the tears forming in both eyes.

Booker, seeing her sister was overcome by emotion, cleared her throat and continued the story. "The whole reason I went into law enforcement was to find my mother and sister. I tracked her to Misty Cove, thanks to Maeviz's father. He's a private detective who didn't charge me, and in exchange—"

"You had to hire his lazy daughter."

Booker nodded solemnly.

"Is your mother here? Have you found her?" Coriander asked.

"She was," Booker continued. "Mom was working undercover for the FBI. At least, that's the information I have." She sighed. "They're never very transparent. You know our father was a criminal. My mother escaped and tried taking him down. When she realized he was too powerful, she asked if there was some other organization she could bring down. They'd been so impressed with her, they immediately sent her the file on a gang of bank robbers."

"That's very noble of her," H.P. said. "I think? You don't sound like you were proud of her."

"It's hard when you love someone with all your heart and they betray you," Lotta said with little emotion. "When Mom decided she wanted to lead The Dirty Half Dozen more than she wanted justice for the victims of their robberies, the FBI cut her loose. She had to serve time just like the other members of the gang. Mom got out of prison and immediately traveled to Misty Cove. I followed her and confronted her."

"What?" Coriander and H.P. said in unison. "You saw your mother? What did she say?"

Booker sat on the edge of her desk and looked at the carpet. "She said she witnessed the murder of a child and it had been eating at her for years. She was going to confess to the FBI and begged me to stay quiet until she did. She was worried about my safety." Booker looked up. "And Lotta's."

"And she was murdered before she could tell them," Lotta continued. "Noraline Angeline tried to do the right thing, in the end."

The image of a body floating in Lake It or Leave It lake formed in H.P.'s mind. It was even worse now that she knew the woman's identity.

"Did Minty poison her?" H.P. asked, forgetting her plan. "I mean, the Pennyhuggers seemed to think he poisoned them."

"No," Booker said. "My poor mother was tortured and shot. What's this about Minty?"

"I'm so sorry, you guys. What do we do now?" H.P. could hear the helplessness in her own voice.

"We set a trap, that's what."

The three stared at Coriander, a woman who couldn't even manage to comb her hair. She seemed an unlikely source for a good plan.

"How? Booker asked.

"H.P., you said your dad thinks you know where the money is stashed. What if we all pretended like you actually do?"

"But I don't know—"

H.P. paused. Her father took her fishing and to the bar while he played pool.

"You'll retrace his steps when he lived here, with you. Then, Booker will announce the money has been found."

"That will pull everyone out from the shadows!"

Booker voice carried an infectious excitement H.P. hadn't heard before.

Chapter Thirty-Six

"Let me get this straight." H.P. rubbed her temples as though she could knead clarity into the mess unraveling before her. "You—Coriander, the Burnt Biscuit Babe—are suggesting we lure an entire gang of desperate criminals into the diner with me as the bait?"

"Yes!" Coriander beamed, seemingly unaware of how absurd the suggestion sounded coming from someone covered in flour. "It's genius!"

"More like insanity," H.P. muttered.

Booker, however, appeared intrigued. She scratched her chin thoughtfully. "It's risky, but not as wild as it sounds. If your dad, Sully the Sinus, is desperate enough to think you've found the money, he'll show up. So will anyone else intending to claim it. I have my suspicions about others in our community.

"Charlie Shine, Minty, and whoever else crawls out

of the woodwork. We can wrap this all up at once," Booker said, almost excitedly.

"And how exactly do we pull that off?" H.P. asked, her voice rising. "I don't exactly keep a stash of ceremonial treasure chests in my pantry!"

Coriander, who'd managed to tangle her hair in her apron string yet again, piped up. "Ooh, ooh! We could get a fake bag of money! You know, like the ones they use in *The Great Biscuit Bake-Off* finales. Except less sprinkles and more... bait."

"And how are we supposed to spread the word about this discovery?" H.P. asked, arching a brow.

"Leave that to me," Booker said. She pulled out her phone and snapped a photo of the chest propped inside the tunnel entrance. "A little, anonymous tip to the right people will get the news out fast."

"You're disturbingly good at this," H.P. muttered.

Coriander clapped her hands again, excitement radiating off her like heat. "This is going to be legendary. I'm already brainstorming biscuit-themed hashtags—'#BaitedByBiscuits,' '#HoneyPieHeist,'—"

"I'm surrounded by lunatics," H.P. groaned.

"Yes, that's what our intel says." Booker Danno lifted her nonfat latte to her lips and sipped casually, as though she'd just informed H.P. that her son forgot his locker combination, again. Instead, she was engaging in a performance to rival Gram Gram's dinner theater performance as Beulah Bubblesworth *in Murder at the Midnight Buffet.*

"Our information indicates that your father hid all the money The Dirty Half Dozen Gang stole in the tunnels underneath local businesses. I'd like to send a team underneath your building."

"Oh, I KNOW where it is." H.P. rested her elbows on the counter, staring directly into Booker's chest while Gwen titled her head to the side and frowned.

"You mentioned that on the phone. Not sure I'm comfortable with your demands though."

"You mean turning it over in a public ceremony? Like the penultimate episode of the *Great Biscuit Bake-Off, Public Ceremony Season?*" That tidbit seemed unnecessary, but Coriander's other ideas were on point so H.P. didn't argue.

"Um... yes, I did. In two days... so I have a chance to find the money and count it. I want every single dollar to be returned to the bank."

"We were concerned the gang would come back to

Misty Cove in search of their lost treasure, but when I met your father, he assured me he was just passing through."

Five Meal Gary, who'd been watching them as he sipped his coffee slowly, slid off his stool. "Don't know who this performance is benefiting, but both o' you ladies need to put more emotion into it."

"But why?" Although H.P. still hadn't tried speaking with him, she couldn't get past the idea that her father hated her. He'd called her his "little punkin' pie;" and a "slice of heaven." It wasn't her fault he ran off. He should still love her to the moon and back.

"No, you're right. I've asked Thud Punchard to be our in-house muscle. He's contracted with the police department before and understands what's expected of him. He'll 'work' here," Booker made air quotes, "until you're out of danger. Completely at the expense of the police department, of course."

That presented a real problem. H.P. just hired Thud to follow Minty and try to ascertain what, if any, evil deeds Minty was planning.

"Thud is more qualified than some law enforcement. No offense."

"None taken." Booker slurped the last of her latte. "Best I've had.

What'd you call this?"

"It's a Misty Cove Mudslide. Made with high quality chocolate milk, chocolate protein powder, chocolate, whipped cream and our coffee, of course."

Booker nodded. "Addictive." She slid off her stool.

"We'll be in touch. I'm sorry this is happening to you, H.P. You don't deserve this kind of treatment."

Before H.P. could respond, she felt, or rather smelled, familiar hot, garlic-laden breath. "Edna! For goodness sake! Just say hello like a normal person!"

H.P. whipped around so quickly, she knocked Edna off her feet.

"Geez! Wish there was an employee handbook so I could sue you for that!"

"Sorry!" H.P. took the old woman's hand and helped her up. "Booker informed me that a robbery will soon take place here!"

Edna squinted as she did when she didn't believe what her boss was saying. "Oh? Is this the kind where a coupla robbers walk through a train and ask the folks for all their cash? Could be a good thing for business if that son of yours could make some fancy posters."

"No, it's not like that at all." H.P. glanced around. In small towns, the tiniest utterances reached the ears and then the mouths of those who lived to spread them. If she pulled Edna into the kitchen, she risked raising Minty's suspicions. "Follow me."

H.P. led Edna outside, where a refreshing ocean breeze lifted her curls as well as her spirits. "Booker says my father is planning to rob us."

H.P. paused, as much for dramatic effect as to make sure Edna understood.

"Well, that's strange. He didn't mention anything when he was here last week."

Gwen, who'd been uncharacteristically quiet until

now, leaned in. "There's one place that'll sell this performance: the cellar. You said there's a tunnel under the freezer, right? We stage a discovery down there. Make it look like the money's been found."

They all fell silent.

"No," H.P. said flatly after she and Edna returned. "Absolutely not. I've been crawling through tunnels, losing sleep, and dodging criminals for weeks. I'm not adding the imminent collapse of my diner's foundation to the list."

Booker crossed her arms, her glasses perched on the edge of her nose. "Would you rather let Sully drag this out? Because he won't stop. None of them will."

The words stung because they were true.

Coriander clapped her flour-covered hands together, sending puffs of dust into the air. "Perfect! Operation Treasure Trap is a go!"

Chapter 37

H.P. stood inside the dimly lit walk-in freezer, staring down at the exposed tunnel opening beneath the floorboards. A single lantern cast long, flickering shadows that danced like ghosts against the walls.

"You're sure about this?" she muttered, directing her question to Booker.

Booker, who was crouched beside the tunnel with a serious look, nodded. "Once word gets out that you've 'discovered' where the money is hidden, they'll come running. I've got deputies stationed nearby and federal agents waiting for the signal. Trust me, H.P.— this ends tonight."

"Trust you? After you staged an arrest that nearly tanked my diner's reputation?" H.P. shot back.

"Details," Booker replied, unfazed.

From the far end of the kitchen, Gwen and Coriander appeared carrying a bedazzled chest. It was decorated with gold spray paint, plastic jewels, and—H.P. swore—bits of glittery ribbon.

Coriander grinned, her face smudged with glitter and powdered sugar. "Ta-da! It's realistic, isn't it?"

"It looks like it belongs in a kindergarten pirate play," H.P. deadpanned.

"Close enough!" Gwen huffed, setting the chest down with a thud. "We'll bury it in the tunnel just far enough to look convincing."

"Coriander, the other day when you told me about your side job—" H.P. winked, hoping Coriander understood. "You never mentioned your mother. Why would they contact you when they knew you were her daughter? What if you told her everything?"

Coriander's eyes did a weird back-and-forth. "When this is all over, I'll tell you why."

Chapter 38

"That's your sixth slice... if I were keeping count. It's so good to see you back to your old self. I was really worried about you, son."

Gwen's mother served homemade pizza to Dex, knowing the Sweetwaters had pizza every Friday night as a routine. Neither she nor Mr. Folds partook in the meal, however. "Too fancy for my taste," Mr. Folds commented. They ate their dinner upstairs on small tables while they watched *Wheel of Fortune.*

"Yeah, I guess," Dex replied with no concern for the wet morsels flying from his mouth. "What was it you wanted to tell me?"

H.P. took a deep breath. Not even a double pepperoni pizza with sausage, Canadian bacon, pineapple, and lime mustard sauce could have prepared him for the conversation ahead.

"Okay, here's the deal. You're not a little kid

anymore, so I think you can handle this very grownup talk."

Dex stopped chewing even though his cheeks were still bulging. "What?"

"My father, your grandfather—"

"The guy Tildie and me found in the alley?"

H.P. nodded. "Yes, that's him. He stayed around town and is up to no good. He and whoever his friends are have planned a robbery at the diner."

Dexter's eyes grew to the size of saucers. "Really? Like the one we saw on that train ride in the Black Hills?"

"No, son. That was pretend. This is real. I don't know when it's going to happen, but for the time being, you and Tildie need to stay away from the diner. Can you both do that?"

He stared at her in disbelief. "Are you joking?"

"I wish I were," she replied wistfully. "Mrs. Folds is over the moon that she'll have someone to bake cookies for and Mr. Bunce said you can study there whenever you need to. You'll go directly to either home and then text Mr. Bunce and me when you arrive. Got it?"

She held her knuckles out, the way kids manifested their own version of a high-five, according to Dex and Tildie. He met her knuckles with his own mustard-covered fist.

"But what if you need me around? Like, for protection?"

H.P.'s heart melted right then and there. Dex was usually as far away from his mother as possible. While she watched with envy as other kids laughed with their parents, her own son seemed to think her every word was part of her strategy to turn him into a weirdo.

"Oh, sweetie. Thud Punchard has been hired by the police department as a decoy. He'll be at the diner every day. But…" She opened her arms, refusing to drop them until he surrendered, and kissed the top of his head as he collapsed into her hug. H.P. drank in that beautiful, sour smell of an unwashed teen.

It was at that moment she understood why Gram Gram insisted on protecting her own son, despite his misdeeds. "Loving your child is for life, Hun Bun. No matter the mud they walk in."

"Dexie, I'm sorry I'm on your case so much. You're a good kid. Great, in fact. I'm so very, very lucky you're mine."

"I don't tell you often enough, but I love you, Mom!"

As he melted further into her chest, she felt something sticky on her neck. It didn't matter. "Dexie, there is nothing in this world more important to me than you."

Chapter Thirty-Eight

The fog rolled in ominously over Misty Cove and the diner became unusually quiet. Minty slipped out, unnoticed, right at closing time. It was more of a relief to H.P. than anything else. She hated confrontation and was hoping Abe and Booker would take care of that challenge for her. H.P., Gwen, and Booker stood silently in the kitchen. The faint hum of the refrigerator was the only sound as Booker leaned against the counter, flipping through a thin stack of papers.

"This is bad," she muttered, her glasses perched low on her nose.

"What now?" H.P. asked, glancing up from the pie crust she'd been rolling out. Gram Gram would be pleased to hear that her recipes were again being featured on the menu.

Booker held up a file, her expression grim. "Minty

Peppermint. Guess who his cellmate was in state prison?"

H.P.'s brow furrowed. "Well, the way this week's been going, I'd have to guess Sully the Sinus Sweetwater." She chuckled to herself about the absurdity of that idea. Despite his poisoned pies, Minty was far too refined to have spent time in a cell with Sullivan Sweetwater.

"Bingo," Booker said, slapping her hand on top of the file on the counter. "I just got the records from an old contact at the state penitentiary. They served three years inside the same cell."

"Makes sense to me," Gwen said. "They were both inside for all those armed robberies, right?"

"Minty very well could have committed robbery with Mr. Sweetwater. But at the time they were housed together, Minty was doing time for poisoning his father; Sully for... well, take your pick."

"So, they were friends?" Gwen asked. She was sitting on a stool with her arms crossed.

"Doubtful," Booker said. "My contacts say Sully treated Minty like his personal errand boy. But here's where it gets weirder." She flipped to another page and tapped a mugshot of a woman with sharp features and a crooked smile. "Recognize her?"

H.P. squinted at the grainy image. "Not really. Should I?"

"That's Shady the Shiv. She was locked up for grand larceny about twenty years ago."

Gwen snorted. "Sounds like the name of a cartoon character, not a felon."

"Trust me, she was no joke," Booker said, setting the paper down. "Shady was one of the point gunmen during the robberies. She stabbed anyone who looked at her sideways, and if you can believe this, she was released early for good behavior. But here's the kicker: her release date overlaps with my mother's disappearance. If Shady the Shiv came to town to kill my mother, she must've known about the diary entry."

The room went totally still, the implications sinking in.

"Wait," H.P. said slowly. "We assume the entire gang converged here to find the money. Besides my father and your mother, who else came here? Have you seen them?"

"Zippermouth Zeb, the gang's most mysterious member, who never spoke a word, got early release for good behavior. Zeb lived a quiet life working as a janitor in a rundown comedy club in Reno. The place specialized in old-school acts—bad magicians, washed-up comedians, and, unfortunately for Zeb, a ventriloquist with a mean streak named Ricky Riddle.

"One night, Ricky got a little too aggressive with his routine, using his creepy wooden dummy, Mr. Chuckles, to roast the audience. When he spotted Zeb in the back, he started heckling him mercilessly.

'What's the matter, buddy? Cat got your tongue? Or did you just never have one?'"

H.P. was enthralled by Booker's story. She had a

hard time imagining her father with this man, who clearly had so much character.

"Zeb was furious," Booker continued. "He rushed the stage and began strangling Ricky. Somehow, Ricky kept his ventriloquist routine going so the crowd thought it was just part of the show. Mr. Chuckles grasped for props in Ricky's suitcase. In an instant, Mr. Chuckles stuck a fork through Zeb's neck. To this day, comedians at the club swear you can still hear faint, ghostly laughter whenever a ventriloquist takes the stage."

"Okay, we've accounted for Nine Nails Nora, Sully and Zeb. Where's Phat Wallet Phyllis?"

"Phat Wallet Phyllis, the gang's money-handler and notorious high roller, kept her love for cash alive after her release: she became an extreme couponer."

"Seems harmless to me," Gwen scoffed. "I'd expect more from someone whose name was 'Phat Wallet.'"

"She scammed grocery stores out of thousands, flipping discounted goods for profit and hoarding every deal like a dragon guarding gold;" Booker continued, "but her biggest score came when she entered the 'Shop 'Til You Drop Sweepstakes' at her local supermarket, a contest promising free groceries for life to the winner. A whole lifetime supply of groceries. To increase her odds, Phyllis submitted over 100,000 entries, stuffing every available ballot box for months. Of course, she won." Booker paused, glancing from H.P.'s face to the door behind her. *Was she expecting someone?*

"When Phyllis arrived at the store, she was ushered to the soup aisle, where a cart was set behind a yellow line."

Gwen sighed. "Why is it always the bad people who come out on top?"

"If only she had." Booker chuckled. "When the whistle blew, Phyllis lurched forward. They neglected to tell her beforehand that she would have to use a cart with one wheel pointed toward Yes We Can, Patriotic Peaches and the other toward the cans of Corn in the USA. Ten seconds later, she'd crashed her cart into a six-foot tower of Peas Out. The cans crushed Phyllis."

"So much for her 'phat' pockets," Gwen snickered. "More like 'phlat pockets.'" She nudged H.P. "Right, bestie?"

H.P. frowned but ignored her friend.

Booker nodded grimly. "It's starting to add up. My mother—the diary she kept in code. Sully's obsession with the missing money. Minty showing up here, trying to poison half the town. This band of thieves has clearly graduated to murder."

H.P. swallowed hard, her stomach churning. "They, or at least my father, left a little girl to die in an armoire. So there was no graduation. It had already happened."

"Wait a second," Gwen said, holding up her hand. "You've accounted for Sully, Minty, Phyllis, Nora and Zippermouth Zeb. We're missing one."

Booker hesitated. "Shady the Shiv. I know. I've been wondering about her myself. Seems like she would have shown up for this gathering. I looked up the whole gang's release dates..." Booker scrolled through messages on her phone. "Aha! She was released a year ago May. Good behavior and all that."

"I didn't come here for sympathy," Booker snapped, although her voice cracked. "I came here to finish what she started. If my mother died because of this gang or that damn money, I'm going to make sure it ends here."

"So, where does Minty fit into all of this?" Gwen asked, breaking the heavy silence.

"I'm not sure yet," Booker admitted. "But his showing up here isn't a coincidence. I can't find any connection to The Dirty Half Dozen Gang. There has to be an explanation. He's got a vendetta against Sully, and his poisoned pies can't be an accident. He must know something we don't."

H.P. chewed on her lip. "And Sully? What's his endgame?"

"Same as it's always been," Booker said bitterly. "Find the money. Take it. Disappear."

"But if he doesn't know where it is," Gwen said, "then why come back here? Why now?"

H.P. pulled out her phone and opened her text messages. "Because of this."

Booker leaned over to read it.

April 17, 25 Years Ago

"If you're reading this, it means the game isn't over. You thought we got away clean, but some debts don't stay buried. Meet me where we swore we'd never go back—

Misty Cove, April 17, twenty-five years from now. No cops, no excuses. Just us. Or else the truth comes out."

"Where did you get this?" Booker asked, her voice shaking. "You should have come to me right away, H.P."

"I'm sorry. I was planning to show you... eventually."

"I guess I shouldn't be too upset. I received a message of my own." Booker licked a finger and thumbed through the file until she found a crumpled page.

"Find the money before Sully the Sinus does. The consequences otherwise will be catastrophic. Leave and don't look back."

"It was taped to the outside of my office door last week," Booker explained. "No name. No context."

"So, someone else knows about the money," Gwen said, leaning back.

"Wait, don't you have cameras all over the police station?" H.P. asked.

"We do." Booker scratched her forehead. "There wasn't anyone on camera. One minute, the door was bare and the next, the note was hanging there. Almost as if a ghost hung it. If I believed in such things."

H.P. felt goosebumps rising up and down her arms. There was only one ghost with those abilities. "Someone must've been afraid to be seen. They messed with your cameras," she said quickly before uttering a loud, barking laugh that startled Gwen. "You know how kids are these days, always coming up with one prank or another."

What are you talking about? Gwen mouthed. H.P. pretended to ignore her friend.

"Or someone's playing us," Booker replied. "But whoever it is, they want to make sure Sully doesn't get his hands on the cash."

H.P. pushed the papers aside, her mind spinning. "I can't believe this many people played us. We've forgotten though, that we're still missing one. Shady the Shiv. I asked before if you knew her real name, Booker?"

"Well, that would be me, Charlie Shine."

Chapter Thirty-Nine

"**D**on't you dare move."

The voice was sharp, commanding, and unmistakable. Charlie Shine stood in the doorway, her wiry hair peeking out from under a Biscuit Babe cap. In her hand, she held a gun, the barrel gleaming in the harsh kitchen light.

"Charlie?" H.P. breathed, her pulse spiking. "What are you doing here? I haven't been anywhere near your private tunnel! Edna even bought BounceMeQuiet soles for her orthopedic shoes so they didn't clomp when she walked. You don't have any beef with us."

"Let's skip the pleasantries," Charlie snapped, stepping into the room with a predator's determined gaze. Her eyes flicked to Gwen, then to Booker, who had just emerged from the pantry. "We're going to take a little trip to the cellar. All of you. Now."

"You've been working *day and night*," Booker said, her voice laced with derision as she descended the stairs. "What makes you think we know something you don't?"

Charlie snorted. "Oh, spare me. You're all connected to him, whether you like it or not. H.P.'s his kid, you're the daughter of a snitch obsessed with taking him down, and Gwen..." She scanned the petite dry cleaner from head to toe. "I'm not sure what your deal is, but I don't trust that face."

Gwen blinked. "Thanks?"

"Did Nails ever tell you how she got her name?"

Booker shook her head.

"Your father ran a huge crime syndicate, moving drugs across the entire country. She tried leaving once and he had one of her fingernails removed. Never grew back."

"She was very brave," H.P. said for Booker's benefit. "That was a bold move."

"And now she's dead because Sully found out she double-crossed us. Well, and maybe Charlie finished her off. Blah, blah, blah." Charlie rolled her eyes. "Let's get this over with. Down to the tunnel and I'll think about letting you live."

Somehow, Coriander Crumb made an entrance without tripping over the broom or starting the napkins on fire. "Mother? Why would you do this to your own child? After all the time we've been apart!" Coriander let out a small hiccup of a sob.

H.P. allowed herself a quick glance in Coriander's direction. The woman seemed calmer than any other time H.P. had seen her.

"Charlie, kidnapping a law enforcement officer won't end well for you," Booker said evenly, although her hand inched toward her hip holster.

H.P.'s eyes were drawn to a transparent hand reaching out from the walk-in. It was longer and wider than a human hand, but the scar from the time Gram Gram cut her hand on the shake mixer was plainly visible. The fingers curled up, beckoning H.P. to come inside.

"Don't even think about it, Officer," Charlie said, waving the gun wildly in the air. "Nothing scares me after spending decades in the tombs, dealing with your type."

Booker's jaw tightened, but she stepped back, raising her hands slightly. "Taking a law enforcement officer prisoner will only bring you a whole new level of prison time, Charlie."

H.P. glanced at Gwen, her chest tightening as she saw the fear etched on her friend's face. "Charlie, you've got full access to the cellar. What more do you want?"

Charlie tilted her head, her eyes narrowing. "You know exactly what I want, ma'am. The money. The stash your dear, old dad hid down there. I've been digging through this tunnel, chasing Sully the Sinus's breadcrumbs for weeks, and I'm done playing games. You're going to show me where it is, or I'll make this messy."

A cool breeze surrounded them and this time, H.P.

heard a voice echo inside her head. *Tell her to lock you in here. I'll keep you safe.*

"Wait!" H.P. yelled, causing the entire group to pause dead in their tracks. Gwen's eyes expressed gratitude.

"There isn't a lot of space down there, at least in our end of the tunnel. Lock us in the walk-in while you search. You'll have free rein."

It occurred to H.P. that Booker had the ability to search to her heart's content anyway. *Give me something, Gram Gram!*

In the trunks your great-uncle gave us. She'll find all the treasure she needs.

H.P. suppressed a smile. "If you take everything off the top shelf, you'll find two deerskin-covered trunks. Those contain all the treasure you'd ever want."

Charlie's eyes narrowed as she moved close to H.P. —so close that H.P. could smell the bitter scent of cheap coffee on her breath. It certainly wasn't anything The Honeypie Diner would serve.

"If'n you knew where the treasure was all along, why didn't you just tell me? Or your daddy? Something smells funny. I think we're all going to the cellar."

"She didn't tell you because she didn't know it was there, Mother." Coriander bravely stepped forward. "Remember the Plentyadollars Savings and Loan job? When I sat in the car and waited with your phone? You said to call when I saw the coppers. I called you when I saw them, and that night, you ordered six large pizzas with all the toppings. I miss those times we had together."

H.P. held her breath, willing her kooky neighbor to continue.

"I don't know what to say, Corrie-bear." Charlie took a ragged red cloth from her pocket and blew her nose so hard, H.P. jumped at the sound. After Charlie finished, she wiped both eyes, where tears had formed.

"Yes, those were good times. Sure, I'd wished your Aunt Bunnie and Uncle Hopper brought you more 'n twice a year to see me, but when they took you and your brother in, that was part of the deal. And now..." Charlie's voice broke. "Here's my baby girl, wantin' to pull a job with her mummy again."

Charlie took the nose of her gun and scratched her forehead. "Me and my gal will go downstairs and find my money together." She pointed toward the cellar hatch door. " Go on, Corrie-bear. I'm gonna take care of these folks and then I'll join you."

"No, Mother. You won't kill them. Remember the bank robber's code?"

All the air left the kitchen as H.P. and her friends contemplated what came next if Coriander wasn't successful in convincing her mother to put her gun away.

"No bodies, no heat," mother and daughter said in unison before bursting into laughter.

"Jankies! What's happening?" Gwen, who had been unusually quiet up until now asked.

"Mom and me always laughed over the codes in the

required reading for The Dirty Half Dozen Gang." Coriander winked pointedly at H.P.

"Larceny for Dummies," Charlie chuckled. "A code in every chapter. No dead bodies makes the coppers wait longer to find the missing loot. Ain't that right, Missus Copper?"

Booker seemed absolutely flustered. "I don't..." she mumbled.

"Okay, my girlie made a good point. I've had a little fun with you, but now I need you somewhere you won't be causing me trouble. I'm likin' the idea of stuffin' you into the cooler. Throw a little salt on you and you'll be nice and cured before anyone's the wiser."

H.P. breathed a sigh of relief. It took every ounce of self-control she had to keep from running to the cooler and the comfort of Gram Gram's aura.

The hostages entered the walk-in without a sound and turned to face Charlie, breathing in the last breaths of fresh air. "Hand your phones to me."

When the women hesitated, Charlie shouted, "Now! Before I shoot 'em outta your manicures!"

H.P. quickly collected the phones and handed them to Charlie.

"Okay, then, you gals enjoy your last few hours. Guess you won't starve in here, it'll be the lack of oxygen that'll do you in." Charlie pushed the door closed and scooted something heavy behind it. "I saw the handle inside. You can't fool old Charlie."

When the sound of her heavy footsteps and

Coriander's annoying voice were no longer heard, the women uttered a collective sigh.

"Don't worry, I'm sure between all of us we can force that door open."

No, please don't, Hun Bun.

Gwen's head snapped around. Although she could see Gram Gram's ghost, she rarely heard anything Gram Gram said.

"Let's figure out our next step while we have the time." H.P. suggested as she peered out the corner of her eye to the bright blue aura that was only visible to her, and possibly Gwen.

"Good idea. I still have my personal phone. I gave her the one we use at the police station because it has extra security. If anyone but me tries to use it, it will emit a high-pitched squeal that won't go away until it's back in my hands."

That's so cool!" Gwen said. "I need one of those for my dry cleaners! Instant business!"

Stall them, my darling. You're in the safest place you can be.

Although it made no sense to H.P., Gram Gram never steered her wrong.

"One positive from having to throw everything out and restock, my produce is the freshest in town. Anyone for an apple?" Without waiting for a response, H.P. opened the box and removed three shiny red apples.

"Not that I'm against food of any kind," Gwen

began, "but I don't know how you could be hungry at a time like this."

"I'm just trying to keep our minds off our current situation is all."

Gram Gram touched her index fingers to her thumbs and moved them away from each other. Her sign to stretch the conversation.

But why? There was a key hanging at the right of Gwen's head. They could unlock the door, shove it open and make their escape completely unnoticed.

"Booker, I bet you have some interesting stories from your time in law enforcement. Can you tell us one now?"

Both women glared at H.P.

"This isn't a campfire storytelling contest," Booker replied sharply. "But yes, I can tell you one." She stretched her legs out in front of her and leaned back against a box of Olivia Orange's Onions. "I began my career as a jailer in the Oregon State Women's Penitentiary. I wanted to right the wrongs of my father, but more than that, I knew my mother was locked up and I needed to know if she ever... you know."

Booker sniffed and glanced at the boxes of dinner roll mix.

"And did you find her?" H.P. asked only half-believing this story. "And did she tell you how much she loved you?"

Booker shook her head. "I bought another guard groceries for two months, all the while eating boxes of ramen noodles. When I finally got the okay to work her cell block, my mother had been transferred to another prison."

"That's an odd coincidence, don't you think?" H.P. spoke in hyper speed. "But I bet you have stories from the prison anyway."

Gwen stood, brushing imaginary crumbs from her plaid skirt. "This has been fun, bestie. And kinda weird if I'm being honest." She stood on her tiptoes to reach the key from its not-so-hidden location.

"No! Wait!" H.P. called. It was too late. Gwen had the key and was reaching for the handle.

Just as Gwen turned the lever, a hot gust of wind blew it shut. H.P. didn't have to look around. She recognized Gram Gram's handiwork.

"Honey Bunny, it's your daaaaddy!"

The women froze in unison.

"How did he get in here?" Gwen mouthed.

H.P. put a finger to her lips, hoping to silence her friend.

Sullivan Sweetwater's heavy boots clunked across the kitchen until he was standing close to the walk-in. H.P. held her breath, hoping her friends did the same.

"Baby girl? I need your help. I know you found my money. Now it's time to return it to your daddy. I worked hard to make a good life for you, sweetie. This is my reward."

Although she hated him for abandoning her and robbing all those banks, there was still a vulnerable little girl insider her that melted hearing him call her "baby girl."

But he killed poor Heather. And left his own daughter without one word of explanation.

They all breathed a sigh of relief when the sound of his boots gradually disappeared.

"We've got to get out of here. I don't care what you say, bestie. The time is now!"

Just as Gwen's hand wrapped around the handle for the second time, a loud blast blew the three of them to the back of the walk-in. Gram Gram used her aura to cushion the blow, wrapping them in her arms and gently lowering them to the ground.

Chapter Forty

The kitchen of The Honeypie Diner looked like a war zone. A thin haze of flour and dust floated in the air, settling over shattered glass and over-turned chairs. The scent of burnt sugar clung to the walls, an eerie contrast to the destruction around them.

H.P. ran a shaking hand over her forehead, smearing dirt across her skin. She turned slowly, taking in the chaos—the broken shelves, the splintered wood, the cracked tile where the force of the explosion had knocked everything sideways. Her stomach twisted. It could have been so much worse.

Booker let out a low whistle, nudging a fallen light fixture with the toe of her boot. "Well, this is gonna take a while to clean up."

Gwen, standing by what had once been the pantry door, grimaced. "Forget cleaning. How are we even alive?"

H.P. knew.

She turned toward the back of the kitchen, her gaze landing on the large metal shelving unit that had once held bags of flour and boxes of canned tomatoes. It had collapsed in the blast, falling forward like a protective barrier. Behind it, the trapdoor to the cellar was sealed shut—buried under the weight of the shelving.

She sucked in a breath.

Gram Gram.

Somehow, her grandmother's spirit had saved them—again.

"She used another favor," H.P. murmured, more to herself than anyone else.

Gwen glanced at her, confusion flickering across her face. "Who did?"

H.P. stepped forward, reaching out to touch the cold metal of the fallen shelves. The truth sat heavily in her chest. "Gram Gram. She kept us from going down to the cellar. She must've known something was about to explode."

Booker frowned. "You're saying she... what? Knocked over a whole shelving unit from the afterlife?"

H.P. didn't answer. She didn't need to. She simply *knew*.

And then, something else dawned on her.

She swallowed hard and stepped around the mess, scanning the wreckage.

There was no way her father could have survived this.

The explosion had originated from below. If the tunnel had caved in, if the trapdoor had been covered... that meant Sullivan Sweetwater was still down there.

Buried.

Gram Gram sacrificed the life of her son to save her granddaughter.

For a moment, H.P. felt nothing at all, just emptiness. Then, slowly, a wave of something she couldn't quite name swept over her. Relief? Grief? Anger? A tangled mix of all three?

She looked down at her watch, her fingers tightening instinctively around her wrist. *Dex and Tildie are still in school*. Safe. Over a mile away.

She exhaled, long and slow.

"He's dead," she said quietly.

Neither Booker nor Gwen asked whom she was talking about. They knew.

Booker nodded solemnly. "Then it's over."

Was it? H.P. wasn't so sure. "But we still haven't found the money he stole, and until we do, someone will always be looking for it."

"There's one place that hasn't been searched," Booker said. "Follow me."

Chapter Forty-One

A s they walked down the street with their ears still ringing, it was evident the blast only affected The Honeypie Diner and Coriander's biscuit shop. Above ground, at least, things were much better than they could have been. Not quite the apocalyptic scene they'd expected to find. Despite that, they didn't encounter one soul. No sign of Sullivan Sweetwater either.

The bell above the door jingled an upbeat sound that didn't fit their circumstances as they stepped into the Biscuit Babe Biscuit Shop. The usual warm scent of honey butter and cinnamon sugar did little to ease H.P.'s nerves. The shop was eerily quiet, lit only by the dim late afternoon sun filtering through the windows.

"Coriander?" H.P. called quietly. When there was no reply, she turned to her friends and frowned. "Really, Booker, I don't understand why this was necessary. Coriander and Charlie were buried in the explosion, just like..." H.P. couldn't even bring herself to say Sully the Sinus's name. Even though she'd only known Coriander for a short time and the woman mostly irritated her, the loss of The Biscuit Babe hurt her heart too.

A loud rustling from the back room startled them. Booker placed one hand on her waistband where she normally carried a gun, but today it was just a plain waistband. Gwen reached for the only weapon she could find— a metal napkin holder and wielded it above her head like a javelin.

To H.P.'s shock, Coriander Crumb and her mother, Charlie appeared with barely a scratch. Coriander's apron was the cleanest it had ever been, and as for her hair, it was almost tame.

"You survived?" Gwen blurted out, eyes wide. "How? That blast just about made a metal pancake out of the diner's kitchen!"

Charlie crossed her arms. "Disappointed?"

H.P. shook her head, still trying to process what she saw. "We thought—after the explosion—"

"We were already halfway down the tunnel when it happened," Coriander explained as her eyes darted back and forth. "Mom and me got the first trunk open pretty easily. It was filled with old clothing and metal miniature toy trucks."

H.P. remembered the only time she saw Great Uncle Festus, he handed her one of his prized cars and the sharp metal cut her small hands.

"We moved on to the second trunk, and that's when Mom heard it ... a ticking sound."

H.P. froze. "Wait. What?"

Coriander's gaze sharpened. "We thought you planted that bomb, knowing the surviving members of the gang would be coming for it."

"What are you suggesting?" H.P. recoiled. "Do you really think I'd blow up my grandmother's diner for some silly cash box?"

Booker stepped forward, her eyes narrowing as a dusting of flour fell from her crisp, white shirt. "H.P. didn't plant anything. If there was a bomb in that tunnel, someone else put it there."

"Someone who wanted to make sure no one got their hands on that money," Gwen added.

A heavy silence fell over them.

"From her days in The Dirty Half Dozen Gang, Mom always knew when something was about to explode. We ran to my shop and barely made it there before we heard the explosion."

H.P. exhaled. "So the money was lost in the explosion?" H.P. asked. Maybe Booker wasn't off base.

Coriander hesitated. "Maybe."

Booker folded her arms. "What do you mean, *maybe*?" Booker's phone rang and she glanced down at the number. "All this excitement and I completely forgot I'm the emergency coordinator in these types of situations. Excuse me for a moment while I have Maeviz notify the volunteer search team members to search for any injured vics." Booker walked outside as her authoritative voice trailed off.

Coriander glanced at her mother. "Are you going to tell them?"

"My father hid the money somewhere else," H.P. blurted out.

A flicker of unease crawled up H.P.'s spine. Something about this seemed wrong.

Coriander met her eyes with a pleading look. "Shoot. I forgot about today's biscuit special, the Strawberry Cyclone. Could you see if any of them survived?"

Charlie eyed her daughter suspiciously before disappearing into the kitchen.

Coriander reached into her large, biscuit-shaped pocket and pulled out a crumpled envelope. "I found this," she whispered as she handed it to H.P. "Hide it before my mom comes back."

H.P. had a million questions, starting with whose side, exactly, Coriander was on. But that would have to wait. For now, she stuffed the envelope into the torn pocket of her uniform. Uneasy minutes ticked by and no one spoke.

The bell over the door jingled again as Booker returned. "Yes, Maeviz, we're currently checking damage at the Biscuit Babe shop. I don't understand why you'd need to meet us, but I appreciate your offer."

Booker looked up and shook her head. "The girl won't lift a finger for months and suddenly she thinks *she's* in charge. Probably bucking for a raise that she's DEFINITELY not getting."

The click of a gun cocking caused everyone in the room to freeze.

"The strawberry biscuits are present and accounted for. Well, all but the six I ate. Little dry for my taste. Now, is somebody gonna tell me the real reason you wanted me out of the room?"

When no one spoke, Charlie rolled her eyes. "Guess we're doing this the hard way. You gals did us wrong, telling us where the loot was and then trying to blow us to pieces. Too bad you got outta that freezer, but this'll work better. You gals will be unfortunate victims of the blast." She motioned with her gun. "Baby," she began, her voice softening, "how's 'bout we take 'em out back? I seen overturned trash barrels and bricks laying every which a-way. It'll make the most sense to leave them there."

"Actually," Gwen cleared her throat. "Gunshot wounds are easily recognizable. No one will believe we were crushed by those bricks."

H.P. shot her a warning look. "Don't help her!" she mouthed.

"Good point, pipsqueak. Bricks to the head it is!"

"No! Wait!" Coriander shouted. "You know how Auntie and Uncle were into the metaphysical universe?"

"Granola groupies," Charlie mumbled.

"They taught us about karma, and that a space

where bad things happened will always be cursed. Please don't curse me!"

"Enough! None of this is getting my money!" Charlie snapped.

H.P. stepped forward, her hands raised in mock surrender. "Charlie, listen to me. I don't know where the money is. If I did, do you think I'd still be standing here, running a diner, dealing with Five Meal Gary's crazy requests and unending ghost chatter?"

"You think I'm stupid?" Charlie hissed, jabbing the gun in H.P.'s direction. "You're Sully's daughter. He wouldn't have shown up in Misty Cove unless he knew where the money is, and he bragged to everyone in prison that he'd left it with you."

H.P. felt the words like a slap. "He left me when I was nine," she said quietly. "My father hasn't been in my life since then."

The only sound was the faint hum of Coriander's large display

refrigerator. Then Charlie let out a bitter laugh. "Nice try. Sully's a rat. He'd claw his way out of hell itself to get that money."

Booker stepped forward, her voice calm but firm. "Charlie, think about it. If Sully's dead, that money is buried with him. No one's going to find it—not you, not us, *no one.*"

At that moment, H.P. noticed a large silver mixing bowl that must've rolled out from the kitchen during the explosion. In one motion, she picked it up and hurled it with all her might at Charlie's head.

Chapter Forty-Two

The dust still clung to H.P.'s clothes, the sour tang of damp earth lingering in her nose as she sat in a debris-covered booth of her diner, staring at her reflection in the window. Outside, the moon hung low, its light barely piercing the fog that blanketed Misty Cove. Dex was spending the night at the Bunce house, and school had been cancelled for the following day. Because Maeviz insisted on helping coordinate the volunteers, Booker waited for her in front of Coriander's shop. Booker walked Charlie to her police cruiser and put her in the backseat, where she wouldn't be able to escape.

"It doesn't add up," she muttered, more to herself than to Gwen, who was perched on the counter, nibbling on a stale piece of cornbread. The source of any food post-explosion was now suspect.

"What doesn't?" Gwen asked, breaking off a chunk and offering it to H.P.

H.P. shook her head. "Sully," she replied, her voice low. "He wanted that treasure more than anything. Why would he install a bomb in the trunk that would prevent anyone, let alone him, from keeping the money?"

"Probably got greedy. He thought you'd already stolen his cash, so he wanted everyone to go out with a big bang?" Gwen opined with a shrug. "That tunnel collapse would've scared the devil himself. He's probably halfway to Mexico by now."

H.P. shook her head, her fingers drumming against the counter. "No. He called it a 'fay-kade.'"

Gwen frowned. "A what now?"

Thud Punchard, who had come in search of H.P. to make sure she was all right, used one thick finger to scroll through his phone. "I know I have the name of the woman who's been meeting your father at the Soused Swine every Thursday evening. Oh. Here it is. Pixie. Pixie Plum."

"That's okay, Thud. I have my doubts he would spend time with anyone connected to his money. He'd be afraid that a stranger would get him drunk and extract the location of his loot. Probably just a one-night hookup."

H. P. shuddered at the thought. "Wait—did you just say 'Plum?' As in Effie Plum?"

Thud scratched his temple. "I believe I said Pixie Plum."

"I need some time alone. I'm going to—"

"I know, I know. You're going to sit in your refrigerator. Never heard of that 'til you came to town. Can I help you walk over all the debris?"

H.P. gulped, temporarily forgetting she sat in the middle of a war zone. "No. Thanks though, Thud. I'll handle this." She pointed to the overturned ketchup bottles and shattered pepper shakers. "You and Gwen help yourself to anything that isn't covered in dust or muck." H.P. took one look around. "That might end up only being the straws."

"I've gotta run. I'm a volunteer first responder and Booker just sent out an SOS. Not the one in the manual though, so I'll need to update her. I'll find you ladies later," Thud replied.

H.P. steeled herself as she flicked the light switch up and down. Nothing. Hopping over pots, pans, knives and broken dishes, she used the light on her phone to guide her toward the walk-in.

"Gram Gram? I wanted to thank you for making such a big sacrifice. It couldn't have been easy."

Gram Gram's aura was a resplendent, sparkling fuchsia. That meant something that made her immensely happy was going on in her world. She was also adorned in a slim-fitting, gold evening gown. In her hair she wore gold flowers, a creation H.P. learned was possible once you reached a specific level in the afterlife hierarchy. Gram Gram's good deeds on the living side meant she came to the afterlife with a surplus already built up.

"You look incredible, Gram," H.P. whispered. "Did you hear what I said? About your sacrificing your son's life for mine? I can't imagine how hard that must've been. Gwen, Booker and I wouldn't be here if you hadn't saved us. Oh, is Sully there with you? Can I talk to him? Maybe now he's ready to apolo—"

H.P. felt a warm breeze pass over her lips.

"Shh... my darling. It was no sacrifice. You are good and kind and loving. My son thought only of himself. And still does. He hasn't crossed over, not that I've seen. It's more likely he crossed you-know-where."

"Oh. Right." H.P. tried to hide her disappointment. She'd held out hope that Sully would join his mother and the three of them would make wonderful memories in the walk-in. "I forgot to ask you earlier; did you find Effie Plum and confront her? What did she say? Did you really let her have it?"

"No, dear heart. I decided to kill her with kindness instead."

"But she's already—"

"Dead. Yes, I know. I don't want to lose my status around her, so for now, I'm employing other means to exact my revenge."

It was so off-brand for Gram Gram. She'd devoted every single day to orchestrating the downfall of Effie Plum. "Well, I'm proud of you for taking the high road. I want to hear every detail tomorrow."

"Of course! I..." Gram Gram paused as her aura changed to a warm, sunlight yellow and swirled down close to H.P.'s face. "Sweetheart, you're positively grey."

"I know. I need to find out what happened to my father and the money. Can you help me with that?"

"Let's see... your father always did like his secrets. He was fascinated by things that weren't what they seemed. Fay-kade. That's what he called them."

"A façade," H.P. clarified, her voice trembling as realization dawned. "That fake wall in the tunnel—it wasn't just a hiding place. It was a distraction. My father never trusted anyone. He would've hidden the treasure somewhere only he could find it. Somewhere only *he* would understand."

"Yes, my dear, sweet child. Your father found hiding places so obvious that no one would suspect them. Search your mind for anywhere he took you as a child. I'm sure you'll find the money there."

H.P. turned to leave. "Did Effie admit she'd stolen your recipes?"

"Funny thing: it wasn't her. It was her son. He wanted revenge for all the years Sully taunted him about his mother losing the pie contest. And do you know that naughty boy poisoned her?"

Chapter Forty-Three

Highway 101, leading outside of Misty Cove, was devoid of its usual midnight traffic—cars and bright-eyed wild animals—as the fog wrapped itself around Gwen's car. The faint scent of burnt biscuits still lingered in their hair.

Gwen's brow furrowed as she chewed on the thought. "So, are you saying that Sully the Sinus—is alive?"

"Yes." H.P. glanced out her window at the reflection of the moon dancing off Lake It or Leave It lake. Her heart thudded in her chest as her mind raced. "The tunnel under Main Street in Misty Cove was never the hiding spot. It was a decoy, a place where he could send his gang members and hopefully blow them all to smithereens."

H.P. shuddered. Her father had no concern for his daughter or anyone else in the diner. What if his only grandchild had been there? And Tildie?

"He made it so obvious with the one letter he sent me from prison," H.P. continued, trying to suppress the anger that was welling up inside her.

"'Remember that ol' fay-kade, Honey Bear? We'll go fishing when I'm out. Promise you'll save our special place for our reunion.'"

"I'm sorry, bestie. I don't get it," Gwen said quietly. "So you weren't supposed to go to a broken-down cabin without him. Maybe he really was looking out for you? He didn't want you falling through the floorboards?"

"You'll understand once we're there.

"That was our special place. He showed me the fay-kade. The tunnel wasn't the treasure's home. It was just a decoy. He wanted his partners in crime to come searching for the two trunks. The one containing a bomb must've been rigged to start its countdown as soon as someone tried to fiddle with the lock."

H.P. had explained, as best she could, what she and Gram Gram figured out.

"Well, if he survived that explosion, he's halfway to Mexico by now."

"I can't promise he's still here, but I know he survived that explosion, and I know how." She dug into her pocket and pulled out the crinkled envelope Coriander gave her. "Read this."

Chapter Forty-Four

A fay-kade.

H.P.'s breath caught.

She'd known all along.

Gram Gram.

Steadily taking tiny steps, H.P. came face-to-face with the last person she'd expected to see.

Her face was shadowed, but her gun was clear as day, pressed hard against Booker's ribs.

H.P. swallowed. "Maeviz."

A slow smile curved the woman's lips. "You've been nice to me, H.P. I hate to involve you in this, but you've left me no choice."

"What, exactly, am I involved in?"

"Maeviz's mother was Phyllis," Booker said, her voice low and calm. "She was part of The Dirty Half Dozen Gang. I was drugged during the poker game, so Maeviz's forced employment didn't happen by accident."

Maeviz's smile widened, her teeth gleaming in the moonlight. "We had a nice chat on the way over." She shoved Booker forward until they were both standing in the moonlight. "Now tell me... where's the money?"

H.P. fought to keep her voice steady. "It's here. But you already knew that, didn't you?"

Maeviz's fingers flexed on the gun. "I don't have time for games, Sweetwater. Open the trunk."

H.P. hesitated. "If I do, you'll see there's nothing inside."

Maeviz's eyes darkened. "Then show me what I *really* want."

H.P. knew, without a doubt, that the second she revealed the real hiding place, Maeviz wouldn't need them anymore.

She just had to stall her long enough to figure out how to survive it.

Chapter Forty-Five

It was just after midnight when H.P.'s car finished bouncing down the narrow, uneven dirt road leading to a small cabin. Faded boards hung on a single nail over the door and the forest had reclaimed most of the porch, with tree roots and moss more visible than the wooden structure, its silhouette jagged in the pale moonlight. A waterwheel had long since rotted, and ivy snaked up the crumbling stone walls. The air smelled damp and heavy, the nearby creek gurgling faintly in the stillness.

"This place gives me the creeps," Gwen muttered, stepping out of the car and shining her phone flashlight toward the entrance.

"It's not what you think," H.P. said cryptically.

"If I didn't know any better, I'd say this is the perfect place to commit a murder," Gwen mused. "But you're not planning to slice me up like a lemon, right, bestie?"

H.P. rolled her eyes. "You know me better than that! Come on. I want to show you something."

With the help of their phone flashlights and the unspoken strength of two women clasping each other's hand,they navigated their way to the front porch. Gwen paused, lowering her phone.

"I'm renewing my objection to this adventure. Not only is this cabin one big gust away from firewood, but there are also all sorts of spooky bugs and animals watching us, just waiting for the right moment to pop out. I can feel them staring at me."

H.P. struggled to comprehend her best friend's words. "Gwen Folds isn't afraid of anything. Forget about the bugs. Follow me."

H.P. found her way to the waterwheel and pushed the fuzzy, green branches aside. She pulled a lever, causing the waterwheel to groan before slowly turning.

"Neat trick." Gwen sighed. "Now can we—"

A door that was previously unseen opened a little more with each turn of the wheel. Inexplicably, whatever lay beyond the door was fully lit.

H.P. yanked on Gwen's hand and pulled her towards the door. As soon as they entered, the scent of... *was it Gram Gram's Lemon Chiffon Pie?* filled their nostrils.

Gwen stared at the situation with apprehension. "This is how every single horror movie begins. Have you not participated in popular culture? Like, ever?"

"Trust me. It'll be fine." H.P. reached a hand to her friend and held it there until Gwen took it. Together, they walked over the threshold and inside a completely different world.

With the room illuminated, it became clear that its contents weren't those of a typical cabin. A plush, camel-colored couch sat on a sky blue carpet. A small glass table with two chairs hugged the wall and in front of them stood a massive fireplace with a roaring fire. On the counter of the small but neat kitchen sat one of Gram Gram's pies. It was as though someone knew they were coming.

"This is the fay-kade. My father told me we were going out here to fish and I told him I didn't want to mess with icky worms and dead fish. But he promised I'd be surprised." H.P. smiled as her mind took her back to the best memories with her father. "We never fished at all. There were board games, a deck of cards, and always one of Gram Gram's Lemon Chiffon Pies. The best part was our talks. Truth doesn't—"

"Get you what you want, Honey Bear," a deep familiar voice said. "Put on a fay-kade—that's pretending to care—that's the name of the game. You smile, you charm, and you get out clean."

Sully the Sinus, aka Sullivan Sweetwater, aka the backstabbing murderer of Heather, appeared from the shadow of yet another doorway, where a bed was visible behind him. "Took you forever to figure it out, Honey Bear. I guess all those years living with your grandmother made you soft." He chuckled to himself.

"The money is here, right, Dad? Can we just give it

to Booker and end this silly game? I've got a wonderful lawyer who'll get you the best deal. You can testify against the others, and..."

The silver barrel of a small handgun appeared as Sully raised his hand. "This game goes the way I say now, Honey Bear. That is, unless you don't want to make it home to your boy."

Chapter Forty-Six

"You had me arrested for your assault because you thought I knew where you'd hidden the money." H.P. said, measuring her words carefully. She was trying to delay the inevitable for as long as possible, although she wasn't sure why. One thing she knew for certain, once Sullivan Sweetwater put his mind to something, he never wavered. "Why would you put me through that?" she continued, "when you could just take your money and run?"

She took in his appearance—dirty red-plaid shirt, faded jeans that hadn't been washed ever, and a scruffy half-beard. An ugly scar down the side of his face was visible now that his grey hair was pushed behind his ears. His appearance looked even more sinister.

"I came to town to get my money, but decided to spend a little time at the lake first. You know, Honey Bear, for old time's sake."

H.P.'s cheeks burned. "I only remember going to

the lake once. To get drugs or something from your friends."

Sully grunted, his way of acknowledging but not confirming her words. "I always knew Nora would be the weak link. Spent many-a-night ponderin' how to do her in, once I got my walkin' papers. Just as soon as I was released, my jail buddies found her for me. I told her to meet me at Lake It or Leave It. Got me a concoction to knock her out, and I stopped at the diner looking for the weapons I'd stashed in the tunnel during high school. Didn't find nothing but an old table so I unscrewed a leg and brought it with me."

"That was you? I thought my son did that and lied! Now I feel awful."

Sully grinned. "Welcome to the crappy parent club, Honey Bear. You gonna let me finish?"

H.P. nodded. The more he talked, the more time there was for someone to realize they were gone.

"Nothing to do once I got there but sit and wait. Nails was still set on turning ourselves in for the death of that kid. There was no way I'd survive another stint in that cage."

"This is all starting to make sense," Gwen said. "The green substance I found under Nine Nails Nora's nine nails was the same green substance Minty was using to poison everyone with his pies."

H.P. said, "And the green substance you found in the pockets of Lotta's lab coats? Was it—"

"Yes." Gwen glared at Sully. "Do you want to explain why you were involved with Nora's daughter?"

Sully scratched his stubble-filled chin. "She came to me. Said she'd been looking for Nails for a long time, to make her pay for leaving her kids with their monster of a father. I told her to meet me at the lake with the poison," he continued in a raspy voice that had become uneven over time. "Ever-thing was going fine. I grabbed Nails and made her inhale the poison. But before I could figger out how to get rid of her, I heard two gals arguing."

"Dr. Kitties and her sister, Booker," H.P. said. "Booker musta figured out why Lotta was here. Lotta's story about trying to find her sister was a big lie. She was here just to set up her mother."

"I dropped Nails into the lake and headed back to town. Didn't realize there was another surprise waiting for me."

Chapter Forty-Seven

"Who beat you to a pulp? And are you taking numbers?" Gwen asked.

Sully squinted as though he were thinking hard. "You're weird, but I like you, little gal."

"Dad! Who beat you up? And why did you blame me?"

"My old celly. I'd heard he was plotting against me, but I thought that was just cell yard talk. When he heard about the money I'd hidden, he wanted a chunk of it. There he was, in the alley, a-waitin' to jump me."

H.P. remembered Minty's scraped knuckles the first day he came to work at the diner. "It was Minty, wasn't it? He was in your gang."

"Nope. He wasn't in the gang. I'd remember."

H.P. frowned, uncertain as to whether she could believe a word her father said.

"I was lying there wonderin' how to form-a-late a

plan. First, I'd have you arrested so you wouldn't get hurt."

H.P. snorted at the thought. "That's ridiculous. You're holding a gun on me right now."

"I remembered where Mom hid the spare key, so I snuck into the

diner and planted the bomb," he continued. "Honey Bear, you've gotta get yourself a better security system. That cock-a-mamie ghost projection don't scare no serious robber."

"How did you survive the blast, Mr. Sweetwater?" Gwen asked. H.P. shot her a look of gratitude. "We heard you go in the tunnel."

"I didn't go in," he said, grinning as though he'd just discovered white bread. "I hollered down the stairs so's it would look like I was coming down and that sneak, Charlie would hurry up 'n' open it. Didn't realize she was smart enough to catch on and vamoose before she became confetti."

"You could've killed us! Not just us, but your grandson too! He's usually in the diner! Didn't you care?" H.P.'s voice wavered. "Don't you have any love left in your heart, Daddy?"

Sullivan ran his free hand through his wavy hair. "Now why do you have to go and make things personal? You're just like my mother. She used to make me feel guilty like that. 'Don't steal from the neighbor kids, son. They don't have two nickels to rub together.'"

"Gram Gram thought you were wonderful, Dad.

Even when you weren't. She just told me last week that you were her favorite."

"Last week? Guess it's a good thing we're ending this conversation soon. Something's not right in your noggin."

There was no reason to make up stories now. Maybe Gram Gram would be there to greet her on the other side. They'd share a hug, a real one. "Did you even care when you let poor Heather die in the armoire? She was just a baby! She even called you her brother!"

Sullivan scrunched up his face, making his bulbous crooked nose appear fake. "She was... my daddy's kid. Momma never knew, but us kids heard all about his philanderin'. Kids all over town with his face and no last name. I felt bad for the kid, sure." His arms dropped to the side as he looked at his feet. For a moment, Sullivan Sweetwater appeared lost in time. Something snapped him back to the present day and he squared his shoulders and pointed the gun. "The kid's long gone. How did you figger all this out, Honey Bear?"

"She's psychic, Mr. Sweetwater," Gwen blurted out. You should ask her about it."

"I know what you're doing, gally. It ain't gonna buy anymore time." His hand squeezed the gun tighter.

H.P. froze, her heart hammering in her chest. "Dad, before you...end us...can you explain why you walked out without a word? I've avoided tacos ever since."

Sully used the hand holding the gun to scratch his forehead. "Do you remember the last time we came out here? I showed you where I hid my secrets and made you promise not to tell a soul."

"And I didn't!" H.P. said, her upper lip quivering. "One of us kept promises."

"After that day, I realized my lips would go a-flappin any time I had too much to drink. Wanted to protect my girl from whatever inside makes me the way I am." He stared at her, hopeful.

"No, Dad. What you did was run away from your problems. The best way to help me would have been to confess to your crimes and do your time. While I do appreciate growing up in a stable home with Gram Gram, I'll never forgive you. Never."

It was as if Sully had been in a trance and now snapped to attention. Once again, the gun was pointed directly at H.P.'s head. "Dad, you could still do the right thing! Please don't do this! I'm begging you!"

Sully's grip on the gun tightened. "I don't want to hurt you and your strange, little friend, Honey Bear. But I ain't going to prison. Not again."

"You don't have to," H.P. said, her voice breaking. "We can figure this out. Together."

"Together?" Sully barked a laugh. "There is no 'together.' There never was. You think the first thing I did when I got outta lockup was to come to Misty Cove because I cared? I was waiting for one thing—

this." He gestured to the duffel bag, his eyes glinting with madness. "I built my life around this. And no one, not even my own daughter, is gonna take it from me." The zipper was half open and H.P. could see the duffel bag was empty.

"You were waiting for an empty duffel bag?" she snapped at him.

"Honey Bear, I was saving that honor for you!" Sully retorted as he looked at the fireplace with a grin.

Perhaps time was still on her side. H.P. felt her stomach twisting. The man standing before her wasn't her father. He was a stranger, consumed by greed. She clasped onto her best friend. If she were going to die, at least she wasn't going alone. She squeezed her eyes shut, waiting for the blast.

Chapter Forty-Eight

The tension was shattered by the sound of an arrow slicing through the air.

Sully gasped, his body jerking as the first arrow impaled his shoulder. The gun clattered to the floor when a second arrow followed, hitting his thigh and sending him sprawling.

"Gotcha!"

Maeviz Dull's voice rang out from the shadows above, triumphant and wild. She emerged from the rafters, her bow still in hand. "I knew I'd put those archery club trophies to good use someday." Her voice was just as monotone as it was when she asked Booker to make change for the candy machine.

Sully groaned, clutching his wounds as H.P. and Gwen scrambled to kick the gun out of reach.

"Maeviz?" Gwen called, her voice equal parts of relief and disbelief. "What are you doing here?"

Maeviz grinned, swinging her bow over her shoulder. "Saving your

butts, obviously. You think I don't keep tabs on suspicious activity in this town?"

H.P. thought back to earlier in the evening when Booker was on the phone with Maeviz. This was certainly a new, more take-charge side of her. It suited Maeviz well.

Sully groaned as blood pooled around him. H.P. knelt beside her father, her hands shaking. "Dad..."

Sully looked up at her, his face pale and drawn. For a moment, the greed in his eyes faded, replaced by something softer... regret, maybe, or resignation.

"You're... just like your grandmother," he muttered, his voice barely audible. "Both of you do-gooders spent your entire lives tethered to that greasy diner. You take the money. Give it to your kid or get out of town. Just don't give it to..."

He coughed, his lungs making a sick, gurgling sound. "You still love your daddy, right, Honey Bear?"

H.P. blinked back tears as she fought the conflicting feelings overtaking her. "You killed a child, Dad. Nothing you did here changes that."

"Let's get the loot and take it to Booker," Maeviz announced. "Before another member of the gang figures out where we are!"

Gwen removed her mustard-yellow sweater and placed it under Sully's head. "You get the money, bestie. I'll tend to your father's wounds."

H.P. barely breathed as she stepped forward. With

trembling hands, she removed two loose bricks from the fireplace and reached inside.

"Close your eyes and reach into my secret hiding place. There, you see? Candy for my Honey Bear!"

She pulled out a small, deerskin trunk, identical to the ones in the cellar but much smaller. The hinges groaned as she lifted the lid, revealing stacks of cash—bills so old, their edges had yellowed. But it wasn't the money that caught her eye.

It was the envelope resting on top.

Her name was scrawled across it in familiar hand-writing. Slowly, she picked it up, her fingers tracing the ink.

"H.P.?" Gwen's voice was soft. "I think he's stable, but we need to get your father to a hospital pronto!"

H.P. nodded. She swallowed as she opened the envelope.

Inside was a letter, yellowed from time. As she unfolded it, her father's voice echoed in her head, as if he were reading it instead of lying on the floor, near death.

"My little gal, Honey Bear, if you're reading this, then I'm already gone. And you've just uncovered a secret that people would kill for..."

H.P.'s breath hitched.

The room seemed to close in around her.

As she kept reading, one thing became very, *very* clear.

Her father had left her much more than just money.

He'd left her the biggest secret of all.

CHAPTER 49

Six Months Later

H.P. looked down at the floor of the walk-in with dismay. "What now? Gram, did you see who threw glitter all over my walk-in? And we just had it cleaned! I'M SUPPOSED TO GIVE A SPEECH IN TEN MINUTES!"

Gram Gram floated down gently beside her. "Relax, darling. It's a special privilege I earned for giving tours. I'll clean it up, I promise. The best part is that I can slide on it to help my loved ones. Only once a minute, or every six months on your side."

H.P.'s eyes widened. "Wait a minute. When Dex and Tildie found my father, Dex came home with glitter on his shoes. Was that..."

"I'm honored to be the M.C. for this celebration," Police Chief Booker Danno said into the mic with her signature cool confidence. "We, the people of Misty Cove, have proven once again that we aren't just a community—we're a family."

316

The crowd gathered on the freshly reseeded lawn in front of the newly rebuilt Honeypie Diner erupted in applause. The spring sun bathed the cove in gold, making the blades of grass glisten like sugar sprinkles in the morning light.

"We repaired more than the walls," Booker continued. "We restored a legacy. We baked our way through adversity—and with no help from Minty Peppermint or his poisoned pies, thank you very much."

Laughter rippled through the audience.

At the front of the crowd stood H.P. Sweetwater, flanked by Gwen, Dex, and Tildie—each wearing a *Pie Saved My Life* T-shirt. Cinnamon Biscuit Maker, now Misty Cove's honorary mascot, lounged on a velvet cushion nearby, a crown of daisies perched between her ears.

The new diner gleamed behind them. It looked almost identical to the original, except for one very deliberate decision: the walk-in cooler had been preserved. It stood at the heart of the kitchen like an ancient oak in a modern forest, its silver door still slightly dented, still humming with secrets.

Because Gram Gram still preferred it that way.

"You all know my sister's arrival in Misty Cove was under false pretenses. She'd tracked our mother down to murder her at the behest of our father. Finding me was a bonus in that she could rid herself of any ties to me at the same time. When I caught up with her, she was packing to leave town. What followed was—"

"An altercation. You mentioned it in the *Puzzles of*

the Pacific Northwest podcast," Five Meal Gary, who had lost forty pounds since the diner's closure, snapped at Booker. "I'm hungry, Chief. Can we move on?"

Booker smiled curtly. "Maybe everyone hasn't heard the entire story, but yes, Gary. My law enforcement training far exceeded what she learned about wrassling a calf to brand it. She's currently awaiting sentencing."

There were whistles and enthusiastic claps from the audience.

"Sandy's Sticks and Rocks, now Sandy's Wood Chips and Second Hand Appliances, is a tribute to our hard work. We all mourn the passing of Sandy Sticks Senior, but he's left this new business in the capable hands of Sandy Sticks Junior."

"Thanks, Chief!" A hand shot up from the back of the crowd, waving at all in attendance.

"Coriander's Biscuit Bar, also renamed, has added wine and biscuit pairings with the extra space created by the blast."

"Come see me for herb biscuits paired with Sassy Lasses Chard-on-ay. It's got a smokey taste from the barn fire last year," Coriander beamed.

After Booker stepped down, H.P. took the mic.

She gazed out over the familiar faces: Edna (begrudgingly smiling) from the front door of the diner, the Bunce family waving in unison, Dex with a disarming half-smile, and even Maeviz—on probation, yes, but surprisingly helpful as the event's volunteer DJ.

"I wasn't sure I'd ever stand here again," H.P. began. "Six months ago, we lost more than three businesses. We lost trust. We lost safety. We lost the people we loved... and we came so close to losing more."

Her voice cracked slightly. "I don't know how to thank you all," H.P. said, her voice breaking. "You didn't have to do this. Any of it."

Booker shrugged. "That's what friends are for."

"Even the bossy ones," Gwen added, smirking at Edna.

"Especially the bossy ones," Edna sniffed, although a slight upturn tugged at her lips.

"But what we found is even stronger: resilience, honesty—and even new friendships." She shot a wink at Coriander Crumb, who promptly blushed and wiped flour from her apron.

The crowd chuckled.

"And although my father..." H.P. paused, "...maybe be gone, I'm choosing to believe he found a kind of peace that he never had before."

"We don't know he's really gone," Five Meal Gary called out with authority. "No body." The crowd booed, seemingly a surprise to Gary. "What?" he asked innocently. "I just said what everybody else was thinking!"

"Gary's right," Booker said. "By the time I made it to the cabin, there was no body. There are lots of possible explanations. No one has seen him since, so we can infer from that he's nowhere near Misty Cove, one way or another." Booker smiled at H.P. "Please continue."

The wind stirred the lilacs and a soft and fragrant scent filled H.P. with a peace she hadn't felt in months. She opened a crumpled page where she'd jotted down everyone she wanted to thank.

"Log and Order, your donation of wood was much appreciated. And Nailed It Construction, the many hours of repair and painting were immensely appreciated. "Oh, and I don't want to forget Shauna, Shandra and Shianne. All the Shingle Ladies Roofing were kind enough to make a bulk order of shingles, so that not only all three businesses were covered, but also my home."

H.P.'s eyes were shiny as she recalled the day every Shingle cousin showed up to reroof her home. Other than sandwiches and iced tea, they didn't ask for anything more. "Everyone in town contributed..." It was no use pretending, she'd have to cry this one out. The water works began as soon as H.P. finished her speech. "Dexter and I made the best decision ever when we moved back to Misty Cove."

Booker handed H.P. a tissue.

"Are you gonna blather all day? The coffee's getting cold!" Edna snapped. "You haven't said anything about our new line of pies, baked by Thud Punchard himself!"

"In a minute, Edna!" H.P. retorted, before turning back to the crowd. "Yes, Thud's Pie in Your Face generously allowed us to be their exclusive client. To all of you who painted, baked, organized, swept, donated, or just dropped by to say something kind—thank you. The Honeypie Diner is open again, and it's more than just a place for breakfast. It's a place for healing. And pie."

The applause that followed was thunderous.

An hour later, after all the speeches had been completed, H.P. was pleased to rejoin Edna in the diner. Peering in the window that served as a place for finished orders, H.P. was relieved to see Thud and both of his brothers keeping up with the orders. Thud had graciously offered to help today and once he explained the boys spent summers growing up in their grandparents' family restaurant, H.P. could barely get an apron on him quick enough.

The kitchen buzzed as pies were plated and passed through the window. "Order up!" Thud called. As he did, his eyes came to rest on H.P. and the menacing look on his face softened. "I was wondering when you might join us," he said, smiling shyly.

H.P. slipped behind the counter, dodging Edna's barked commands and Gwen's chili-scented elbow. "I'll give you a break in a minute, Thud."

She paused at the walk-in, resting her hand on its cool metal. It was an odd feeling of security.

"You did good, Hun Bun," Gram Gram's voice echoed softly as H.P opened the door.

"Couldn't have done it without you, Gram."

Gram Gram shimmered into view beside a rack of

lemons. Her aura was brighter today—light pink, with flecks of gold.

"Did I mention that Lincoln from the Afterlife Express has asked me to co-host an eternal radio show?" she asked proudly.

"That tracks," H.P. smiled. "Just don't forget your number one granddaughter."

"I could never do that."

As Gram Gram faded, H.P. stepped out of the cooler with warmth in her heart. She almost ran over the top of her neighbor.

"Coriander! You scared me!"

"Honeypie! Where are you, you sexy beast?"

Grudgingly, H.P. set her plate down and moved through the sea of people until she found the culprit. "Coriander, what brings you here today? I assumed your place would be packed to the gills as well!"

Dressed in an only-slightly-soiled pink apron with flour smudges dotting her face like blobs of makeup waiting to be blended, Coriander was positively glowing. "I just spoke with my friends from the FBI and thought you might like an update. Care to step outside?"

She didn't want to leave when everyone inside had donated their time, but she was also very curious. Once they were in the alley, the noise level dropped by half. "Okay, make this quick. Poor Thud has been here all morning and he needs a break."

"Well, Mr. Peppermint, aka, Minty, aka—"

"Yes, Coriander, I know who he is!"

Coriander looked taken aback but continued. "His sentencing in federal court was yesterday. He'll be spending another twenty years in prison. Before the ink was dry on the order, he asked the judge if he might work in the prison kitchen." Coriander winked knowingly. "Scary, right?"

"What about your mother? I know you were waiting for the FBI to give you what they'd promised —a deal for your mother."

"Mom's gonna be staying at a supervised facility downstate. For, uh, 'therapeutic biscuit research.'"

"Good," H.P. said warmly. "And you've done an outstanding job of saving us all. Thank you, Coriander. You'll always have a booth here."

Coriander wiped her nose with her sleeve, gave a sloppy curtsy, and disappeared into the night.

Later that afternoon, the air above Misty Cove glittered with the promise of a new summer as H.P. locked the front door of The Honeypie Diner for the night.

The town celebration had wound down hours ago, leaving behind empty pie tins, stray balloons, and the comforting hum of community well-loved. She smiled to herself, feeling the weight of the past six months fall away like the last stubborn snowflake of winter.

Inside, Gwen spun in a slow circle behind the counter, a half-eaten biscuit in hand. "You know," she said oblivious to the crumbs she spewed over the clean floor, "I'm thinking of opening a side hustle. Gwen's

Gadgets and Ghostbusting. Misty Cove's first super-natural cleaning service."

H.P. laughed, wiping down a chair. "Better include glitter clean-up in the package."

"I'll make it a deluxe add-on," Gwen said solemnly.

Abe entered from the kitchen, sleeves rolled up, a smudge of flour on his cheek. He handed H.P. a pie server with a playful flourish. "Official Pie Queen duties, Your Majesty."

She curtsied low and mock-regally accepted it. Their fingers brushed briefly—enough to send a warm fizz up her arm.

Later, H.P. sat alone in a corner booth, a slice of Lemon Chiffon Pie in front of her. The small deerskin trunk sat beside her—empty now, save for the letter Sully had left. Inside, her father's scrawl was messy but unmistakable:

"Honey Bear, the real treasure ain't in bills or coins. It's in family, in second chances, and in finding folks who don't run out on you."

H.P. traced the words, her throat tightening. In the end, Sully had given her one final, unexpected gift:

My little gal, Honey Bear, if you're reading this, then I'm already gone. And you've just uncovered a secret that people would kill for. There's a ledger contains the real names and aliases of dozens of prominent figures who used Misty Cove's secret tunnels to

Smuggle alcohol

Escape criminal charges

Launder money through small businesses

Those who thought about talking about it ended up drinking sludge at the bottom of Lake It or Leave It.

Use it or don't. Just don't tell your grandmother I know.

Love you to the moon,

Your Dad

As she'd unfolded the yellowed page, $20,000 fell to the floor. The exact amount needed to replace her roof. Besides a dry floor, Sully gave her a much more valuable gift. He'd reminded her that despite everything—the lies, the theft, the betrayals—she still had a chance to choose differently. She burned the note and never thought about it again. This town and its' current residents were her extended family now.

Misty Cove wasn't just her home.

It was her heart.

Lemon Lavender Chiffon Pie

INGREDIENTS:

Crust:

- 1 1/2 cups graham cracker crumbs
- 1/4 cup granulated sugar
- 6 tablespoons unsalted butter, melted

Filling:

- 1 tablespoon dried culinary lavender
- 3/4 cup granulated sugar
- 1 tablespoon grated lemon zest
- 1/2 cup fresh lemon juice
- 1 envelope unflavored gelatin
- 4 large eggs, separated
- 1/4 cup water
- 1/2 teaspoon cream of tartar
- 1/4 cup powdered sugar
- 1 cup heavy whipping cream

Instructions:

1. Prepare the Crust:
   - Preheat the oven to 350°F (175°C).
   - In a medium bowl, mix the graham cracker crumbs, granulated sugar, and melted butter until well combined.
   - Press the mixture evenly into the bottom and up the sides of a 9-inch pie dish.
   - Bake for 8-10 minutes or until golden brown. Let it cool completely.
2. Infuse the Lavender:
   - In a small saucepan, combine the granulated sugar and dried lavender. Use your fingers to rub the lavender into the sugar, releasing its oils.
   - Add the grated lemon zest and 1/4 cup of water to the sugar mixture. Bring to a simmer over medium heat, stirring until the sugar dissolves.
   - Remove from heat, cover, and let steep for 10 minutes.
   - Strain the mixture through a fine mesh sieve to remove the lavender buds. Set aside.
3. Prepare the Filling:
   - In a small bowl, sprinkle the gelatin over the fresh lemon juice to bloom for about 5 minutes.

- In a medium saucepan, whisk together the egg yolks and the lavender-infused sugar mixture. Cook over medium heat, stirring constantly, until the mixture thickens and coats the back of a spoon (about 5-7 minutes). Do not let it boil.
- Remove from heat and stir in the bloomed gelatin until fully dissolved. Let it cool to room temperature.

4. Beat the Egg Whites:
   - In a large bowl, beat the egg whites and cream of tartar with an electric mixer on medium-high speed until soft peaks form.
   - Gradually add the powdered sugar and continue beating until stiff peaks form.

5. Whip the Cream:
   - In a separate bowl, whip the heavy cream until stiff peaks form.

6. Assemble the Pie:
   - Gently fold the cooled lemon mixture into the whipped cream until well combined.
   - Carefully fold in the beaten egg whites until the mixture is smooth and no streaks remain.
   - Pour the filling into the cooled pie crust, spreading it evenly.

7. Chill and Serve:

- Refrigerate the pie for at least 4 hours or until set.
- Garnish with additional lemon zest or a few sprigs of lavender, if desired.
- Slice and enjoy your Lemon Lavender Chiffon Pie!

Also by Joann Keder

The Story of Keilah

Secrets and Sunflowers

Franniebell and Purple Wonder

Be the first to hear about new releases! Sign up for my newsletter here:

http://www.joannkeder.com

About the Author

Joann Keder is a USA TODAY Bestselling author who writes award-winning novels full of heart, humor, and just enough trouble to keep things interesting.

After spending her 40 formative years on the flat, windy plains of Nebraska (where the gossip travels faster than the wind), Joann relocated to the Pacific Northwest—and promptly agreed with her soul that it was time to start writing down all the stories taking up space in her head.

Today, she brings to life unforgettable women, their wonderfully quirky companions, and the crooked, scenic routes they take toward healing, hope, and occasionally homemade scones and cookies. Her award-winning novels are a mix of mystery, wit, and heartfelt mayhem.

When she's not writing, Joann enjoys walking among trees that don't bend sideways, savoring good chocolate, and spending time friends and family. And yes, they will all eventually find their way into a story.